I. Sofia-_____

LOVE CHILD OF
COLONEL FITZWILLIAM:

a perfect world in the moon

I, Sofía-Elisabete,

LOVE CHILD OF COLONEL FITZWILLIAM:

a perfect world in the moon

ROBIN ELIZABETH KOBAYASHI

ISBN: 978-0-9985716-3-8 (epub)
ISBN: 978-0-9985716-4-5 (mobi)
ISBN: 978-0-9985716-5-2 (print)

Cover design and illustrations by www.brunovergauwen.com
Interior design by booknook.biz
Interior moon image design by www.sailorschifferli.com
Interior image © siridhata/Shutterstock
Elizabeth Bailey Assessment Services, www.helpingwritersgetitright.
co.uk

For Madison Nii

Table of Contents

Foreword

I AM A LOVE CHILD, born in the year 1810, and a love child I would be for ever. You see, once you're a love child, you can never be anything else in this unforgiving world. I know not why this is so – why a child born to parents who aren't married to one another should be treated unfairly. But I don't care one jot what people say about me.

Yes, yes – it's true that I wasn't just a love child. I had the great misfortune to be an abandoned love child, one that had been cast off into a foundling turnbox wheel, yet survive I did. In my childish heart I consoled myself, believing my real parents to be the most perfect people, and it became my secret wish to find them.

A small child I was at the time, with magical powers where I could make things right again whenever my enchanted world got tangled up in misery and sorrow or whenever the all-knowing grown-ups didn't make any sense. Oh, to believe in that child again! And now, here I am, seven years wiser, bereft of my magical powers, trying to make sense of it all – of this thing, this really big thing that happened to me in 1815, when I found my parents and then I lost my parents.

Chapter One

A Voyage To Inglaterra

My First Memory, thinks I, was of an old, wrinkled nun named Sister Matilde as she and I rode her burrinho, a burrinho named Bento, meaning 'blessed', in a land far away, in the mountains high above Monchique. She prodded Bento with her heels and cried out 'Allez! Allez!' in French, for she was born an age ago somewhere near Paris and had fled France during the revolution. Together we merrily sang 'Arre burrinho, Arre burrinho' as we rode down the green hillside, atop of which stood the ancient but poor Convento de Nossa Senhora do Desterro – Our Lady of Exile – much of it in ruins after the great earthquake of 1755.

'Minha Sofinha, if you are a good little girl,' Sister Matilde tapped me on the nose, 'I shall reward you with a lemon ice or a fresh fig.'

'Ice! Ice!' cried I with joy, because no three-year-old wanted to eat a squashy fig if an ice could be had.

In the market-town of Monchique, Sister Matilde placed me near the door of the tenda, the grocer's shop, where I stood beside the other beggars. I kissed my palms, and I held out my hands to passers-by, many of whom became seized with pity for this anjinha, this tattered little angel adorned with wild jonquils in her hair, and they gave me a réis.

I was born in Lisbon, on the third of June, 1810, amidst the turmoil of warfare, where thousands and thousands of country peasants crowded into the city to escape Napoleon's Le Grande Armée. My papai, being a brave British officer, suffered an injury in Sobral, and while he recovered in Lisbon, he learnt of my existence and then he disappeared. 'War and circumstance separated us,' he used to say. Should you wonder, I am no longer a bebê, being now a proper young lady of twelve years. But I have excellent recall and a prodigious mind, as papai is wont to tell me. 'My daughter is "la jeune savante" – the young scholar – and as learned as her governess,' he often boasts to his family and connections.

Yes, yes – I know what you are feeling. How came I to live in Inglaterra? What happened was this. One dreary winter's morning, a nun at the foundling hospital in Lisbon heard the loud cry of an abandoned bebê. She rushed to the roda dos expostos – the foundling turnbox wheel – where she discovered me, shivering from the cold. And so I came to live with this nun, Sister Matilde, who sheltered me at the Convento do Desterro, one hundred and sixty miles south of Lisbon. I learnt how to say my prayers, and once, while we celebrated Mass, God told me He would send a guardian angel to watch over me. My angel was beautiful and kind, and she wore a red capa or cloak. She called herself Elisabete, but I called her Sister Lisbet, because all guardian angels were nuns who worked for God; at least I thought so, given that I lived in a convent.

It was from there, in July 1813, at the grand age of three, that I took my leave of my homeland. Sister Lisbet told me I must go and find my papai, he being 'so very lost', which is how she described him to me and what I came to believe. He had been missing for three whole years. How could a grown-up get lost? My wee brain struggled to understand this mystery. Sister Lisbet found two Irish nuns who would take me to their convent in York, and with Sister Matilde's blessing, the Irish sisters and I embarked for Inglaterra, setting sail from Lagos. I had no fear, even when we entered the treacherous waters of the Bay of Biscay and got caught in a gale near the Spanish coast. 'Wet betokens luck,' Sister Lisbet whispered to me as the waves and wind knocked our sea-boat about.

From Falmouth to York, I searched and searched, I waited and waited, I prayed and prayed that I would find my papai. Unbeknown to me, he had journeyed to Lisbon to search for his little girl, but I had already gone. Ai de mim! Ay me! The following year, as my fourth birth-day approached, my papai visited Pemberley, his cousin Darcy's estate in Derbyshire, to do a bit of rusticating, for he had been brought low by my disappearance. One day, when his health improved, he received the broadest of hints from Sister Lisbet to come to York. And so hie to this ancient city he did. He brought with him his cousin Darcy and his good friend Mr Bingley who knew of our convent and guided him to us. Oh que gosto! What joy! I had found papai, and I gave a thousand thank-you's to God.

'Papai, why are you crying?'

'Oh, filha da minha alma, daughter of my soul.' And he began to sob again.

'Are you not happy to see me?'

'I am extremely happy to see you.' Papai chucked me under the chin. 'I thought *you* would never find *me.*'

'Sister Lisbet helped me find you.'

This gave him a shock. 'Sister Elisabete? The nun I met at the convent in Lisbon?' He looked round but couldn't see her standing by his side.

'You must have faith,' I shook my finger at him. I thought him curious for not having a strong faith like mine.

'Yes, I should, poppet.'

'What's a pop-head?'

'A poppet is a child who is dearly loved,' he tried to explain.

I gasped. 'Do you love me?'

'Do I.' And he kissed my hand.

'Papai, may I have a burrinho?'

He gave a hearty laugh. 'Why, you imp.'

Having found papai, I would live with him for ever, unaware that I could no longer stay with Sister Lisbet at the convent. When Sister

Lisbet told me this, that she had fulfilled her mission to find my papai, I stamped my feet – left-right-left-right. Ai de mim! 'I shan't give you up, Sister Lisbet, I shan't,' insisted I, for I had changed my name from Sofia to Sofia-Elisabete to honour the good sister.

Mother Coyney at the convent knew not why I wept. She reasoned with me that I must needs leave the convent if I wished to become a proper young lady. I sobbed again while Sister Lisbet tried to hush me. 'Calai-vos, calai-vos,' she soothed me with her melodious voice. Sister Lisbet revealed to me that she would always be one dream away whenever I needed her. She gave me a silver cross to wear, and she promised to give me a macaw, a macaw named Graça, who could speak in Portuguese. A talking bird? I asked her if I could have a talking burrinho instead. 'Tut, tut,' she shook her head at me.

There, at the convent, papai introduced me to my cousin Darcy, a tall and pretty gentleman indeed, and to Mr Bingley, a most handsome and friendly gentleman who had married the sister of Mrs Darcy and who had travelled with papai to search for me in Lisbon. Papai said that Mr Bingley's father used to celebrate Mass here, when it was a secret convent, and once upon a time, our Mr Bingley, being a mere boy then and mischievous, got stuck inside the priest hole until a nun heard him blubbering and rescued him. Bing, Bing, Bingley-O! How I adore him, let me count the ways. He has reddish hair, a handful of freckles on his cheeks and long, silky eyelashes framing his fine blue eyes.

'Bom dia o senhor.' I curtseyed prettily to him.

'Bom dia. Que bella menina!' Mr Bingley bowed to me.

To be sure, his sweet compliment in Portuguese pleased me, and so I kissed his hand again and again.

Papai cleared his voice. 'Poppet, let go of his hand now. Poppet, did not you hear me?'

But I had not done yet flirting with my new friend.

'Vem cá. Come here.' Papai picked me up, and pressing his lips on my cheek, he blew on it – hooooooonk – to give me a wet and loud kiss.

'Gah!' squealed I, having never been kissed before.

'Well, now, that is my special gooseberry kiss,' papai teased me.

'Gooseberry' seemed a curious word at first to me, but it turned into a special one whenever papai is funning with me or distracting me with a kiss. Ever since then, I have been wild for anything gooseberry – gooseberry fool, gooseberry pie, gooseberry jam.

For many months thereafter, it was just the two of us: me and my papai. We lived for a bit at Pemberley, where cousin Darcy gifted me with a piebald burrinho, a burrinho I named Pie, the only problem being that Pie would live at Pemberley and never with me. Even the macaw Graça, whom papai had brought back with him from Portugal, would live at Pemberley for ever. Methinks the macaw wouldn't want to leave this place. Graça and Bixby, cousin Darcy's favourite dog, became boon companions, and one could often see Bixby gambolling on the hillocks, the macaw perched on his back.

Cousin Darcy became fond of Graça and she of him. He taught the macaw all sorts of words in different languages, and curious folks would come from miles away just to hear the macaw speak. One day, Graça surprised us with 'jig it', which gave Mrs Darcy much mirth because her reserved husband loathes to dance. But in those rare instances when cousin Darcy feels inclined to dance a jig, he would always joke, 'I am of a mind to jig it', and dance he would, amazing everyone as he tripped about.

My papai, on seeing how scraggy I was, determined that I should be fattened up with mighty English roast beef, maccaroni and potatoes. Having never eaten meat before, I found it not to my liking, and I would toss my scraps of beef to Bixby who sat under the table. Thereafter, papai would cut up the food on my plate into tiny, uniform pieces, and he lined them up, the meat on one side and the vegetables on the other, like two opposing armies meeting on the battlefield. I would spear each piece with my fork, and once I had vanquished them all, papai would award me my victory 'goose-grog' – my gooseberry fool.

I gave a thousand thank-you's to God that I no longer experienced pangs of hunger. I no longer had to imagine that the cup of water Sister Matilde had given me to fill my stomach was a bowl of sopa de peixe when there was no food to be had at the Convento do Desterro. And I no longer had to go with Sister Matilde to beg for alms. But

I shan't forget the day when we found three new-born infants in the roda – the foundling turnbox wheel – of the Convento and how Sister Matilde raised her arms heavenwards, praying for food and for the poor and desperate parents to come back for their children.

One night at Pemberley, after the house had quieted, I closed my eyes, and I willed myself to float in the air, and float I did, from the nursery to papai's bedchamber one storey below. Once I had planted my feet back on the ground, I threw off my hateful night-dress, and I climbed into the warm bed with my papai. The next night, papai awaited me this time.

'Sofia-Elisabete, we shall be in a heap of trouble when it becomes known you are giving Nurse the slip every night.'

'I hate the nursery.'

Papai groaned. 'Did not the good sisters tell you that you must wear a night-dress in England? You cannot sleep in a state of nature like you did in Portugal.'

'I hate the night-dress.'

'You silly gooseberry.' Papai sighed. 'What to do? What to do?'

'Please papai,' I tugged at his sleeve. 'Nursey snores.'

Papai gave up. 'Well, go to sleep for now.'

'I'm not sleepy.'

'Vem cá. Come here. I'll sprinkle magic dust into your eyes, and you shall meet with the dustman soon enough.'

In the morning, Nursey gave me a scolding, and she warned me the bugbear would gobble me up for being naughty. When I asked her what a bugbear was, Nursey told me that a goblin in the form of a bear lurked in the woods and preyed on naughty wicked children. Not knowing what a bear could be, because we never had ursos in the south of Portugal, it bewildered me as to why Nursey was worked up to a perfect fit of frenzy at a little bug which anyone could squash with his hand. Que estranho! How strange! These folks in Inglaterra have odd customs.

My first memory of a curious scent, thinks I, was that of papai as I slept near him. My papai brings to mind a hodgepodge of cloves and cinnamon and heavy dew and bark and musty earth. He calls it his manly perfume, the truth being he never likes to bathe much. Me? I don't like to bathe either. I am my papai's daughter after all. One day, just before dinner, papai asked me if I had washed my hands.

'I must have done,' I twisted my hands behind my back.

Papai lectured me on the evils of lying. 'Right-about-face, soldier, and quick march upstairs to wash your hands.'

The next day, before we supped, for my papai always let me dine at table when the Darcys were from home, he asked me if I had washed my hands.

I showed him my hands. 'They don't look dirty, so why do I need to wash them?'

This diverted papai at first, but he became stern, like the colonel he is. 'Wash your greasy hands or I shan't give you a dish of your goose-grog.'

Ai de mim! I rushed upstairs, struck with panic that I wouldn't get my share of gooseberry fool.

Our tranquil days at Pemberley seemed destined to last for ever, until one day we received an unexpected visitor. Lord Matlock, he being my papai's father, rode his black stallion to Pemberley in search of his son. He galloped towards Darcy's Lake all in a fury, having sighted papai there, angling for a carp named Callidus, a whale of a fish who is rumoured to be sixty-five years old and who rules the lake.

'Pater?' Papai gazed in astonishment at the imposing figure of Lord Matlock astride his black stallion.

'Son.' His countenance grim, Lord Matlock dismounted his horse. 'Why have you not visited Matlock? I have ridden here myself to see if there is truth to the rumours I am hearing.' For the first time, his lordship noticed me playing with my doll near the bank of the lake.

'Pray what rumours would that be?'

Lord Matlock prodded papai with his riding-whip. 'Unlike you, I will not dissemble. I am speaking of the rumour that you and your by-blow are living here at Pemberley.'

'She is my daughter, and it took us a long time to find each other. I will not give her up.' Papai tugged at his cravat.

'So it is true,' thundered Lord Matlock. 'Are you out of your senses?'

What to do? How could I, Sofia-Elisabete, end their quarrel? I placed myself inside a skiff, and I willed a gust of wind to push it towards the centre of Darcy's Lake. I cried out for papai again and again, when, to my amazement, Lord Matlock dove into the lake, and he swam like a madman to rescue me by towing the skiff back to the dock.

His lordship scrutinised me, now that I stood safe on land. 'I wonder how you got into the skiff?'

'I climbed into it.'

'But how did that rope become loose?'

'I made it loose.' I giggled at his puzzled face.

'Oh, and did you perform magic to make the skiff drift to the centre of the lake?'

I nodded. 'I told Wind to help me.'

'Why did you put yourself into danger, child?' He rubbed his forehead and frowned.

'I stopped you and papai from fighting.'

He admitted defeat. 'You are definitely a Fitzwilliam and so much like your father when he was a boy. Heaven help me!'

Ever since that time, me and my avô, which is what I call my grandfather, have taken a great liking for one another, he teaching me how to blow soap bubbles with a pipe, I teaching him some Portuguese words and customs, such as when I kiss his hand and bless him – 'a bênção meu avô'. My avô wished more than anything to protect me from Lady Matlock, who no doubt would cut me up; at least that's what I heard him say. Would she use an adaga, a dagger, to cut me up? Surely papai would protect me from this bruxa, this Lady Matlock, and give me a magical amulet to ward off this witch.

The unfortunate day arrived sooner than I wished when we received something called a 'summons' from Lady Matlock. Papai hired a post-chaise, which got us to Matlock. From there, we met

Lady Matlock's barouche and four, which conveyed us to papai's ancestral home. No one greeted us except for the butler.

I tugged at papai's sleeve. 'Where is my avô?'

'Your avô is busy in the metropolis far away.' Papai grimaced. 'There is nothing for it then; we must face an inquisition on our own.'

I wished to know what he meant, but he shushed me. We followed the butler into the stately entrance-hall, after which we climbed up-up-up a mountain of a staircase to a drawing room, where an ancient lady awaited us.

'Pray, how old are you?' Lady Matlock peered down her nose at me as I stood before her, she being seated in a high, throne-like chair.

'I am four, which is nearly five, your ladyskiff,' pronounced I in my best polished English. My papai whispered to me to say 'your ladyship' next time.

'Not yet five? Impossible, you love brat.'

'What's a love brat, your ladyship?'

'Why, it is you.' Lady Matlock sniffed the air. 'How dare you defile this ancient hall with your presence here.'

'But you summoned me, your ladyship.'

'O fie!' Lady Matlock fluttered her handkerchief impatiently. 'But now that you are here, pray tell me something that will amaze me, for I hear that you are uncommonly clever for someone so young.'

I glanced at papai, who urged me on. 'Well, ah, cousin Darcy's dog can kill fifty rats in five minutes.'

'Phoo! Phoo!' Lady Matlock waved me off in disbelief.

'Truly,' I assured her, having seen Bixby the spotted terrier carry out this feat. 'My papai bet on Bixby and made a cart-load of money.'

Lady Matlock narrowed her eyes at me. 'What exactly do you want from our noble family? Are you already so fond of money? Is that why you bedevil me? For shame!'

'All I wish for is…a soap bubble pipe.' I blew air bubbles at her.

'Absolutely not.'

'I wish then for…a frog.' I placed my hands on my knees and jumped about most frog-like to impress her.

'What nonsense.' Lady Matlock rapped the floor with her walking-stick. 'You, love brat, will be scorned by persons of rank for ever.'

'Can I still have goose-grog?'

'Do not be ridiculous. I shall degrade myself no longer to the natural daughter of a low creature.'

I shrugged at papai, wondering what Lady Matlock meant.

'You may kiss my hand before you go,' commanded the grumpy Lady Matlock, her outstretched hand before me, her lips twisted to one side.

How silly she looked. Grown-ups always look silly when they're grumpy. So I did what any mischievous child would do. I grasped her hand to kiss it, and I blessed her with 'a bênção minha boba'.

Papai gave me a stern look as he tugged at his cravat. After he bowed over Lady Matlock's hand to kiss it, we took our leave, my papai steering me with one hand atop my head.

'You saucy girl, calling Lady Matlock a fool,' he scolded me in a low voice as he led me out of doors. 'As penance, you will be put on fatigue duty when we return home, and your chore this time will be…'

'Look papai! It's Sister Lisbet.' I knew this would distract him, because he paled whenever I mentioned her as if he had seen a ghost. I made good my escape, running round the barouche and four while papai chased after me, and when I attempted on my own to clamber up the step, he tapped me on my shoulder with his glove.

'Ahem…Sofia-Elisabete, you're in a heap of trouble now,' declared he, as he lifted me into the barouche.

And so ended our visit with the snappish Lady Matlock and how I came to know that a love child I was. Later, as our post-chaise rumbled away from the town of Matlock, papai placed me on his lap, and he explained to me that he had made me out of love but had not been married to Marisa Soares Belles at the time I was born, and that she had abandoned me at a convent in Lisbon.

This confused me. 'Who is she?'

'She was a lindissima, a young beauty, I had met once when I was in Lisbon during the war.' Papai bit his lip as he glanced out the carriage window.

'Where did she go?'

Papai assumed a grim look. 'I believe 'twas Brazil or perhaps Spain.'

'Why?'

'Humph. She was in love with Don Rafael and wished to dance the bolero every night with him.' His face darkened with fury of a sudden.

'Papai, may I learn the bolero?' I thought this would please him.

'Permission denied,' said he in sharp tone.

'But papai...' Hot tears filled in my eyes.

'O, ho! I dare say *you* shall never dance the bolero.' He shuddered at the thought and thereafter closed his eyes.

After a few minutes had passed, I tugged at his coat sleeve. 'Papai?' whispered I, wondering if he was still cross with me and if he would tell me more about the mysterious Marisa Soares Belles. I thought he had fallen asleep when he didn't respond, but then he muttered to himself that he shan't apologise to anyone for having a love child nor will he ever give me up or send me back to the convent. Still, this touched me to the quick. With mingled feelings of gratitude and disquietude, I kissed my papai's hand to bless him.

Chapter Two

Destiny

My First Mother, thinks I, was she who gave birth to me, a bolero dancer by the name of Marisa Soares Belles. I dreamt of her often, this lindissima, she being a young beauty of eighteen years adorned with ribbons and spangles and a bright red flower in her dark hair. At the mid-night hour under a cold sleepy moon, she placed a baby girl in the roda – the foundling turnbox wheel at the convent – and she took her leave without a backward glance, snapping her castanets and dancing a spritely bolero under the beams of moonlight. 'Olé!' cried she, her arms raised in a graceful, defiant attitude. And here, at that very moment, my dream ended, but I dared not speak of it to papai out of fear he would become cross with me again.

After we quit Matlock – and with little regret, as papai would tell me, for he so much disliked his mother – we journeyed to the city of York, where we rented private apartments at Mrs Beazley's boarding house, a timber-framed dwelling on Blossom Street near the crumbling Micklegate Bar. Papai said this was our half-pay home, what with the war being over and he being on half-pay. Together we strolled the tree-lined New Walk along the River Ouse, where I observed many a mother and father promenading with their brood of children. A cloud of wistfulness enveloped me, when I seized upon a brilliant idea.

'Papai, can we buy a new mamãe?'

Papai laughed. 'Where would we buy her?'

'At the grocers.'

'O, ho!' Papai pointed his walking-stick at Mr and Mrs Hart, they being fellow worshippers at my chapel, as they strolled arm in arm in front of us. 'You shan't ever see me living in the Land of Henpeckism, ordered about by a wife. You see before you a manly man, unshackled and free, and in that state I shall remain until I die a fusty old bachelor.'

The Harts must've heard papai's speech, because they turned round, casting him a look of disdain, and when he tipped his hat to them, they acknowledged him not. Papai thought the whole thing a joke – he, a son of an earl, being given the cut by the 'middling sort'. I wondered what a middle person was, and I recalled Lady Matlock having mentioned that I had sprung from a low creature.

'Papai, am I a low or middle creature?'

'Truthfully, you are neither because you are *my* creature.' Papai winked at me.

The day next, after papai reclaimed me at the convent school where I was a day-pupil, I begged him to take us to Tuke's Grocers, a Quaker-run shop on Castlegate where we could buy Tuke's Superior Rock Cocoa – pure cocoa and sugar shaped into cakes – which Cook would use to prepare chocolate for breakfast. My papai, being obliging most days for his sweetest little girl in the world, as he was wont to call me, hired a hackney and away we went.

There, at Tuke's, I stood before the display of chocolate, pretending to admire the superior rock cocoa, cocoa coffee and rich cocoa, the earthy-beefy-sweaty-honeyish aroma tickling my nose. Beside me, and far more interesting, stood Mr Tuke's young niece, who busied herself with arranging the cakes of chocolate. I scrutinised this gentle Quakeress with her kind grey eyes.

'Miss Tuke, how much are you?'

She started at my question. 'I beg your pardon, little miss?'

'I wish to buy a new mamãe.'

'Well, now, mammas can't be bought.'

I waved her off. 'Papai bought a fresh, young thing once...'

Miss Tuke gasped. 'Bless me!'

'...for six bob. I heard him say so.'

'Poppet? There you are. Off we go...' Papai grasped my hand. 'Now, there's an odd thing. I could swear the lovely Miss Tuke just gave me the cut.'

On the ride back to Blossom Street, I observed the poor children begging on the streets.

'Look papai.' I pointed out the window of our hackney. 'That girl has only one shoe. And that boy over there. And that little girl, too.'

'Methinks that is the only shoe they've got.' Papai patted my hand.

This bewildered me. 'Can they buy another shoe at whippa-whoppa-gate?'

'Whipmawhopmagate? They are too poor to do so, my dear child.'

I wiggled my toes inside the new leather shoes with ribbon rosettes that papai had bought for me the other day at Whipmawhopmagate, and I struggled with my conscience about giving up one of my pretty shoes and having to walk lopsided. In the end I decided that would not do. There must be a better way, given my destiny to be a nun like Sister Matilde, for I had resolved to join the sisterhood and ride a burrinho. Ai de mim! How I wished my destiny was chocolate instead. I imagined myself roaming the streets atop my piebald donkey, with my tin pail filled with the delicious chocolate that I would feed to the poor and hungry children who gathered round me, eager to fill their empty bellies. I congratulated myself on a brilliant plan, but how would I learn the secret of making chocolate?

Enter Agnes Wharton.

In mid-July, 1814, papai announced we would decamp to Scarborough, a seaside town on the Yorkshire coast, our travelling companions being the Bennet family and our cousin Georgiana Darcy, she being my papai's ward, for he was joined in guardianship of her, this younger sister of cousin Darcy. I heard Mr Bennet joke with papai that we would lodge with Mrs Wharton, a really ancient and cripply widow who was nearly connected to the Bennets. When we arrived at a three-storey, red-brick house on Queen Street, no one stood outside the door to greet us. Just then, the door swung open, and a shadowy figure standing in the interior called out to us.

'Why is everyone still dawdling on the street? Come in! Come in!' beckoned the crusty old widow. 'Symcox, where are you? Show them into the parlour.'

An ancient, decrepit butler tottered his way to the vestibule, and he led us to a neatly-furnished parlour.

Mrs Wharton seized his ear trumpet, and she held it to his ear. 'I ought to dismiss you for making me answer my own door,' she scolded him.

The impertinent butler burst into a guffaw ere he shuffled his way out.

Mrs Wharton gave a friendly laugh. 'Ah, well, he never listens to me.'

I gaped at Mrs Wharton, who, being an ancient forty years of age, was still a handsome woman with reddish brown hair and sparkling green eyes.

Puzzled by this, I tugged at papai's hand. 'Is she the old tabby we come to see?'

Papai coloured as he tried to hush me.

'Old tabby?' Mrs Wharton held up a quizzing glass to inspect papai up and down, he doing the same to her sans quizzing glass, because nothing could intimidate a British officer like him.

'Papai, you looked at her bubbies.' I giggled into my hand.

Papai picked me up in his arms to give me a quick gooseberry kiss. 'Your papai is an army man, and he cannot help himself,' said he in a half-whisper.

I discovered then that grown-ups often do not make any sense, and there was nothing for it but to ignore them when that happened. Later, at dinner, papai stole many a glance at Mrs Wharton, as if she had bewitched him. I know this to be true, because the next day, I owned that I overheard the two of them whispering about what a lovely time they had last night. Ere long papai began to do strange things, such as getting his hair dressed, bathing twice in one week and wearing sandalwood scent.

'Papai, are you flirting?'

'Flirting, you say?' Papai coloured. 'Where did you learn such a word?'

'I heard Mrs Wharton say so.'

'Well, now, you see before you a man who's flirting with Mrs Wharton and proudly so.'

On Sunday papai escorted me and Mrs Wharton to the Catholic chapel on Auborough Street where we celebrated Mass and where I thought I had a revelation. 'Sister Lisbet, you came back for me,' I embraced Mrs Wharton, who was all astonishment. Papai flinched at the mention of Sister Lisbet as he always does for some reason, and he turned so very pale. I had no sooner caused a scene during the middle of Mass, than Sister Lisbet appeared before me, and she begged me to hush. 'Calai-vos,' she whispered into my ear, and she promised to tell me a secret soon about Mrs Wharton.

One evening, when we had joined a party of pleasure to the town of Whitby, something singular happened. Snug in the cradle of papai's arm, I pretended to sleep while he and Mrs Wharton held hands, gazing at the Northern Lights, which only they and I could see. That same night of our Northern Lights, Sister Lisbet appeared in my dream, her red capa flowing about her, her red roses tumbling from her hands, and she told me the meaning of the Northern Lights, but I shan't tell anyone what it is – what she said of papai's and Mrs Wharton's destinies being united. Besides, you would never believe it unless you have a strong faith like mine.

Things being so, it bewildered me when papai announced in early August that we would decamp for Pemberley, thereby abandoning Mrs Wharton in Scarborough for ever. I made a fuss, but papai, with an officer-like coolness, remained firm and determined. 'Adeus, Mrs Wharton.' I sobbed in her arms, for I had to come to adore her. Adeus – that's how we bid farewell to folks in Portugal. Then, a few weeks later, papai ordered me to pack my bags to decamp to York. All this decamping made my head spin like a teetotum, like a wooden top.

Enough, I told myself. I bundled up my doll, and I ran away. 'Adeus, papai, adeus!' But Bixby picked up my scent, and he led papai to the stables where I had hidden myself under the straw next to Pie, my loyal donkey. Papai laughed as he pulled me out feet first.

'Come here, you silly gooseberry.'

'I a'n't goin',' insisted I. 'It i'n't fair.'

Papai cupped his right ear. 'Did I hear you talk like a stable-boy?'

'I talks like you.' I sat with my arms folded, petulant as ever.

'O fie! I a'n't one to talks like a stable-boy.'

When papai advised me of the real reason for our leave-taking, namely, to meet up with Mrs Wharton for York races, I threw a handful of straw up in the air with glee and cried out, 'Adeus, Pie-O! I am for York.' Now, having returned to York, I decided 'twas time to give a broad hint to my papai, so I began to call Mrs Wharton my mamãe, and sure enough, papai proposed to her, not once, but twice. Ai de mim! She rejected him both times, telling him that he was not ready for marriage and that he suffered from fits of jealousy. Furthermore, his 'honeyed' words, 'Oh, hang it, I love you, Aggie', would not convince her otherwise.

After mamãe returned to Scarborough without us, papai announced his need of French courage now that he was no longer cagg'd. I asked him what his cagg was, and he told me of a vow he had made of not getting drunk on brandy for six months. He shook his finger at me. 'Don't you know – my cagg is out?' He sat in his bedchamber, singing a song in praise of the mighty roast beef of old England, and he swore again and again like a drunken soldier. 'Ready. Present. Fire!' And he would gulp down more of this stinking thing called French courage.

The next morning, having witnessed and smelt the effects of the wicked liquor on my papai, I wrote two letters using my best penmanship: one to cousin Darcy, and one to mamãe. I begged them to help me, because my papai was a 'stinkin human bean'. Our landlady sent the letters by the post, and thereafter I prayed. Several days later, when cousins Darcy and Georgiana arrived at our boarding house, they heard me howling like a monkey, but unbeknown to them, I had been stung by a bee, and papai had been sucking the venom out from my wound.

'Unhand her, you foul fiend.' Cousin Darcy snatched me from papai. I could hear him and my papai shouting at each other as Georgiana carried me away.

'Now see here, Darcy,' papai tried to reason with him.

'You cannibal,' thundered cousin Darcy. 'How dare you hurt your own child.'

'*You* are a dolt,' retorted papai.

'Did you spit on my bespoke waist-coat? Well, now, prepare yourself to die, cousin.'

Ai! They had no sooner begun to fight at fisticuffs, than mamãe arrived at the boarding house. She tried to talk sense to them, but they much preferred to argue and wrestle. 'Men!' declared mamãe as she came down the stairs.

Their bout finally at an end, cousin Darcy and papai joined us in the parlour, unashamed of the red marks on their faces from having knocked each other down. Mamãe insisted that papai stop drinking and gadding about with a miscreant named Mr O. P. Umm and that he speak to Father O'Shaughnessy, or Father O as we called him. But papai refused. 'I shan't speak with a priest,' he stamped his foot. My heart sank to my toes. Mamãe rose to leave, and I began to weep, believing we would lose her for ever. She had not taken more than three steps, when papai grasped her hand, and he confessed that he had sinned, and sinned again, and again and again, and that he promised to speak to Father O.

'Papai, how many times have you sinned?'

He grimaced. 'Too many times, my girl.'

'God will forgive you,' I consoled him.

'Let us hope He will.'

And so we decamped once more, both of our cousins Darcy and Georgiana joining us, to return to Scarborough where papai could speak with Father O. It was then that mamãe surprised us by taking us to Bunberry House, her estate in Hackness, where she oversees a Catholic school for poor girls and where Father O celebrates Mass with them each month. While my cousins and I strolled in the garden, we overheard papai's outburst on the other side of the yew hedges.

'I beg your pardon. But you do...who do...what?'

'Hush, Colonel. I said I have been financing trade with countries on the continent, and I have used the profits to sustain the school and maintain the estate,' mamãe revealed to him.

'My God! You're a smuggler.'

'Nay. I am a tradeswoman.'

'I would rather you be a ruthless pirate,' grumbled papai.

'What? And not give you quarter every Sunday night?'

'You minx,' thundered papai. 'Your feminine arts and allurements shall not beguile me this time.'

Just when their big row became interesting, Georgiana led me away to the main house. 'Não, não, não,' protested I, but obey Georgiana I did. At the parlour window, I stood on the watch, and from there I espied, with a glad heart, my papai and mamãe in the garden embracing each other. To be sure, all would be right in our world again. Nevertheless, I wished to hasten matters, so I summoned up my magical powers to cast a spell on my papai and mamãe to make them marry soon.

After dinner, we walked the trod to River Cottage, a hermitage on the estate, where we bedded down for the night – mamãe and Georgiana and I in one bedchamber, papai and cousin Darcy in another bedchamber, and Father O in the library. The soothing gurgles of the River Derwent promised us a deep slumber, when, of a sudden, papai cried out, 'Riflemen! Riflemen!'; for, he had many a nightmare about the war. The next morning Father O and papai disappeared down by the river bank to have a long talk, and while they were gone, I discovered that mamãe knew the secret of chocolate.

Mamãe believes every woman, rich or poor, should learn how to care for themselves, which meant cooking, cleaning, &c. Here, at River Cottage, she reigned as mistress, housekeeper and cook. My cousin Georgiana expressed shock at seeing mamãe in the kitchen, but not I. Unlike Georgiana – she being a young lady of quality who

would never go near the kitchen, much less know how to cook – I
and the other foundlings at the Convento do Desterro had gathered
onions, garlic, chile, potatoes and cabbage to prepare our sopa de
peixe, a meagre soup, each day.

I stood there entranced at the kitchen-door as mamãe stirred the
shavings of rock cocoa with fresh milk and some spices in a pot
over a charcoal fire. She brought the pot to the table, where she
began to mill the mixture, and once she had tossed some flour into
the mixture, she milled it again. When she returned the pot to the
charcoal fire, she added several drops of a magic potion that she kept
in a phial, and she stirred the mixture.

'Mamãe, what's in the magic bottle?'

'It's a secret.'

'What's the secret?' persisted I, my curiosity insatiable.

'Love and forgiveness,' revealed she.

When Father O and papai returned from their river talk to join us
for breakfast, papai joked that he was in need of sustenance. I thought
he was right, given his red-rimmed, watery eyes and haggard face. I
kissed his hand to bless him, as was our habit each morning and each
evening, and he mustered up a grin for me, but soon thereafter he
closed his eyes, his lips quivering ever and anon. Father O clapped
papai on the back. 'God bless Soofia-Eee. All childher are special.'

I sat at table next to papai, impatient for Father O to get on with
it and say grace, for I was a naughty child. Oh, how I coveted the
silver pot sitting there on the table and the mystery therein. Once
papai poured me a cup of chocolate and the liquid cooled enough
for my tastes, I greedily slurped half of it down. When I had done,
I proudly displayed my chocolate moustache to him, thinking he
would find it droll, but he only sighed with an impenetrable sadness
ere he wiped my moustache away.

While we breakfasted, papai glanced many a time at mamãe,
and she at him, and with each forkful of food he ate, his humour
improved.

'Who prepared the eggs if we do not have a cook here?' Papai
swallowed a piece of poached egg.

'I did,' Georgiana proudly revealed.

'W-w-what? Is it safe to swallow?' Papai winked at his ward.

'I can assure you that Miss Darcy's poached eggs are safe,' mamãe defended Georgiana's skill.

Papai humphed. 'Well, now, Georgiana, seeing how we have no servants, shall you be scullery-maid and clean the dishes?' papai teased her.

'Colonel, do you know what a pail of slops is?' Mamãe's eyes sparkled with mischief.

Papai hesitated, casting a suspicious look at her. 'Is this fatigue duty?' Whenever papai didn't want to do something, he would always call it fatigue duty for some reason.

'The Colonel an' I will gladly clean the kitchen for ye,' offered Father O.

'We will, Father O?' Of a sudden papai checked himself, grinning at me. 'Ay, to be sure we will.'

It seemed papai would do almost anything for mamãe – even empty the pail of slops and scrub the kitchen – if only she would accept his hand. Ai! Two whole months passed ere my magic spell finally took hold. Papai seemed far less troubled, now that he read the Bible each morning and met often with Father O to discuss his long list of 'frailties'.

Papai proposed again. And mamãe accepted his hand this time. She smiled and patted my cheek when I said my spell had worked. She explained that unlike his first two scanty proposals, his third proposal convinced her that he no longer desired to possess her, having understood that she belonged to God, as did we all. For some reason, knowing this gave him peace, as he said, and this peacefulness, in turn, helped to restore his faith in himself, and as Father O would remind him, he had the power, the love and a sound mind to address his weaknesses. My wee brain struggled to understand this grown-up talk, but I gave up. With an inward shrug, I remained convinced that my magical powers had brought change.

Father O, with a gladness in his heart, received papai into the Catholic Church, and thereafter my parents got married, first at

St. Mary's, the Anglican church, by the vicar there, and then at the Catholic chapel at Bunberry House. To our amazement, my avô attended the wedding ceremony at Bunberry chapel, this despite Lady Matlock's objections to the marriage and me – I, Sofia-Elisabete, whom she still referred to as a foreign love brat and the natural daughter of a low creature. I had a new mamãe, but Lady Matlock's cutting remarks reminded me of my unfortunate destiny, one where I was connected with the mysterious bolero dancer, this Marisa Soares Belles, who lived in a land far far away. And so I was.

Chapter Three

Bugbear in the Old Wood

MY FIRST FOOT-RACE, thinks I, was with my pug-puppy on the sands of the North Bay here in Scarborough. A girl I would always be, yet that didn't stop me from wanting to do boyish things, or what papai calls hoydenish things, such as climbing, jumping and romping. One time, while papai lay under his favourite Scots pine in our garden, amusing himself with his great and deep thoughts as he was wont to say, my own great thought was for my puggy and I to jump over him each time we circled the pine tree, and noisily so, for I had burst into a fit of giggles. 'Silly gooseberry, I shall court-martial you,' papai teases me whenever I act hoydenish. But, truly, I cannot help myself.

In May of 1815, after papai had returned from doing war business with the Lancashire Militia, he announced, 'We are for the old wood where no doubt Sofia-Elisabete shall entertain us with her hoydening', to which I shouted, 'Goose-grog! I hope they have goose-grog.' You see, I rather wished to spend my fifth birth-day with Pie and Graça at Pemberley where I could eat a cart-load of gooseberry fool. 'No-no-no,' papai shook his finger at me, 'to the Fitzwilliam Hunting Lodge we go, to visit your grandfather.'

Papai promised that Cook at the lodge would make gooseberry fool for me, she being the best cook in the world. He cast his eyes heavenward – the savoury and sweet memories tumbling round in his head no doubt – as he praised the singularity of Cook's apple charlotte. 'O apple of my eye.' 'O sweet charlotte.' 'O the goodly apple.' Mamãe goggled her eyes whenever papai would request that dessert, it being clear to her now why he favoured it so. 'Ay, ay,' cried she, knowing she would need to cajole the receipt from this Cook.

We would spend a month in the old wood, as the country-folk called Sherwood Forest. Things being so, I wished to bring Tin-Key with us, but papai warned me that our dear little puggy might be mistaken for a wild animal and end up stuffed and nailed to my avô's trophy wall at the lodge. Reluctantly, then, did I agree to leave Tin-Key with Mackie, our trusty footman at our Scarborough abode. I hear you cry, 'What is a Tin-Key?' I named my pug-puppy Tin-Key in honour of my papai, who, with his ear made of tin, has the ability to sing in a key of his own, as mamãe frequently reminds him.

During the long carriage ride, papai serenaded us with 'O, the month of May, the merry month of May, So frolic, so gay, and so green, so green, so green.' Mamãe, she being greatly vexed with papai's singing, knew not what to do at first, for a proficient in music she is, until she learnt to sing along with him to drown out his voice. On the third day of our journey to the old wood, whilst papai serenaded us with 'Oh the roast beef of old England, and old English roast beef', I tugged at his sleeve with urgency.

Papai cast a grim look at me. 'Pray tell me you visited the Necessary House before we quitted the inn.'

'Não. You said quick march to the carriage.'

'Well, now, perhaps I did.' With a waggish grin, papai gazed at mamãe. 'Surely you wish for mamãe to help you?'

'Não, não, não,' protested I.

'Oh, hang it! Fatigue duty again.' Papai rapped his walking-stick for the driver to stop.

Later that afternoon we reached our destination of Fitzwilliam Hunting Lodge, an estate situated on former Crown land that had been sold to my avô, Lord Matlock. While my mamãe stood there admiring the rustic lodge framed by ancient oaks, I broke from her grip to get a better look and see at the turret atop a small rise. This folly, this enchanted tower, whispered to me in some kind of forgotten language that I must needs clamber up the hillock to explore its mysteries. Ai de mim! Someone had secured the door with a padlock. My avô explained to me that a bugbear resided therein who would gobble up any naughty wicked children, particularly those who came near his magical abode without any grown-up protection. Que estranho! These bugbears have strange customs.

'Meu avô, I'm not afraid of Bugbear.'

'O, ho!' My avô tapped me on the nose. 'You are a courageous one.'

'I bet a ha'penny I can squash him,' bragged I.

'Done! I'll take your bet,' replied he.

Upstairs in our apartments, mamãe led me to the dressing room, where she instructed me to call for her when I had done. While I sat within, I overheard my papai and mamãe romanticking themselves in the next room; for, they had been separated for two whole months while papai did his war business in Lancashire, and they had pined for each other every day.

'My dear Mrs Fitzwilliam, we are finally together in the wilds of England.'

Mamãe laughed. 'Are you flirting with me?'

'I am, indeed. Perhaps you would indulge me in one of my wandering fancies to-day?'

'Pray, what fanciful thing would that be?' she teased him.

'Come here, my Senga,' said he in an audible whisper, 'and be merciful and quick about it.'

I rapped the wall three times with my knuckles, for they had forgotten that I sat within, and not for the first time, believe you me.

'Mamãe, I'm ready for you,' I shouted with all my might. This displeased papai, to be sure.

'Y-y-yes, my child…I shall be there in a minute…'

'Pray be merciful and quick about it, mamãe,' commanded I.

The next day, while my papai and mamãe were romanticking themselves on a stroll through the old wood, my avô promised to take me to a faeryland. We rode out on a mare, passing through the pretty village of Edwinstowe, and then the wilds of Birkland, and from there we rode on another mile or so to Budby Forest where fifty thousand hawthorns bloomed. Hoisted atop my avô's shoulders, I picked ever so many of these sweet-smelling blossoms from the branches to surprise my mamãe with. We settled ourselves on a log covered with snowy-white blossoms, whereupon my avô recited the tale of Robin Hood and his Merry Men. I sat thus entranced with the plucky deeds of the brave outlaws.

'What say you of Maid Marian?' my avô inquired.

'Gah!' exclaimed I. All this romanticking with her outlaw I could do without. 'I want to be Robin Hood and shoot arrows.'

My avô laughed. 'I'll teach you how to swim instead, just like I taught your father when he was a boy.'

A few days later, whilst my papai and mamãe walked out to shoot hare, my avô took me to the Great Pond. My avô knows everything about the art of swimming – how to plunge oneself into the water like a frog, how to breathe under water like a carp, how to avoid drinking down a great deal of water like a horse and so forth. Once I had mastered some basic tricks, such as swimming on my belly and treading water, I learnt a diverting trick – the flying boulder – by jumping high into the air, tucking my knees to my belly and pinching my nose ere I landed in the water. And each time I performed a perfect flying boulder, my avô would clap his hands in approval.

'Raaaawwrrr!' roared a filthy, stinking man with a long beard, who appeared from nowhere to attack my avô. The two of them tussled for a long while until my avô, being a strong man, shoved his foe into the water.

'Meu avô, who is he?' I gaped at the shabby man who clambered up the bank.

'Eh? Oh, I've named him Yahoo. He lives in the hermitage, and I dare say he enjoys attacking me as much as I do him.'

I gasped. 'Is he a bugbear?'

'Well, now, you might say he is my bugbear.' For a moment, my avô looked as guilty as papai did when he had fallen asleep during Mass and Father O had given him a severe rebuke for doing so.

When the time came for us to quit the Great Pond, I skipped merrily alongside my avô while he sang in his rich baritone:

When Robin Hood was about twenty years,
With a hey down, down, and a down,
He happened to meet Little John,
A jolly brisk blade right fit for the trade,
For he was a lusty young man…

In the shadows of the ancient oaks, I could see Yahoo dodging us all the way back to our abode, but I feared nought with my brave avô at my side. I rushed up the stairs in the lodge to change my clothes, when I came to a sudden stop, my brain tingling with my magical powers. That is when I observed my parents speaking in a hushed tone, enough so to raise my suspicions that I was in the midst of some romanticking going on.

'What rotten luck to tussle with a stinking tatterdemalion instead of tussling with you,' papai wrapped his arms round mamãe. Apparently, Yahoo had wrestled with papai as well.

'My poor dear was attacked by a strange hermit.' Mamãe wrinkled her nose. 'Pugh! You really do need to bathe.'

'I will, but only if you help me, Senga.' Papai gave her a lopsided grin.

Mamãe knew that if she did not help him, he would not bathe for at least a week and only on a Sunday morning before we went to chapel. With a wink, mamãe led him by the hand into the dressing room. Soon she got him into the bathing-tub, and I could hear them laughing and then their low murmurs and after that complete silence and then the laughter started up again. I wondered why they thought it so amusing to bathe.

At dinner-time, I begged papai to let me sit up to supper, which I often did when we were at home, but papai lectured me it would not be appropriate for a child to dine at table with an earl. I stamped my way upstairs, vexed at being cast off, when I seized upon a brilliant idea on how to get rid of my dinner of pease, beefsteak and maccaroni, now that I wasn't hungry. Having accomplished the evil deed, I sneaked downstairs to the drawing room to eavesdrop on everyone.

'As like as two peas are to one another...' my avô muttered to himself.

'Pater, did you say something?'

My avô cleared his voice. 'You, son, were a holy terror as a young lad.'

'Is that why you washed my mouth twice with soap when I was seven years old?'

'O fie! I never washed your mouth with soap.'

'My papai hates soap-suds,' I chimed in, giving everyone a start.

'Sofia-Elisabete, you ought to be in bed,' papai scolded me.

My avô lifted me to his knee. 'Do you know, while we dined, a most curious event took place outside the window? I could swear 'twas a tempest of pease, beefsteak and maccaroni. Who'd have thought that possible?'

I commenced my tale with relish. 'While I supped upstairs by myself, I heard the strangest thing. Mr Pea bet Mr Beefsteak to jump out the window. Then Mr Beefsteak bet Mr Maccaroni to jump out the window. And then Mr Maccaroni bet Mr Pea to jump out the window. "Done! Done! Done!" they all cried. So there was nothing for it. They threw themselves out the window to win their bets.'

Papai shook his head, and he berated me for my hoydenish behaviour and bad habit of lying. 'A child fabulist has sprung from me,' complained he.

'What's a fabulist?' asked I.

'It's someone who invents stories.'

I shrugged with raised brows. 'But papai, the truth is so hum-da-dum-drum.' Well, upon hearing that, papai threatened to escort me upstairs if I didn't go to bed. I lingered a moment or two in the passage to spy on them again.

Papai inclined his head towards mamãe. 'I fear she's quite like her lying mother, who sent me to the wrong convent in Lisbon when I was searching for...'

'Oh, nonsense,' mamãe interrupted him. 'Our Sofia-Elisabete is just a child with a lively imagination.'

I climbed up the stairs, wondering if my first mother was a hoyden and a fabulist like me. A week passed, and by then, I had long forgotten about it.

The third of June arrived, it being my natal day, and I wished to go swimming with my avô, but papai had invited his friends, the Robinsons, to join us at the lodge for a picnic instead. According to papai, he had met Tom Robinson nearly two years ago at the Black Swan in Edwinstowe when papai, who had disguised himself as a common labourer, spilt ale on Tom, and Tom, in turn, had planted a facer on him. And that is how grown men amuse themselves and become great friends, methinks.

These Robinsons lived in Edwinstowe where they owned a grocer's shop. There were five of them in all – a hugeous father, a sweet mother, two boys named Pico and Pequin, ages ten and eight, respectively, and a toddler called Poppaye, who looked, well, Poppaye-ish. But we Fitzwilliams could not help but be curious about the names Pico and Pequin. Mr Robinson explained that he named his sons after places mentioned in a certain tale – one where a Spaniard journeyed to the moon with the aid of his flying gansas or geese. Oh, how I wished to fly on a gansa to the moon. But Pico scoffed at me, claiming that no girls could survive the long and difficult journey to see the Man in the Moon, nor would they be safe from the moon men.

The Robinson boys taught me how to play ancient games, such as blindman's bluff, leap frog, buck buck and running the gauntlet. They taught me how to speak like a Notts boy, and so I taught them a few choice words in Portuguese, including 'Viva!' when you greet someone. The dinner-bell having rung, we raced one another to the festive table that Cook had set up out of doors, it being laden with fish, flesh and fowl, pyramids of this, that and the other, and my favourite gooseberry fool, all nicely dished up.

'D'yer eat this ivry day?' Pico goggled at these platters of food, particularly the mound of maccaroni.

'Yi, don't you?' It hadn't occurred to me that the Robinsons were poor. Could they not eat the food in their grocer's shop if they so wished? Surely they never went to bed hungry.

Pequin picked up one of the hairy gooseberries. 'I've niver seed a goosegog afore.'

'Niver?' I had thought all English ate gooseberries.

Once the dinner concluded, the men smoked their pipes, and the women played with Poppaye, while we children stole away to the surrounding old wood. Boredom having set in, the Robinson boys took out their sling-stones, and they began to hurl rocks at an imposing, ancient oak tree. 'Retreat!' warned Pico, and he tossed his sling-stone into my hands, for he had heard my papai's rapid approach. Convinced that I was the culprit, papai lectured me that I should not sling rocks at Matlock's Favourite Oak because it would upset my avô.

'But papai, I wasna slingin' stones. Pico an' Pequin...'

'I don't care who did the slinging. A proper young lady must not do it,' commanded he.

'But papai, I dunna know how to sling. I dunna...'

'Confound your buts and dunnas. Obey me at once.' He held out his hand for the sling-stone, which I gave to him with alacrity. When he strode off, angry as can be, I stuck out my tongue at those two connivers who fell a laughing at me for getting scolded. I saw how it was. Boys got to run wild, slinging stones, whereas girls could not.

'Yer in the suds now, nincompoop.' Pico guffawed as if he had uttered the wittiest thing in the world.

'Pah!' taunted I. 'Yer niver gettin' yer sling-stone back.'

'My papa will clot yer papa if he doesna give me my sling-stone.'

The next week my avô proposed a jaunt to Creswell Crags where we could explore the secret caves that sheltered Robin Hood and his Merry Men from the law. My heart filled with joy at the thought of another boyish adventure with my avô, but to my ten-fold dismay, he invited the Robinson boys. I got into the carriage where I sat in between the two miscreants, Pico and Pequin, who pinched me and pulled my hair when my avô did not attend to us. 'Yow!' I rubbed my sore head. To distract my tormentors, I begged my avô to tell us another tale of Robin Hood, and so he did. We learnt how Robin Hood set the prisoners free at King John's Palace in Clipstone while King John searched the caves at Creswell Crags for the bold outlaw.

'I'm goin' to be Robin Hood someday,' remarked I.

Pico laughed at me. 'Yer just a slip of a girl.'

When we reached our destination, we clambered up the hillside to inspect one of the caves. There, I suffered a goodly amount of time trapped inside the small cave while my captors pestered me with spiders and other horrid creatures.

'Yer canna get out, Robin Hood, 'til yer eat it,' Pico dangled a gigantic spider in front of me.

'Why, you rascal.' I picked up some magic dirt, and I threw it at Pico, thereby enabling me to escape from the cave. I ran to my avô, who awaited me with a proud grin on his face.

To my great relief, we returned to Edwinstowe where our carriage conveyed us to the grocer's. I bid the Robinson boys farewell with 'adeus', hoping I would never see those two imps ever again. Unfortunately, that was not to be.

One sunny day too soon thereafter, Mr Robinson and those aforementioned imps arrived at the lodge. Pico said the men were going to fish for trout. 'Yer a namby-pamby girl an' canna goo wi' us,' taunted he. I gave him a monstrous glare. I ran as fast as I could up the hillock, where I pounded on the turret door with my fist. 'Let me in you silly Bugbear,' cried I, my eyes filling up fast with hot tears. I turned round to discover that papai had followed me up to the folly, and in a fit of rage, I saluted him with a volley of oaths that he always used when he thought I couldn't hear him.

'Saucy girl! I counted four oaths in your string of invectives. That's four fatigue duties for you.'

'I dunna care.' I turned away in a pout, and I stamped my feet – left-right-left-right – for I detested chores more than anything.

'Do you wish to make it five?'

'It isna fair. He's my avô,' insisted I. 'I knowed him first.'

'When you can speak the King's English again and behave like a proper young lady, pray let me know.' Having said that, papai turned a crisp, right-about-face, and he marched off with long strides. He, being at odds with my avô for some reason, had declined to join the Robinsons on their fishing excursion.

'It isna fair to be a girl,' muttered I. And that is why I determined to run away and hide somewhere. I slid my way round the turret where no one could see me. Leaning against the wall, I closed my eyes, and I willed myself to drift upwards – higher and higher and higher – and when I opened my eyes, I found myself standing atop the turret.

I knew not how long I was up there, but it seemed as if I had no sooner accomplished this grand feat, than I heard papai calling my name. I own that I took delight in hearing the concern in his voice, because surely he now believed how wronged I had been. Ere long my mamãe joined him, as did my avô, who had returned from his angling adventure with the Robinsons. 'Where are you? Sofia-Elisabete, where are you?' Their voices rang with worry.

I peered down at them through an arrow-slit on the parapet. 'Meu avô! Meu avô! You have come home at last.'

The three of them glanced up at me. I do believe I gave them a good fright, for they certainly seemed shocked to see me high atop the turret.

'Dear God, no.' Papai gaped at me in disbelief.

In an instant my avô opened the turret door, having found the padlock unlocked. Their loud footsteps echoed in the folly as he and my papai charged up the winding staircase, uttering oaths at each other and blaming the other for not remembering to lock the door.

'Sofia-Elisabete, I shall court-martial you,' bellowed papai, he still being of a snappish humour.

'Bugbear chased me up here,' claimed I.

'I dare say you are lying.' Papai scowled, and he sprang forward to catch me. 'Vem cá. Come here.'

I ran away from papai as fast as I could. 'Avô! Avô!' I sought the safety of my grandfather's outstretched arms. 'You believe me, don't you?'

He stooped down to scrutinise me. 'Child, how came you to be here?'

'I knocked at the door – tap-tap-tap. Bugbear called out, "Come!" And so I let myself in. Bugbear chased me round and round. But I squashed him good and hard.' My tale was so brilliant I had convinced myself that this had really happened, yes, indeed.

'Now why would Bugbear chase you? Think carefully little one.'

The gleam of reproach in his clear blue eyes cut me to the soul, and thus I hesitated for a long moment.

'I...was...naughty?'

'That'll do.'

Having understood my avô's censure, I covered my face with my hands to hide my shame. I began to weep a hundred – nay, a thousand – nay, a million – tears, for most assuredly my avô detested me now, and I would never get to do flying boulders or other boyish things with him ever again. To my great surprise, however, he grasped my right hand, and he placed a ha'penny into it. With a wink, he gathered me into his warm embrace where all was forgive and forgot.

Chapter Four

Tree on the Hill

My First Drum, thinks I, was an adufe, or pandiero quadrado, in the shape of a square, its two goat skins stitched along the sides of the frame. I clutched the adufe with my thumbs and the pointing finger of my left hand, while the rest of my fingers beat the rhythm on the skins, the seeds rattling pleasantly within. I imagined myself a true adufeira, just like Catarina Baptista, she being a popular adufeira from Trás-os-Montes who came to live one day in Monchique. It was she who taught me the adufe rhythms – ritmo de passo and ritmo de roda – whenever I begged for alms. When I took leave of the Convento do Desterro to find my papai, Senhora Baptista celebrated by playing her adufe as I rode by her on the streets of Monchique. She sang an old song of her adufe not being played with her hand but with a golden ring, a gift from her heart:

> *Este pandeiro qu'eu toco não se toca com a mão,*
> *toca-se com anel d'ouro, prenda do meu coração.*

Here, in Scarborough, without an adufe, I beat my fingers on the tea-table, the bedpost, the cover of a book – whatever I could find and whenever my papai and mamãe weren't attending to me, because they forbid me to drum my fingers. To be sure, papai would still my hands if he caught me. He would mutter something about it being impolite, not to mention hoydenish. But then, one afternoon, it being the day of the summer solstice, 1815, I heard the strongest of heartbeats – tah-tah da-dum, tah-tah da-dum – summoning me below stairs.

I sneaked out of doors, into the small kitchen garden, where I beheld a most astonishing sight. My papai's valet, MacTavish, wore a brass drum, the shape of a gigantic pot, resting high up on his left hip. This drum, so similar to the caixa used by the Portuguese military, hung suspended from a leather strap that he wore over his right shoulder. With a stick in each hand, he beat the drum with the air and spirit of a valiant soldier, making a tempest of sounds of which I had never heard before.

'Viva! MacTavish,' I greeted him when he had done. 'Is that your caixa?'

'Ay, ay – 'tis my bres drume.'

MacTavish told me that when he was just a lad of nine years, he enlisted in the army as a drummer boy after lying about his age. He came from a poor family of ten children, and his parents reasoned that one less bairn to feed would mean more parritch an' broo of broth for the others. He and two other young lads in the village enlisted at the same time, eager to wear a smart uniform and to eat tasty chum in the army – mighty English roast beef – these sorts of things being promised to them by a jolly Captain MacAdoo, who, by beat of drum, raised volunteers for a regiment of Foot Guards.

A drum-major taught MacTavish and the other lads the drum signals – march, alarm, approach, assault, battle, retreat and so forth. Why, there were even drum beats to signal the taverns to stop serving ale to the soldiers, or to signal the idle women, they being camp followers, to take their leave. And every so often they had to drum out a miscreant from the army with the Rogue's March. According to the drum-major, the French Army enlisted boys as young as seven years to be drummer boys, and many years ago, the British Army had done the same.

'I'm five, and that's nearly seven.' I counted on my fingers. 'Could I be a drummer boy?'

'Ye're a wee bit bairn wi' wee bit han's. Listen,' he removed his drum, 'Ah'll tell ye a' aboot Mary Ann Talbot instead.'

I learnt the strange story of Miss Talbot, who claimed that, as a youth, she had been disguised as a foot-boy against her will by a certain Captain Bowen, and she had served in the army as a drummer boy. As an eyewitness to the siege of Valenciennes, she observed many a soldier on both sides swallow fire. She said the drummer boys had been ordered to keep a continuous roll despite the cries and confusion on the battlefield.

'Och! The lass murgullied the drume roll, nae doot.' He shook his head.

'Murgullied?'

'The lass bungled the drume roll. 'Tis true that only lads make gude drummers.'

I scoffed at his maxim, when nothing could stop the rhythm that poured out of my soul. I snatched the sticks from him, and I began to beat the skin of the drum in the same pattern he had done and without bungling it. This shocked MacTavish to see a wee bit lassie striking a bres drume. But soon he clapped his hands and stamped his feet to the beat – tap-tap tah-too, tap-tap tah-too, tap-tap tah-too, tap-tap tah-too. Amazed by my brilliant display of primitive drumming, MacTavish promised to teach me the drum signals, but only if my papai agreed to it.

The day next, I advised MacTavish that papai had granted my request to become a drummer boy and that I could commence my lessons that very afternoon if I didn't practise more than half-an-hour. I tried my utmost to sound convincing, knowing that my papai and mamãe had walked out and that their stroll would take – oh yes – exactly half-an-hour.

MacTavish looked askance at me. 'Ye're a bardy bairn. Ah'll speak wi' the Colonel aboot it.'

'But you cannot now,' I shook my finger at him. 'Papai is doing his manly duty. He took mamãe for an airing.'

Fortunately for me, MacTavish's suspicions gave way to his passion for drumming. 'Ah'll meet wi' ye oot in the yaird,' said he.

There, under our Scots pine, my first lesson covered something called 'technique' – a fancy word, methinks, for holding the sticks properly and for standing upright with my left heel jammed into the hollow of my right foot. In the upper or left hand, one must position the stick firmly between the thumb and two middle fingers and rest it on the third finger above the middle joint, while in the lower or right hand, one must hold the stick with the whole hand, the little finger gripping it firmly like one does with a sword.

Next, my maestro demonstrated how to perform a long roll – rat-tat tat-tat, rat-tat tat-tat – and a stroke roll. He placed his bres drume on a footstool where I could reach it and practise the rolls. And once those beats became easy and familiar to me, he taught me how to close a roll with two heavy strokes with the upper hand, followed by two strokes with the lower hand, quickening the strokes each time till the roll was closed – rat-tat tat-tat t-rrr-r-r-r rrr-r-r-r-rrr.

Eager for my second lesson, I met with MacTavish the following 'Soonday', and he taught me the open flam and the close flam – a-ra a-tat-a-ra a-tat – all of which I learnt quickly. To challenge me, he demonstrated two drum signals – advance and retreat. He had no sooner done so, than papai stalked into the garden. Unbeknown to me, papai had returned early from his stroll with mamãe.

'Sir!' MacTavish saluted him soldier-like with a pull of his cap.

Papai cast a severe look at me. 'Sofia-Elisabete, did I not refuse your request to become a drummer boy? 'Tis not proper for a young lady to be a drummer.'

'Please, papai, please.' I stamped my feet – left-right-left-right – in a most unladylike manner.

'Permission denied, again.' He turned to rail at his man. 'Confound it, MacTavish! I am the master of this house, yet I find I'm running down the stairs and then back up the stairs because of your drum signals. I've no idea if I'm supposed to be advancing or retreating.'

'Colonel, Ah've faithfully discharged my dooty an' teached the lassie a guid drume beatin',' MacTavish spoke with his usual dry manner.

'What duty?'

'Sir?' MacTavish shrugged, his eyes twinkling.

Papai turned round to scowl at me. 'Why, you rascal pup. Prepare to be court-martialled little drummer boy.'

Alarmed, I tossed the sticks to MacTavish, and I took to my heels, my papai uttering a dreadful oath or two behind me, for he had stepped on one of Tin-Key's turds in the garden. 'Confound it! That pug is getting turnspit duty,' thundered he whenever he stepped on Tin-Key's turds. Mamãe would always joke that the entire town could hear him and that the town-folk would say, 'Hark! The Colonel must've stepped on another turd to-day.'

I duly appeared for my court-martial in papai's study, where he questioned me concerning my bad habit of lying, not to mention my hoydenish behaviour. In my defence, I pleaded that I never really lied, but rather, I helped the truth along whenever it needed it. To be sure, this argument neither pleased nor persuaded him, and so he withheld my goose-grog at dinner that day, and the day next and the day after that.

'Papai, I wish for goose-grog again. Please?' begged I. But my bitter complaints over the loss of my goose-grog failed to sway him.

'It is your punishment,' he reminded me. 'The alternative would be a good flogging with the cat o' nine tails, so which would it be, drummer boy?'

'By gock, the army this is not,' mamãe shook her finger at papai. 'You daren't tease her in such a coarse manner.'

'But...' Papai had no sooner uttered a word of protest, than mamãe held up her hand to silence him.

'Now, then,' she turned to me in earnest, 'your father will never use the cat on you; for, if he does, I shall use the cat on him.'

Papai waggled his brows at her. 'Madam, I wonder if perhaps you meant the wildcat?'

Mamãe goggled her eyes and pointed her chin at me for some reason, and I wondered why parents must act so silly at times.

One afternoon, while Maddison, my mamãe's maid, and I strolled near Quay Street, I observed papai leaving the chemist's and placing a flask inside his coat pocket. I waved, I jumped, I hallooed to gain his attention, but he acknowledged this hoyden not and thereafter ducked into The Golden Ball for a prime ale – the best thing for his health as he was wont to say. When the time for dinner arrived and we had taken our places at table, I discovered the reason papai had been skulking in town.

'Colonel, where were you this afternoon?' mamãe inquired with an arched brow. 'Gadding about as usual?'

'Mrs Fitzwilliam, you are looking at a man who takes pleasure in gadding about.'

'I saw papai gadding about to-day.' I giggled at papai who nearly spilt his wine on the table.

'Oh? Where was this?' wondered mamãe.

'Near Quay Street. Papai went to the…'

'My dear Sofia-Elisabete,' exclaimed papai. 'You shall ruin my little surprise.'

'What surprise? Oh, tell me, tell me, papai,' I gazed at him with curiosity.

Papai gulped down his Madeira, and he became thoughtful. 'I am now of the mind…to grant your request to learn the drum signals – yes, yes. I shall purchase a small drum more appropriate for your wee stature.'

I jumped down from my chair with alacrity to kiss papai's hand. 'You're the best of papais,' I told him. With great tenderness of feeling, he chucked me under my chin. Mamãe bit her lip, and she tapped her fingers hoyden-like on the table, no doubt wondering why papai had changed his mind of a sudden.

Ere long papai presented me with a small drum and small drum sticks with small buttons on the ends. MacTavish tightened the calf skin head to create a crisp sound. He slung the drum strap round my neck, and he checked the length of the drum carriage, ensuring it rested on my left thigh such that when I bent my knee, the drum balanced on it.

Equipped with my wee drum, I mastered the drum rolls – faint roll, faint stroke, hard roll, hard flam, stroke and flam, half drag, single drag, double drag, &c. – and the drum signals, including the Rogue's March, Troop, Retreat, General, Dinner Call and the Taptoo. MacTavish declared me a musical prodigy, a true musitioner, and he taught me the drum beating for the 'Grenadier's March', 'The Female Drummer' and 'Rule, Brittania'.

Mamãe took great pride in my drumming skills, and she would sometimes ask me to beat the Dinner Call to save our old butler from having to search for papai out of doors, where he sat under his Scots pine thinking those great thoughts of his. Like a true army man, as soon as he heard the Dinner Call, he would hasten within. 'Where are my pease on a trencher and mighty roast beef?' he would joke.

Once, when papai disappeared in the evening and mamãe wished him home, she shook me awake. 'We need to find your papai,' whispered she. I rubbed my sleepy eyes, wondering why mamãe seemed beside herself with worry. In the gloom of the night, we drove up and down the streets in our hired hackney, with a window let down, she peering into the dark alleys near Quay Street, I beating the Taptoo – the signal to retire to quarters. Sure enough, papai shuffled out of a public-house. Mamãe told him to get into our hackney, and get into it he did, albeit against his will. 'I shan't be henpecked, I shan't,' grumbled he. I thought I had dreamt it all. But the next morning when I awoke, papai lay splayed on the ground near my bed, stinking of the wicked liquor. I never did ask mamãe about our nocturnal quest, and I think she preferred that I didn't.

With my parents at odds with each other for several days, I turned to spying on MacTavish. One afternoon I hid behind the Scots pine, from where I secretly observed MacTavish flirting with Maddison. He followed her round the garden, beating his drum most passionately and singing 'Hot Stuff', an army song. When he had done serenading her about stuff, he issued her a challenge.

'Dance a reel wi' me, lassie,' he pressed her. 'Are ye afraid o' my Scottish might?'

'Ye doan't freeghten me wi' yer wee stuff,' Maddison replied with an insolent coolness ere she stalked away.

'Viva! MacTavish.' I jumped in front of him, which made him start. I begged him to show me the drum beating for 'Hot Stuff', but he coloured and said I was too proper a young lassie to learn an army drinking-song, and besides, my papai would drumhead court-martial him in the garden if he did. This confused me, when the song rallied the British troops, did it not? 'Advance, Grenadiers. And let fly your Hot Stuff!'

'MacTavish, did you let fly hot stuff in the war?'

'Na.'

'Did your friends let fly hot stuff?'

'Na, na. Blown to atoms, they were, by an exploding shell.' MacTavish explained that drummer boys had to assist with carrying the wounded to the regimental surgeon and thus they were exposed to fire on the battlefield. And that is how his young friends had perished and never got a chance to become soldiers. He and his friends had gone to war for the glory of Britain and a' that, but instead, he had buried what had remained of them. When he became old enough to serve as bât-man to an officer, they assigned him to the Colonel – the Colonel having been a lieutenant colonel at the time – and he has served the Colonel ever since.

I wrinkled my brow. 'Twas difficult for me to understand how one could lose friends in an instant from a shell. With an inward shrug, my thoughts soon returned to drumming and my wish to be the best drummer boy – nay, the best drummer girl. Now that I understood drum notes and their proportion to one another, and the rules relative to time, I practised the method of carrying the drum while marching a quick step behind 'Drum-Major' MacTavish as he strutted to and fro like a coxcomb, marking the beat with a cane that he held high in his right hand.

One Sunday, as MacTavish and I marched round the garden beating our drums, we nearly stumbled upon papai, who lay sprawled underneath his Scots pine, dreaming with his eyes half-closed.

'MacTaveeshhh, pray lead me to...to...the front door. I do believe the house is backwards,' papai rose to grip his man's shoulder. 'I wish to be at home now.'

'Sir, ye're at whome, just nae within.'

'Confound your Scotticisms, MacTaveeshhh, I wish to be at home,' demanded papai.

'Sir, ye're in Scarbro' an' at whome already.'

'No-no-no…impudent scoundrel,' papai wagged his finger at him. 'I know a Scots pine when I see one. I dare say I am not within.'

'Exackly, sir.' MacTavish sighed as he removed his bres drume. 'Aweel, aweel, did ye meet wi' Mr O. P. Umm to-day?'

'To be sure I did.' Papai nodded slowly. 'He is a great friend of mine.'

'Ay, a raal jintilman that one,' MacTavish drily said.

MacTavish led papai to the house, where I could hear papai bellow, 'A-a-a-aggie, I'm with-i-i-in now.'

The next evening Father O came to see us, or rather, my papai, the two of them settled in papai's study for a long while. I had never seen papai brought so low, and it frightened me. When I asked why papai seemed unhappy, mamãe turned grave as a judge, and she motioned for me to sit by her.

'Human happiness is transient – it comes and it goes – and such is life,' advised she.

This puzzled me. 'Where does it go?'

Mamãe became wistful. 'It goes inside your heart, where you keep it safe, and where you are reminded of it from time to time until you wish for it again.'

'Do things remind you of Elias?'

'Very much so,' mamãe drew her arm round me. 'My son died, but I have many a happy memory of him. After I had mourned him, I wished for happiness again when I met you and your papai.'

'Will papai wish for happiness again?'

'Oh, indeed,' mamãe brightened. 'We each of us must endure life's changes with fortitude, faith and prayer. Your papai sometimes forgets this and loses his faith. He may be flawed, but he loves us with all his heart. So "let us God's word obey, 'love one another', be happy whilst we may."'

And that is what I did. I waited and loved, I waited and loved, until papai regained his health and happiness. It seemed as though an age had passed ere he could muster a smile or tease me again with a gooseberry kiss. It occurred to me that papai's gloom was connected to that hateful man, Mr O. P. Umm. 'Adeus! says I', because I never wished Mr O. P. Umm to return to our Scarborough abode.

One morning, after breakfast, papai suggested that he and I go for an airing. While we strolled the sands of the serene North Bay, a bright white arc appeared on the horizon in the thinning fog bank.

'Look, papai, it's a Scar-bow. Viva! Scar-bow.'

Papai turned sentimental. 'Perhaps it portends a new resolve for me.'

'Will you be happy again?' I wondered aloud.

'O, filha da minha alma,' he reassured me, the daughter of his soul. 'Don't you know – I recently discovered, whilst we sojourned in the old wood, that I have a half-brother and half-sister?'

My eyes became wide with wonder. 'Hurrah! How lucky you found them.'

'I guess I am rather lucky,' mused he. 'That's why they call me Lucky Fitzer.'

'Papai, I wish I had half of a brother.' Methinks I had uttered something clever to make papai laugh for the first time in many weeks.

As we continued our stroll on the sandy strip, hand in hand, my attention became drawn to the waves nearby that rolled to and fro gracefully upon the shore in a rhythm of their own. Could I ever produce that soothing sound on my drum? Determined to find out, I gathered some twigs, imagining how much softer it would sound than a drum stick. I then recalled the adufe and the seeds that rattled between the two skins. With great care, I scooped up two handfuls of pebbles and crushed shells that papai stored in his pockets for me.

Once I had described to mamãe what was fixed in my mind, she sewed tiny pouches for the pebbles and shells, and she tied each pouch to a sturdy stick. She gathered the twigs I had brought her, tying them into two bundles shaped like whisks. 'Let us surprise your papai on his birth-day next week,' suggested mamãe. Together we practised in secret one of our favourite songs, my mamãe and I singing the beautiful melody while I worked out a unique drum beating using my different sticks.

The day of my papai's birth-day having arrived, Father O toasted him at dinner, wishing him many happy returns of this day, and we feasted on dressed lobster and papai's favourite apple charlotte. When we had done, mamãe beckoned everyone to the drawing room for a musical performance. She helped me with the strap of my drum, whereupon we began to sing 'Tree on the Hill', the pebbles and shells creating a pleasant sound on the skin of my drum and marking the rhythm in 4/4 time – p-rum p-tush p-rum p-tish, pa-da dum-dum ta-tishhh, pa-da dum-dum ta-tishhh.

> *On yonder hill there stands a tree;*
> *Tree on the hill, and the hill stood still...*

For an interlude, I switched to the twig whisks, which mamãe had placed on a small table near me. I stroked the whisks in a crescendo roll, followed by a diminuendo roll, bringing to mind the advance and retreat of a zephyr that makes the needle-like leaves quiver on a Scots pine. Papai always said it is then that the wind can be heard. 'Its susurration is ancient and divine and, for me, salubrious,' he would explain. He called it his wind music, and he claimed that it inspired many a waking thought for him and that these waking thoughts blended into his dreams.

> *And on the branch there was a nest;*
> *Nest on the branch, branch on the tree,*
> *tree on the hill, and the hill stood still...*

Using the pebbles and shells this time for a second interlude, I conjured up the crackling of an egg shell as the baby bird secured his freedom and was born, marking his natal day.

> *And in the egg there was a bird;*
> *Bird in the egg, egg in the nest,*
> *nest on the branch, branch on the tree,*
> *tree on the hill, and the hill stood still...*

I closed with a good roll using the twig whisks, evoking the sound of a sudden rush of windswept pine needles on the ground. Twwwoooooshhh. And then, slowly, I scratched the surface of the skin of the drum several times with the whisks – tsshk tsshk tsshk – to recall the scattering of a few errant pine needles. Our performance at an end, I removed my drum, and I curtseyed very prettily to my adoring audience of two. 'Bravo!' papai cheered me. He hoisted me up to kiss my cheek, and he teased me by tapping my nose with one of the twig whisks. With his shiny eyes and broad grin, he summoned up an earthly happiness, albeit a fleeting one, which did not signify; for, the eternal joy of music was now and for ever locked deep in his soul.

Chapter Five

World in the Moon

MY FIRST ROPE DANCE, thinks I, was with my cousin Anne de Bourgh, whom I called cousin Annie. Papai referred to her as our crazy country cousin, she being an eccentric who lived with Lady Catherine far away in the land of Kent. There, the mother and daughter lived on an estate called Rosings, its manor-house boasting over a hundred glazed windows, its grounds bedecked with parterres and curiously clipt hedges. One day, though, Annie had had enough of Xanthippe, it being the name she used for her overbearing mother, and with cunning and dare, she ran away, escaping somehow in her ladyship's elegant equipage. And come to Scarborough she did in the beginning of July 1815, for she had convinced herself that she was in love with my papai.

All remained calm the first evening because mamãe, being a good hostess, made her guest feel welcomed. However, the next day, mamãe departed for Bunberry school to attend to her students, and while she was from home, the quarrels began. They started after dinner to be exact. We had retired to the drawing room, when Annie announced her intent to exhibit for us. With a sigh, papai motioned to the pianoforte and advised her to have at it then. On a sudden, Annie executed a kind of sideways somersault – like a human wheel

– where she landed on her hands, her feet high in the air, and she
ended the trick on her feet. I thought it brilliant, whereas papai
thought it ridiculous – nay, scandalous – and he goggled, as did I, at
the buckskins that she wore underneath her skirts.

'What the deuce! Did you steal my buckskins? I shall never wear
those again if they are,' thundered he.

With a smirk at papai, Annie introduced us to two comical-
looking puppets – a girl puppet and a mamma puppet.

'Hurrah! A puppet-show.' I clapped my hands.

Papai shook his head in disbelief. 'One wonders, Miss Hoyden,
how long you can hide in Scarborough before Lady Catherine
finds you.'

'You daren't write to my mamma,' squeaked the girl puppet. 'If
you do, cousin Fizzy, I shall tell everyone our little secret when you
mistook me for your chambermaid.'

'Stop calling me Fizzy.'

'By the bye, cousin Fizzy,' the girl puppet tapped her chin. 'I
cannot help but wonder why "Senga" is embroidered on the inside
of your buckskins. I do believe that's an anagram, a half-palindrome,
for "Agnes", is it not?'

'Confound it!' Papai coloured a deep red as he strangled the girl
puppet. 'Those were my favourite buckskins that Mrs Fitzwilliam
gifted me with.'

'Gak…gaaak…gak,' the girl puppet half-choked.

Mamma puppet shook her head. 'Tut, tut. It seems I was in the
right, nephew, when I warned you against this marriage to an old
widow. Why, she's at least seven years older than you, is she not? You
don't wear the breeches in this house. For shame!'

'If you weren't such an old tabby, I would knock you on the head.'
Papai shook his fist at mamma puppet.

What a hullabaloo it was. Now, believe it or not, papai did not
have the heart to send Annie back to Rosings, even after she stole
his favourite buckskin breeches and goaded him to madness with
her puppets. Nor did he do so after she tossed a handful of quaking
pudding into his face, when he claimed that women like her knew

nought of life except how to make a pudding. And nor did he do so after she thumped him on the backside with a bed warming pan, when he told her to make herself useful by scrubbing the kitchen-pots.

I hear you cry, 'Why ever not, when she's a little crack-brained?' What happened was this. The rector, Mr Collins, appeared at our door like a common thief-taker, he having been sent by his patroness, Lady Catherine, to seize her spinster daughter as if she were a common criminal. He stood thus with handcuffs to remove Annie by force from the premises until papai, who felt a thousand pities for his cousin, placed her under his protection, claiming that Lord Matlock, my avô, had decreed it so. Annie, with tears in her eyes, expressed surprise at papai's show of mercy, and from that moment on, she embraced him as her champion.

Annie became a member of our family, and she proved to be the best of cousins to me. Together we did many a hoydenish thing, much to papai's despair. Annie taught me how to turn a somersault, how to stand on my head and how to cross my toes. She taught me the art of mummery, assuring me that our second-rate mummery would bring papai immense pleasure and happiness, and given his wide-eyed wonderment, I think it did. She taught me her favourite songs – 'Pease Pudding Hot' and 'The Jolly Ploughman' – and we would sing 'too-ran-nan, too-ran-nan, too-ran-nan nanty na' all day long, which drove papai to distraction.

But the most diverting thing she taught me was how to walk across a rope without falling. She had discovered the secret of rope dancing from Maddison, my mamãe's lusty maid, and she revealed that secret to me, having first obtained permission from mamãe, who declared that the tight rope must be no higher than ten inches and be strung across the lawn to prevent injury. At first, we obeyed mamãe's rules. I learnt how to walk across the rope this way while playing my drum. Later, whenever mamãe quitted town to attend to her students at Bunberry school, Annie raised the rope three feet high, and I practised 'roasting the pig' by laying myself upon the rope, holding it with my hands and with my feet crossed, and ever so swiftly, turning round and round.

'Cousin Annie, did you run away from your mamma?'

Annie nodded. 'To be sure I did. Ever since I was a child, she never let me do what I pleased unless I begged for permission first. Enough, says I.'

'I've run away two times, Annie.' I recalled how I had hid in the Pemberley stables and later atop my avô's turret.

'Twice?' Annie questioned me with raised brows. 'Well, when you run away next time, just make sure your papa knows exactly where you went. Always leave a note on your pillow. That's the first rule for running away. And when he comes to get you, tell him your demands.'

'My demands?'

'Tell him what you want and how you won't return home unless you get it.'

One afternoon, mamãe and Annie presented me with a set of proper boy's clothes to march in and play my drum. 'Such foolery,' exclaimed papai, because only boys were breeched at this age. Mamãe, who could be just as headstrong as any man, refused to give up her idea. She and Annie had sewn me a white cambric shirt trimmed with ruffles, and nankeen breeches that buttoned above the waist onto a short red jacket with two rows of brass buttons. To complete the ensemble, they had bought a striking red military-style cap with tassel from the milliner, white stockings from the hosier and black slippers with straps from the shoe-maker.

'You daren't cut her hair, or else...' papai shook his finger at mamãe.

'Or else what?' mamãe teased him, a pair of scissors in her hand. 'There, there, now, I promise you I shan't cut off all her hair. I simply wish to give you a small lock as a remembrance of this special day.'

'Her hair is so silky and soft.' A tear formed in papai's eye as he beheld the lock in his hand.

Mamãe snipped another small lock for Annie, who would be departing two days hence, because my cousin wished to return home to Rosings. Annie had exchanged letters with her two pied ponies, both of whom missed her deeply, at least that's what I think she wanted me to believe, but we both knew that a lonely Lady Catherine had written her the letters, expressing her wish to see her daughter again before she, her ladyship, died someday, whenever that would be. 'Adeus, cousin Annie!' cried I. Upon her leave-taking in late July, I lost my first true friend, and the sorrow of it made me most melancholy. Papai worried about me moping round the house, and during breakfast one morning, he hinted at a grand surprise for me.

'Oh, tell me, tell me,' begged I.

Papai's eyes twinkled. 'We shall host a certain important personage.'

'Papai, who is it?'

'It's Pico Robinson.'

Ai de mim! My heart sank to my toes upon hearing that my tormentor Pico Robinson would visit us in Scarborough and thereby ruin what remained of my summer.

Mamãe poured me another cup of chocolate. 'Is it not great news?'

'Não, não, não.' I pushed the chocolate away.

'My dear girl,' papai set down his morning newspaper. 'What are you about? You were great play-fellows with Pico and his brother during our stay in the old wood.'

'I hate him hugeously. Please, papai, please make him go *whoam*.'

'Manners, Sofia-Elisabete,' he scolded me. 'He is your cousin.'

'He *isna* my cousin.' I scowled at papai.

'Tom Robinson is my half-brother,' papai revealed to me. 'How lucky you are, for did you not wish for half of a brother? Well, now, you have half of a boy cousin, who, being our near relation, is just as good in my mind.'

I gaped at papai in disbelief. 'Gaaaaaahhh,' shouted I, and I took to my heels. I bounded up the stairs to my bedchamber, where I beat a defiant To Arms – the drum roll for raising the alarm that the enemy was upon us. Papai berated me for my unsoldierly conduct, and for the first time ever, he said he would confiscate my drum as punishment. At first, I knew not what he meant. When he took away my drum, only then did I realise that my drum was being sent to gaol.

'It i'n't fair.' I ran the length of the passage after papai. 'It's my drum! It's my drum!' I sought the comfort of mamãe's arms where I complained of my mistreatment, but she instructed me on something called etiquette. She said that a true Christian politeness comes from a pure heart – one that is good and kind.

'If you wish to be a proper lady, you must exercise the goodness of your heart every day and extend the gentle courtesies of life to everyone, including Pico,' advised she.

I turned away in a pout.

'Listen to me, child. Pico is our guest. A good hostess must always see to the comfort and happiness of her guests, and she must never insult them or be rude to them,' continued she.

'He calls me nincompoop.'

'Rudeness must not be met with rudeness,' returned she.

But I refused to subscribe to her maxims.

Ere long my half of a cousin Pico, he being a whole five years older than me, strutted into our drawing room all dressed in the style with his fancy high-waist blue breeches and blue jacket – these things having been paid for by my avô. He bowed genteel-like, presenting mamãe with a nosegay. She complimented him on what a handsome boy he was.

'How are ter?' He grinned at me, his eyes gleaming with mischief, his plans set into motion on how best to torture me with spiders – I was sure of it.

I sneered at him, which only made him laugh, and when I deigned to give my half of a cousin a quick curtsey, he laughed at me again. Papai boasted of the wonders of Scarborough, and he remarked how glad I was for Pico's visit. 'Sofia-Elisabete has many an exciting adventure planned for the two of you,' added he. *Impossible,* I told myself. I shot a confused glance at papai, wondering why he was allowed to lie, but I was not.

Later, after we had supped, mamãe did the unthinkable and asked Pico to entertain us with a story. I suppose she had no choice when she aimed to be a good hostess to our guest. We sat near Pico, who struck a silly pose leaning on the side of the chimney-piece, as he recited his favourite story, one that had been written an age ago by Francis Godwin, Bishop of Llandaff, about Domingo Gonsales's strange voyage to the world in the moon. Listening to Pico's boyish version of the tale, I realised he was a brilliant story-teller, and I begrudged him nought, for did I not pride myself on being a diverting and charming story-teller whenever I chose to be?

Pico recounted how the young Spanish nobleman, Domingo Gonsales, defied his parents and ran away from home to go warring, much to their unhappiness. 'He fought the Prince o' Orange an' his troops. "Gie me yer munny," demanded Gonsales, but the prince's trooper replied, "I'll gie thee nowt." So Gonsales dispatch'd him good wi' his pistol – the man's blood flowin' like a riv'let – an' Gonsales plunder'd the man's munny an' other stuff worth two hundred ducats.'

'Papai, why did he patch the trooper's clothes?'

'I shall tell you later,' whispered papai, but I knew this meant he would never tell me.

Pico described how Domingo Gonsales returned to Seville and got into a heap of trouble. 'Gonsales fought a duel wi' pistols an' he killed the man – booffft! – so escape to Lisbon he did. Munny he needed now, so he left his wife an' brats to go a-tradin' for diamonds, em'ralds an' pearls in the East Indies, but on the way whoam he took ill.'

'Mamãe, what's an emerald?'

''Tis a green gemstone,' mamãe showed me her sparkling green wedding-ring.

Pico continued on, telling us how Domingo Gonsales did some rusticating for a year to improve his health and how he puzzled his wits together to become the first flying man. 'Gonsales lived on the Isle of St. Helens, wheer he found huge flocks of wild gansas wi' claws like an eagle. He harness'd twenty-five gansas to carry him inside an engine he had made.'

'Papai, what's an engine?'

'It's a machine, a device,' papai told me. 'His might have resembled a wooden chair – something for him to sit on.'

Pico described how Domingo Gonsales set sail for Spain, when an English fleet attacked his ship. Afore his ship crashed on the rocks an' smashed everyone to a million bloody bits, Gonsales, who had harness'd his gansas to the engine, escap'd by flyin' to Cape Verde. "Lo there!" cried he. Stinkin' savages wi' long staves charg'd towards 'em, an' so the gansas took flight again, this time to the top of a pike, fifteen miles high, above the clouds, the gansas a-puffin' an' a-blowin' an' ready to burst from a' the hard work.'

I turned to papai. 'Are clouds soft and furry?'

'Perhaps one day I shall take you to see a cloud, my dear child.' Papai winked at me. 'Go on, Pico.'

'Well, after a bit o' rest for the gansas, summat odd happened. "O my stars," shouted Gonsales. The gansas struck bolt upright, an' they drifted higher an' higher, floatin' in the air. Gonsales believ'd that wi'out his true Spanish might, he would ha' died o' fear.'

'But where did they float to? Oh, tell me, tell me,' pleaded I.

Pico revealed that Domingo Gonsales and his gansas floated in the air for what seemed an eternity – but was just eleven days – surrounded by a sky lit up with bright stars. On the twelfth day, they descended on the world in the moon. 'He came 'pon the Lunars – moon men, moon women an' moon children – who spoke in tunes. Fal de ral de ra. Some o' the moon men stood ten feet tall, an' some o' the ancient-lookin' ones were one thousand years old an' they stank o' rotten cheese.'

Pico told us of a perfect world, a paradise, where the Lunars knew not pain, hunger, murder or thievery. 'Thieves? Pfft.' They needed not lawyers, as there was no contention amongst them. 'Lawyers? Pfft.' They needed not doctors that much, as the air was pure and temperate; for, it never rained, and never did a wind blow on the moon. 'Doctors? Pfft. The Lunars, being good Christian folk, lived wi' love, peace an' friendship. If a moon child grew up wick'd, they'd trade him for a child in America, which is wheer they got the tobacco for the moon men to smoke.'

And so Pico concluded the story of Domingo Gonsales, who journeyed back to earth, it taking him a whole nine days to do so. 'He landed in China, near the city o' Pequin, wheer a devilish set o' men arrested him for being a magician. But he learnt to speak summat called Mandarin wi' the hopes he could return to Spain.' Pico bowed to our applause, declaring his intent to see the world and have mighty adventures just like his hero Domingo Gonsales did.

That night, after we children had gone to bed, I dreamt of a voyage on the high seas, and when our vessel hit a gale, Pico and I climbed atop a gigantic gansa to fly to the world in the moon. 'Viva!' That is how I greeted the moon children who gathered round us, dressed in their moon-coloured clothes. 'Pray let us exchange Pico for a well-behaved moon child?' I suggested to them. And so we did. A pretty moon boy climbed atop the gansa with me, and we descended to earth where we landed in the countryside near Seville, for my aim had been off. There, I found a pot of chocolate ducats half buried in a field, and I bought us pão hespanol and butter that had been made in Alcalá. We lodged that evening on an old palheiro – a haystack with a wood pole in the centre – and when the sky darkened and the bright moon appeared, we could make out Pico-in-the-Moon. My cousin would live there for ever, or at least for one thousand years, unless the Lunars exchanged him for a child in America given his wicked humour and bad manners.

The next morning at breakfast mamãe continued her attentions to Pico, and she surprised him with his favourite hasty pudding all nicely dished up with a hole in the middle containing the melted butter and treacle. We never ate pudding for breakfast, and so it bewildered me why all of a sudden my parents thought it the tastiest thing in the world.

'O tasty hasty! O hasty tasty!' Papai winked at us. 'Observe my technique. I shall spoon some pudding from the brim of the plate, after which I shall plunder the sauce hole – mind you, without demolishing it – and as quick as can be, I shall devour the spoonful of hot pudding. Mmm…what triumph.'

'Papai, I bet a ha'penny that I shan't ruin my sauce hole.'

'Done! I'll take your bet.'

I grasped my spoon, and I set about to fortify my sauce hole with extra pudding.

Pico scrutinised the walls of my pudding fortress. 'Yer need a drawbridge for yer castle.'

'A drawbridge?'

'A bridge for the troopers an' their hosses to cross to get into the castle.' With his spoon, Pico smashed a part of the wall surrounding my butter and treacle, and the buttery brown liquid spilled forth, like a muddy moat oozing in my dish of pudding.

I gasped at his treachery. 'Why, you...you dunderhead.'

'Manners, Sofia-Elisabete,' papai reprimanded me. 'Apologise at once to your cousin.'

'Não.'

Mamãe cleared her voice. 'Sofia-Elisabete, must I remind you what a good hostess is?'

A dark cloud hovered over me, but my countenance soon brightened. 'I apologise, cousin Pico, for calling you a dunderhead. I ought not to call you a dunderhead. A dunderhead...'

Papai groaned at my insolence. 'Yes, yes – but I still win the bet. Where is my ha'penny?'

I, Sofia-Elisabete, being no stranger to losing bets with my papai, removed a ha'penny from my pinafore pocket. Papai snatched the coin from me, and he tossed up the coin ere he placed it inside his waist-coat pocket.

To my astonishment, Pico expressed his wish to play at being drum-major, he having heard from MacTavish that I was a true musitioner. 'An excellent idea, indeed. The two of you shall become good play-fellows,' mamãe rejoiced at our truce, and she urged papai to give me back my drum. Eager to show my parents that I could be a good hostess, if I turned my mind to it, I dressed in my stylish nankeen breeches and red jacket to impress my guest. But Pico laughed at me and my boy's clothes. 'Yer a rum 'un,' declared he.

Pico commanded me to beat my drum and to march behind him. So obey him I did. On a sudden, papai stalked into the garden to confiscate my drum, this time as punishment for drumming out Pico from the army with the Rogue's March. 'It's my drum! It's my drum!' cried I, as I ran round and round the garden. *Enough,* I told myself. I refused this time to give up my cherished drum. 'Manso! Be still!' papai caught me by the arm. The two of us struggled over the drum, he winning the battle in the end, given his might.

I stamped about and I sulked, I stamped about and I sulked, making sure everyone knew when I was sulking. That's the trick, you know, to get one's way by being a highly visible sulker and not hiding oneself in one's room or behind a curtain in the drawing room. Papai, who soon tired of this stamping about and sulking, ordered me to walk out with Maddison and Pico, for they were going to the harbour in the South Bay to buy turbot and soles at the cobles that arrived on the sands each day.

In my childish mood, I shuffled down the street behind my two companions. Once we reached the sands Maddison set about to inspect the fresh fish for our dinner, while we children took turns peering through a spyglass to count the number of sails in the harbour. When it came my turn again, I started at the sight of someone who resembled Sister Lisbet. I had not visited with my guardian angel in a long time. Had she forgotten me?

'What did ter see?'

I boggled for a second. 'I believe 'twas a dolphin.'

'Liar.' Pico snatched the spyglass from me. 'Gad zookers! It's Domingo Gonsales.'

There, on the pier, stood a Spaniard, mysterious and magnificent in a wide-brimmed hat pulled down to mask his face. He wore an embroidered jacket, breeches, black buckled shoes and a brown capa that he flourished like a torero in the bull ring ere he flung it over his left shoulder. Beside him, reaching for his arm, was a handsome señora dressed in a black velvet jacket and white silk skirt fringed with lace, her hair adorned with a high comb and a red flower, her white lace veil billowing in the wind. Who was this elegant lady? Why she had come to Scarborough, a most unlikely place for a Spanish noblewoman, especially one who looked like an angel on earth?

Pico and I raced each other to get to the pier first to meet his hero Domingo Gonsales. The two foreigners expressed their amusement at seeing me, a half-boy dressed in boy's clothes, approach them without an introduction. Pico performed a gallant bow, as did I. We stood there shyly with our caps in our hands, when, suddenly, Pico blurted out, 'How are ter?'

'Buenas tardes,' the Spanish lady dipped her chin. 'I am Doña Marisa, and this is my cortejo – my escort – Señor Gonzalez.'

I goggled my eyes at the man. 'Are you really Domingo Gonsales who flew to the moon?'

Señor Gonzalez lifted the brim of his hat to wink at me. 'No, but seeing how I am Sábado Gonzalez, I must surely be his primo, his cousin. What are your names?'

'I'm Pico, an' this is my cousin, Soofia-Eee.'

'Pico?' Señor Gonzalez stared at Pico's nose and then he laughed for whatever reason. He turned to peer at me. 'Are you a boy, un niño, or a girl, una niña?'

'I am a drummer girl,' declared I.

'A drummer girl?' Señor Gonzalez turned to his lady.

'Sofia es una tamborilera.' Doña Marisa fanned herself, her graceful movements enchanting everyone.

We learnt that the *Lapwing,* the packet to London, would sail on the morrow if the winds veered round, and our new Spanish friends would be gone with it. Doña Marisa explained that they came from the land of Seville, having travelled a great distance to find a special someone in Scarborough, and that their destination was now la luna – the moon! As we walked out on the sands behind them, Pico revealed a secret to me that he would serve as foot-boy to Señor Gonzalez and that he would sail away with them. He, Pico Robinson, was wild for adventure.

'Yer a namby-pamby girl an' canna goo wi' us,' taunted he.

I wished for adventure on the moon as much as he. 'I bet a ha'penny I can.' I stuck my tongue out at him.

'Done!' cried he.

I ran up beside the noble lady. 'Doña Marisa, please may I be your foot-boy?'

'Sí, I wish for you to be my foot-boy.' Doña Marisa smiled at me prettily, her eyes as bright as emeralds.

'Truly?' I bounced on my toes in excitement.

'Very much so. Hmm…Perhaps I should cut your hair tomorrow, so no one will know you are una niña.' She smoothed my tangled hair with her hand.

'Doña Marisa, may I bring my drum and tight rope?'

'A tight rope? Por qué?'

'I'm a rope dancer.' Methinks my explanation diverted Doña Marisa, who gave a hearty laugh and patted my cheek.

That evening, I dreamt again of the mysterious bolero dancer who had given birth to me. In my dream this time, she appeared as a friendly senhora dressed in a black velvet jacket, red sash and white silk skirt. She placed me as a bebê in the roda – the foundling turnbox wheel at the convent. 'Adeus, my child,' whispered she, patting my cheek. She took her leave, her castanets strongly marking the rhythm as she walked away, when she came to a sudden stop, her arms raised in a graceful attitude. 'Olé!' cried she, and she beckoned me with her pretty smile and bright emerald eyes. When I awoke the next morning, my secret wish to know who she was – a secret that I hid inside of my heart out of fear of my papai's wrath – now overwhelmed me for some reason.

Come mid-day mamãe told us that she was going to chapel for choir practise and that we should obey my papai. Pico and I shared a look, and once mamãe took her leave, we rushed upstairs to fetch our bundle of things and to dress ourselves – I, of course, in my boyish clothes and red capa. I left a note that Pico and I would fly up to the moon on gansas and that I wished for papai to come and get me there. Finding no one about, I sneaked into papai's study to locate my drum. Where could it be? Apre! Hey day! The drum sat on papai's desk as if it had been expecting me.

I met my fellow runaway out in the garden where I looked for my tight rope. But I had forgotten that one end of the rope was tied to our Scots pine. There, sitting in the shade with his eyes closed, papai leant against the pine, his mind travelling on some great highway of deep thought, as he was wont to say. Pico shook his head in bewilderment. 'I've niver seed a man who likes a tree that much or even thinks that much,' whispered he.

And so, without further ado, we connivers scurried down to the pier where Señor Gonzalez awaited us in a coble, the afternoon tide having begun to rise. 'Adeus, Scarborough!' cried I, my heart brimful of emotion as we were rowed out to sea. Once aboard the *Lapwing*, Señor Gonzalez led me to Doña Marisa's windowless fore-cabin where I would serve as her foot-boy.

Doña Marisa's sweet fragrance of blossoming myrtle filled the interior of the tiny cabin, reminding me of my homeland far away. While she hummed a Portuguese modinha or love song, she brushed my hair, dividing it into five locks, ere she tied each lock with gold thread. I closed my eyes while she snipped each lock, and when she had done, I glanced at the strange boy in the looking-glass.

'My papai will be angry with me.' I began to sniffle. 'He will take away my drum for ever.'

'No te preocupes. You needn't worry. Mira!' Doña Marisa held up a letter. 'I have already written to your father to explain everything.' She enclosed a lock of my hair ere she sealed the letter.

'Doña Marisa, are we going to la luna now?'

She became thoughtful. 'Sí, la luna. We shall go to the world in the moon.'

This piece of news cheered me, knowing I would see the moon at last. 'My papai will like it there. No one is sad or sick or angry on the moon.'

Doña Marisa's brow clouded. 'You believe that your father shall come for you?'

I nodded at her, knowing papai would read my note. And when he came for me on the moon in eleven days – because that's how long it took Domingo Gonsales to get there – I would make my demands, and believe you me, I had quite a few of them.

'Sí, cómo no. He will meet us there.' Doña Marisa half-smiled at me. 'Until then, we shall have many magical adventures together.'

We up anchored and set sail on the beauteous blue of the North Sea. I waited on deck for the gigantic gansas to fly us to the moon, but the gansas never did come for us. Perhaps the gansas wished for my papai to join us so that we could travel together to the moon? Once there, papai would surely be cured of his sadness and whatever else ailed him. But as the days passed, I began to wonder if papai was lost again.

Chapter Six
The Magic Oranges

My First Waterzooi, thinks I, was in Rotterdam, where we sojourned for a sennight while Doña Marisa took to her bed. My lady, or minha Senhora, which is how I sometimes addressed her in Portuguese, became terribly ill of a sudden. She blamed it on the insufferable heat and on the foul odours that arose from the canals. One day, she began to feel better. 'Tengo hambre,' said she. And so I, being a good foot-boy, hastened to fetch her a bowl of waterzooi, a fish and vegetable stew made with egg yolk, cream and broth. She pushed me away, grumbling about the disgusting fish odour, and thereafter buried her head half-way into a pot. 'Tonta!' her maid chided me, and she thrust the stinking pot into my hands.

Señor Gonzalez believed that his lady's mysterious illness began in London, where she bought livery for me and Pico, and that her condition worsened in Harwich, where we sat idle, waiting on the winds for five days. When the winds finally veered round, Captain Bridge, the commander of the *Prince of Orange*, led us in prayer, as was his custom, and only then did he give the signal to weigh anchor and to unfurl the sails. We were nearly three days out at sea in what became a miserable North Sea crossing for us passengers on a crowded packet-boat.

There, becalmed at sea, we floated in murky waters. I waited on deck under a cheerless sky, praying that the gansas would take us to the moon. But the gansas never came, nor did my papai. Things being so, I worried anew. I wished to speak with Doña Marisa concerning our voyage to the moon, but she refused to leave her cabin, except for an airing once or twice on the arm of her cortejo, Señor Gonzalez. Whenever I approached them, he would wave me away; hence, I sat on deck, wearing a gloomy face.

'There's them Spaniards,' Pico half-whispered to me. 'A pair o' landlubbers they are.'

'What's a landlubber?' asked I in my disagreeable mood.

'It's a looby who doesna like the sea, yer looby.' Pico pinched me.

'Yow!' I rubbed my arm, scowling at my cousin.

Pico proclaimed it a grand voyage, heedless of my misery. He befriended the Chief Mate, who told him many a brilliant story about Captain Bridge's derring-do's during the war, including the time the Captain attempted a dangerous landing amidst ice floes.

'The *Prince of Orange* shot the ice, and close to Cuxhaven pier it got, but it grounded on a sandbank, and the ice floes threatened to capsize it,' recounted the Chief Mate. 'We would have perished at sea if it had.'

'Gad zookers,' exclaimed Pico. 'What happened next?'

'There was nothing for it but to pray the *Prince of Orange* hadn't suffered damage. Once the tide ebbed, the Captain delivered the mail and collected the war despatches at Cuxhaven,' recalled the Chief Mate. 'Thereafter, we returned home, where the London papers called him a hero because everyone was desperate for news of the war.'

'Huzzah! Captain Bridge for ever.' Pico's broad grin diverted the Chief Mate.

That evening, I stood on deck, gazing at a big orange moon near the horizon.

'How many moons are there?' wondered I aloud, for I had seen the moon wear different colours – grey, blue, red, yellow, orange.

'There's many a kind of moon,' the husky voice of Captain Bridge interrupted my musings. 'Crescent moon, half-moon, full moon, gibbous moon, new moon – oh, and waxing or waning some are.'

'Are they different colours, Captain?'

'Oh, ay!' He winked at me.

In my mind the earth had all sorts of moons circling round at different times. But only one appeared each night, they each of them taking turns, or perhaps they stood watch at different times? I wondered which moon Domingo Gonsales had visited.

That night, I had trouble sleeping. Where, oh, where could those gansas be? Ai de mim! Having given up my hope to fly on a gansa, I determined that we must fly on our own to a moon. I closed my eyes to summon up my magical powers. A rush of wind swept me higher and higher and higher, but I dared not open my eyes or the magic would end. On a sudden, the flapping of a great many wings drew near, and I landed with a thud on a mound of soft feathers. I leant on the gansa's neck and wearily so, relieved that the gansas had come for us at last and we would reach a moon. And there, wrapped up in the warmth of my gansa, I dozed peacefully for the remainder of our flight.

'Wake up! Land ho!' Pico shook me.

I found myself sitting on a dock. I rubbed my sleepy eyes, wondering if our gansas had, indeed, taken us to a moon.

The tide having been favourable, we tacked up the reddish waters of a river to reach Helvoetsluys, where lived town-dwellers called Dutch. Doña Marisa pressed a lace handkerchief to her nose – 'qué mal olor' – and she declared this place unhealthful, for the canals here stank during the summer. The foul odour did not signify much to me. Why, everyone knows a moon stinks of cheese. I raced with Pico down the path to explore the small merchant-town with its clean streets, its gabled houses with peculiar mirrors hanging near the windows and its curious, round people – the men dressed in bulky breeches, long coats and three-cornered hats, the women dressed in short petticoats shaped in the form of diving-bells, and lined, straw hats that resembled small umbrellas.

'Pah! The men smoke on the streets, just like the moon men who smoked ivrywhere,' observed Pico.

'Look! Look!' I pointed. 'A moon boy is smoking a pipe.'

'Ivrybody smokes, 'cept the namby-pamby girls.' Pico snickered.

'Fie! I can smoke. I'm a foot-boy,' replied I.

'Yer still a girl, an' yer canna smoke,' rejoined he.

We continued on our way, mindful of the Dutch labourers driving wagons and sledges. I thought it strange to see work horses treated with such kindness, for they each of them walked with a lively step. But the strangest thing to me was that no one begged on the streets. And none of the poor children walked about shoeless or one-shoe'd like the children I had seen in York. Here, the children wore wooden clogs shaped like little canoes. No misery. No poverty. No cruelty to animals. The Dutch must surely belong to the race of moon-folk; at least I thought so.

At the entrance of Hobson's, an inn frequented by English, I came upon an elderly Dutch man serenading his horse between puffs of his pipe. ''T sijn de starren (puff), Neen mijn lief (puff) wilt noch wat marren.'

'Viva!' I greeted him, wondering what he had sung in his musical moon language.

'Goedemorgen,' returned he, as he fed the horse a slice of 'brood'. As a token of friendship, he gave me a slice of brood, which I thanked him for, and he taught me how to say 'danke je'.

I peered at the old man. 'Are you the man on the moon?'

'De maan (puff, puff)?'

'De moon?' I tilted my head to one side.

'De maan. Ja (puff).' He resumed his serenade, ''T is de maan…'

Oh que gosto! What joy! I had reached a moon paradise. And so I congratulated myself on having spoken with my first moon man and eaten my first moon bread. Later, after I had breakfasted on my first moon eggs at the inn, Señor Gonzalez, with Captain Bridge by his side, summoned Pico.

'Gracias for your service as foot-boy,' Señor Gonzalez placed his hand on Pico's shoulder. 'However, I can no longer employ you. You must return home with Captain Bridge.'

Pico groaned in misery. With a grip like iron, the Captain led Pico away, unmoved by my cousin's pleas and angry complaints. Oh, to be rid of my tormentor at last. I own that this piece of news made me happy at first. There, on the wharf, sat poor Pico dressed in his black and orange striped livery and cocked hat, soon to be exiled in his own country, while I, Sofia-Elisabete, a true explorer, would seek adventure on a moon.

'Adeus, Pico!' I waved my cap at him.

Doña Marisa sighed. 'Pobrecito.'

'We still have your foot-boy, mi amor.' Señor Gonzalez gave her a secretive smile.

We embarked on board a trekschuit, a moon barge towed by a horse at a small trot. Riding astride the horse was a moon lad – the luckiest lad here on this moon – who got to blow a horn whenever he needed to signal for the raising of draw-bridges or to warn of passing barges on the canal. The moon land beyond as far as I could see appeared flat with no hills in sight. Here and there a spinning windmill or a farm-house with green shutters dotted the flat landscape. And everywhere I looked, the trees were laden with apples in the most brilliant hues of green and red. No wonder the moon-folk did not starve; for, they could eat as many apples as they wished.

The weather being fine, as it always is on a moon, the three of us – Doña Marisa, Señor Gonzalez and I – sat on a bench near the stern instead of inside the roef, the main cabin, where the moon men smoked their pipes, their constant companions. Señor Gonzalez, being the dutiful cortejo, shaded his lady with her parasol, while I, being the dutiful foot-boy, fanned her whenever she required a breeze. 'Tengo hambre,' said our lady, and so her dutiful cortejo sliced up a big red apple for her to eat.

'The Dutch have the sweetest apples on earth, but there's nothing sweeter than a Valencia orange,' Señor Gonzalez spoke with pride.

'Ah, but nothing can compare to a magic orange,' returned she.

My eyes widened with wonder. 'A magic orange?'

'Ah, sí. There once lived a wealthy man named Senhor Soares,' Doña Marisa began. 'He owned a quinta, a large country house, which was surrounded by a thousand orange trees. Harvest after harvest, his laranjeiras produced the best, the sweetest, the juiciest oranges in all of Portugal. He bragged to everyone that the nectar of a Soares orange was as sweet as a spoonful of wild honey that melted on your tongue and dissolved into your heart.'

I wrinkled my brow. 'My oranges never tasted like honey.'

'An orange is not an orange unless it comes from Valencia,' claimed Señor Gonzalez.

Doña Marisa nodded her agreement, and she continued her story. 'There was only one thing that Senhor Soares, a widower, treasured above his precious oranges, and that was his beloved daughter, a lindissima named Jacinta, who wore orange blossoms in her long black hair, which she plaited and coiled high atop her head.'

'Did her mamãe love her?' wondered I.

Doña Marisa shook her head. 'She died shortly after Jacinta was born. One day, a handsome Spanish nobleman named Don Luis de Luna arrived at the quinta. He had journeyed from Cádiz to inspect Senhor Soares's laranjeiras, because no Spaniard could believe that the Soares orange could best a Valencian orange. Don Luis became enchanted with Jacinta, and they secretly met one evening under their trysting tree, one of the orange trees in the Soares grove. He tantalised Jacinta with an orange that he held in his hand, heedless of her admonition that "an orange is gold in the morning, silver at noon, and lead at night".'

This confused me. 'Why is the orange gold?'

'An orange tastes best in the morning, and, as such, it is better for your health and digestion to eat it then,' Señor Gonzalez told me. 'Whereas noon-time is the second-best time of the day to eat an orange. But one should never eat an orange late at night when it could harm your health.'

I scratched my head. 'Why did Jacinta wish to hurt her belly then?'

Doña Marisa sighed. 'Jacinta was in love with Don Luis. So she peeled the orange, and when she divided the segments in half for them to eat, she found nestled inside a brilliant and rare orange diamond worth many, many gold escudos. Qué maravilla! In exchange for this exquisite diamond, Don Luis gave her an ancient key, telling her it was the key to his heart.' Doña Marisa clasped her hands as if in prayer, her gaze heavenward, her lips curved up in a blissful smile. How silly she looked.

I wondered at her fascination with this thing called a diamond and a really old rusty key. 'Did the diamond make the orange taste bad?'

'Ay, Dios mío!' Doña Marisa frowned, and she pressed her handkerchief to her forehead.

'Foot-boy, have you ever seen an orange diamond?' inquired Señor Gonzalez.

When I shrugged at him, Doña Marisa proudly showed me her ring, in the centre of which sparkled an orange diamond, the colour of fire.

'Did you find it inside an orange?' I asked her.

Señor Gonzalez chuckled, but he abruptly stopped when Doña Marisa gave him the evil eye for whatever reason. It was then that I noticed a diamond ring on Señor Gonzalez's finger.

'Señor Gonzalez, was your diamond inside an orange?'

He grunted. 'Dios mío! I had to peel many an orange for a lady to get this diamond.'

'Picaro!' Doña Marisa called him a rogue.

'No te preocupes, mi amor. I shall peel oranges only for you – now and always,' said he in an audible whisper to her.

His promise having pleased her, she resumed her story. 'Thereafter, the two lovers continued to meet in the evenings under their trysting tree, where Don Luis enticed Jacinta with an orange, and each time she divided the orange in half, she would find an orange diamond nestled inside. But alas, on the evening of their twenty-second tryst, the enchantment ended, and no more glittering orange diamonds were to be had. Don Luis took his leave with alacrity, never to return to Portugal, he being all the richer with twenty-one orange diamonds tucked away in his bolsa.'

'He didn't love her,' declared I.

'That dog,' muttered Señor Gonzalez.

Doña Marisa shushed her cortejo. 'Poor Jacinta. Finding herself with child, she feared her papai's wrath, for he would surely send her away to live in a convent…'

'I lived in a convent when I was a bebê,' remarked I. 'There's a wheel for the foundlings that goes round and round…'

'Sí, sí,' Doña Marisa interrupted me. She pinched the bridge of her nose for several seconds as if she suffered from head-ache. When she had calmed herself, she concluded her tale. 'One starry night, Jacinta leant against the trysting tree, contemplating her sad lot, when a drunken Gallego labourer stumbled upon her presence. Unbeknown to them, Senhor Soares had seen them standing together underneath the trysting tree. He raged at his daughter, declaring her ruined and lost for ever to him. He forced her to choose between a vow of poverty, imprisoned behind the bolts and bars of a convent, or a vow of poverty, married to a poor Gallego labourer. Jacinta determined that her fado, her fate, was to marry this poor Gallego, and marry him she did, and several months later she gave birth to a girl – a girl christened Maria Isabel but whom she would always call Marisa.'

A girl named Marisa! My eyes became round as saucers. I begged her to tell me more about the girl Marisa, but alas, she pronounced that I would have to wait, and if I were a good little girl, perhaps she would tell me another tale. Sensing my disappointment, she explained that we must needs disembark – 'Mira! We have reached Rotterdam.'

We floated into a maze of canals, passing under many a picturesque draw-bridge, when we came upon a landing-place near a tree-lined promenade. From there, we hastened to find lodgings at the Maréchal de Turenne, an inn kept by an Englishman who took pride in its Dutch cleanliness – gleaming windows and floors, polished furniture and grates, snowy-white linens and what not – for everything was clean and perfect on a moon.

Fatigued, Doña Marisa disappeared into her bedchamber for what would be a sennight, to be attended by Josefina, her lady's maid. With Doña Marisa indisposed, and there not being much need for a foot-boy, I was allowed to do as I wished. But soon I became bored. Oh, how I missed Pico, the master planner for our adventures. I wandered outside the inn, where I sat on a bench and moped.

'Goedemorgen, jongetje,' the maid greeted me, and pretty and charming she was in her white mob cap, short blue petticoat, white apron and wooden clogs. Armed with soap and a pail of water, she proceeded to attack the street with her scrubbing-brush, and with such great violence, to wash it clean. Between her bouts with the dirty street, the maid Grietje told me that she came from nearby Gouda, where she had learnt the secret of making stroopwafel.

'Jongetje! Little boy! Want you a stroopwafel?' Grietje reached into the large pocket tied to her waist. She handed me a small cloth, wrapped inside of which were two thin wafers with a syrupy filling in between.

'Danke je.' My countenance brightened now that I had a sweet and sticky treasure. 'Do you have gooseberry tart?'

'Ja, ja – kuisbessen-taart.'

Soft giggles erupted behind us. Twin girls, who appeared to be the same age as me, inclined their heads together, speaking in audible whispers of 'een kus, een kus'.

Grietje laughed. 'Niesje and Kaatje want kissen you.'

'I'm not a boy. I'm a girl,' declared I, having forgotten that I wore my nankeen breeches and red jacket.

'Jongetje, jongetje,' the twins chanted as they skipped round me. I stamped my feet – left, right, left, right – but to no purpose. They considered me their beau, their namorado, and they insisted on calling me Hendrik. They followed me everywhere, these children of the innkeeper. Soon, however, I found that being Hendrik brought me unexpected pleasures. Hendrik voiced a command, and the twins obeyed him. Hendrik strolled the Boompjes Quay, a promenade along the River Maas, and the moon men would nod at him, as if they all belonged to the same moon men fraternity.

Hendrik requested stroopwafel whenever he wished for one, and the kitchen maid would make it for him. As the boy Hendrik, I had become golden.

One day, while we children sat near the entrance of the inn, Hendrik lazing with his feet atop the bench and eating stroopwafel, the twins playing with their dolls – cleaning them, dressing them, grooming them, for Dutch girls' hands are never idle – I espied a familiar-looking boy wearing Dutch boy's clothes and smoking a pipe along with other Dutch boys his age. When this boy sauntered towards me, puffing on his pipe and setting his three-cornered hat a bit jauntily to one side on his head, only then could I credit my eyes.

Pico boasted to me, 'I gave old Captain Bridge-y the slip (puff-puff).' He had earned some coppers by guiding English travellers in Helvoet, traded his livery and cocked hat for Dutch costume, clay pipe and tobacco, eaten apples that he snatched from orchards, slept on a flat boat in the canal and thereafter footed it to Rotterdam in hopes of finding work of some sort.

'What's that yer eatin', Soofia-Eee?' Pico licked his lips.

'I, Hendrik. Want you a stroopwafel?' pronounced I in the curious English spoken by the Dutch.

'Yi, Hendrik.' Pico gobbled up the stroopwafel. 'Wheer's them Spaniards?'

'Doña Marisa took to her bed,' I told him.

'Landlubber.'

'I gave her waterzooi...'

Pico made a face. 'Pah!'

'...and she put her head into a pot.'

Pico convulsed with laughter. 'Yer a rum 'un fer givin' her that stink o' fish stew. Give her erwtensoep – pea soup. The travellers always ask fer it at Hobson's.'

Eager to be in Doña Marisa's favour once more, I fetched a bowl of Dutch pea soup for her dinner, but she grumbled that it smelt like green canal water. And bury her head into a pot again she did, just like with the waterzooi. 'Tonta!' Josefina shook her finger at me, and she handed me the stinking pot when her mistress had done with it.

The next day Pico announced he was in 'need o' munny'. He formed an idea for us children to turn somersaults near the road where the carriages passed by. We rushed to the roadside with childish glee, and when Pico gave us the signal, we rolled head over heels – once, twice, thrice. Sure enough, the foreign travellers in the carriages laughed at our tumbling act, and they gave us five sous. Feeling emboldened by his success, Pico directed me to beat my drum while we sang a few verses of 'Rule, Brittania' for some red coats, who cheered for good old England and tossed us a generous handful of sous.

When, on the following day, we gathered on the roadside to perform our tumbling act, and for me to beat my drum, something singular happened. An assortment of painted wagons drawn by old horses approached us. On closer inspection, Pico counted fifty or so brown-skinned, dark-haired men, women and children who rode in the wagons or walked besides the horses, and one fine-looking man, he being the leader, the 'duke', who rode astride a horse.

'Waterloo teeth! Waterloo buttons! Waterloo musket balls!' the gipsies shouted. This caravan of gipsies had come from Brussels, where they had scavenged stuff from Waterloo, all of which things they offered for sale. Not understanding the meaning of this, I asked Pico why Waterloo had a goodly amount of stuff, and he explained that this stuff had once belonged to soldiers – tens of thousands of them – who had perished in a bloody battle a few months ago. This confused me. Did not moon men live for a thousand years?

I questioned the twins. 'Is this a moon?'

'De maan? Ja, ja – de maan,' the girls replied together, for they always agreed with whatever Hendrik said.

'Yer dunderheads, this isna the moon.' Pico seized my cap, and he rapped me on the crown of my head with it.

He had no sooner done so, than Grietje came to retrieve the twins. 'De Zigeuners,' exclaimed she with disgust, as she hastened the girls away, their wooden clogs clattering on the broad stone street. The gipsies ignored her rudeness, as if they had become used to such treatment wherever they roamed. But the whole thing struck me as odd. Were not peace and friendship a part of the creed of good moon-folk?

Captivated by the exotic gipsies, Pico and I followed their roving caravan. They encamped at a field a quarter of a mile from town, where they sold medicines and lured the curious with fortune-telling. When the gipsy acrobats strung up a tight rope, I quick marched to the scene, eager to join them. I shifted my drum to my back, and before anyone could stop me, I climbed up the ladder to reach the rope.

With my fingers and toes tingling, I balanced myself on the taut rope. There, six feet above the ground, with one of the gipsies standing underneath me to catch me, I turned fearless. I rope danced half-way across, beating my drum, and to much applause, for I had attracted a wide crowd. 'Hoezee!' the onlookers cheered. Buoyed by their encouragement, I handed my drum to the gipsy and thereafter amazed everyone with my best trick – roasting the pig – by laying myself upon the rope and swiftly turning round and round ere I dropped into the gipsy's arms. 'Hoezee! Hoezee! Hoezee!' the crowd chanted.

My triumph complete, the gipsy lifted me high above his head. With the broadest of grins, I waved to the cheering crowd. How I wished to be adored so for ever! And how those coppers rained down on us! Puffed up from my brilliant feat, I searched for Pico to show him the five sous I had earned, when I observed him take to his heels to hide behind a wagon.

'There you are, foot-boy,' Señor Gonzalez grasped my arm. 'You have made Doña Marisa most anxious.'

'Señor Gonzalez?' I started at the sight of him. 'I rope danced with the gipsies and…'

'Los gitanos?' He glowered at the gipsy rope dancers, and with a fling of his capa over his left shoulder, he commanded in a sharp voice, 'Vámonos!'

He strode back to town, with me scurrying behind him, when a Dutch official demanded to see our passport. 'I am Señor Gonzalez, escort of Doña Marisa, and we travel with servants,' explained Señor Gonzalez, showing our papers. The official cast a suspicious look at him and then at me with my drum perched on my back, until Señor Gonzalez pointed out that our passport had been signed by the Dutch minister in London and countersigned by the Dutch minister in Rotterdam.

Once the official had returned our passport and let us alone, Señor Gonzalez grumbled 'voto a Dios'. He complained that he had been stopped ten times since our arrival in Rotterdam. When I asked him why, he mentioned that an age ago this country was known as the Spanish Netherlands until the Dutch revolted, led by their king, William I of Orange, and that is why many of the Dutch still disliked the Spanish. Yet, somehow that didn't discourage the Dutch from trading with the Spanish. 'Dinero, dinero, dinero. They love our money,' concluded he in ill-humour.

Señor Gonzalez declared his need to be quit of this 'foul-smelling' country, and when we reached our inn, he advised me that we would be departing Rotterdam two days hence. This struck me into a panic. If Pico was right that Rotterdam and its town-folk didn't belong to a moon world – what with everyone hating each other and arguing over money and killing each other in a war – how, then, would papai find me? Ai de mim! Cousin Annie had forgotten to tell me the rule for running away when I could not be found.

My mind in a muddle now, I rushed out of doors. I found myself at the bank of the green canal, and there, in my lonesome and pitiful state, I wept for half-an-hour, for I had been too long from home. Oh, how I missed my papai, my mamãe, my puggy and my Scarborough home and everyone else and everything in it. 'There's nothing more beautiful and noble than the sight of Scarborough,' papai would often say to me.

I remembered how mamãe would dress me in my pink night-dress with whimsical embroidered roses – each rose having a pair of eyes to watch over me while I slept – and the warm home feeling it always gave me when she put me to bed. I remembered how papai and I would ramble the sands of the North Bay and how he would let me run barefoot, and when I had done prancing up and down the shore, he would tickle me by brushing the grains of sand from in between my toes. With a grieving heart, I trudged back to the inn, now that my crying spell had come to an end.

It occurred to me later that I must needs bother Doña Marisa, the landlubber-ish invalid, to write another letter to papai. The next afternoon I tap-tapped at her door, this time bearing a gift of hot and fresh stroopwafel. To my dismay, Josefina refused me entrance, no matter how much I pleaded with her. 'Vete!' she dismissed me with a wave of her hand. In her bad English, she told me I was a 'no good penny', sure to return with food to make her mistress ill, whereupon she shut the door in my face, cutting off my cries of 'Minha Senhora! Minha Senhora!'

Vexed at being cast off, I stamped down the stairs, carrying my basket of stroopwafel. I, Hendrik, ordered the twins to bring me paper and pencil, and so they did. Together we wrote a letter to my papai. I told him Rotterdam was no good and push on we must to the Land of Cuckoos. I knew not where this cuckoo-land might be, but the twins had heard their papa speak of it with Señor Gonzalez. I drew a large heart, inside of which I scribbled the word 'mamãe' for my dear mamãe in Scarborough. At the bottom of the letter, the twins sketched a picture of themselves, writing their names Niesje and Kaatje under each of their likenesses.

I folded up the letter, and I addressed it to 'Colonel Fitzwilliam, British Army'. Surely the army could find him on the road somewhere, searching for me and the perfect world in a moon. I asked the twins to get me a wafer to seal the letter with, but they knew not what I meant. Then I remembered the stroopwafel. I broke off a small piece, wondering if it would do. I removed one side of the wafer to reveal the warm, syrupy filling, and I pressed this sticky wafer onto the letter to seal it.

'What are you zuinig.' The twins nodded with approval.

'Ja, I am thrifty,' declared Hendrik, impressed with himself.

We sat within, facing the large window in front of the inn, Hendrik beating his drum, the twins playing with their small knitting needles and balls of bright orange yarn. I kept a look-out for a red coat by glancing at the two spying mirrors that hung outside the window, these framed mirrors giving me a clear view of all that passed on the street. We heard a Frenchman shout out, 'Vive l'Empereur!' By and by, the disgruntled prisoner came into view, hooked to a pole and steered to gaol by a guard. Next came a match girl with a pole slung across her shoulders – the large balls of stick matches dangling from each end of the pole. Half-an-hour passed when I sighted a British officer striding towards us, his gait crisp, his air of authority so similar to my papai's. I ran outside the inn, where I saluted him soldier-like with a pull of my cap. He halted before me, curious about this foreign drummer boy.

'Your name, drummer boy?' asked he with an officer-politeness.

'I am Drummer Boy Hendrik. Do you know Colonel Fitzwilliam, the son of Lord Matlock?'

'Och! I do, indeed.' The officer grinned. 'I, Captain O'Sullivan, served under him in Portugal.'

I gasped. 'What was he like?'

'The former lieutenant colonel, now Colonel Fitzwilliam, was and is a worthy, excellent officer, a valiant soldier and a warm-hearted friend beloved by all who know him.'

I stood proud, with my chin lifted. 'Captain, could you give him this letter?'

The Captain examined my childish scrawl and the sticky wafer seal ere he placed the letter inside his coat pocket. 'Depend on it, drummer boy, I shall fulfil my commission.'

'Thank you, Captain.' My heart filled with gratitude.

The officer set off, happy to have this commission, methinks.

When the morning arrived for our leave-taking, Niesje and Kaatje began to weep, and miserably so, until Hendrik deigned to let them kiss his cheek three times, which seemed to ease their sorrow. Hendrik, being a brave boy, never shed a tear. The twins gifted me with a pair of wooden clogs, each clog bearing their names on it so that I would not forget them. In return, I gave them a picture I had sketched of us riding the wafer sails of a windmill that I had named 'De Stroopwafel', having learnt that all the windmills in Holland are christened with names.

'Vaarwel!' Grietje and the twins waved at me as our diligence rumbled away. 'Adeus!' cried I, with mingled feelings of loneliness and wistfulness at the loss of my Dutch friends. I waved back at them for a long while, because I, along with the snappish Josefina, had been placed in the basket seat located at the rear of the carriage. 'Siéntese!' Josefina chided me, each time I stood up to wave. When we lost sight of the inn, only then did I allow the hot tears to tumble down my cheeks. Dressed now in my striped livery and cocked hat, I took up my duties again as foot-boy to Doña Marisa, whose sickly countenance, by the bye, still looked a bit green to me, like the colour of pea soup.

Chapter Seven

The Officer and the Water Maiden

My First Truth, thinks I, on this voyage to a moon world, was not so much an inward feeling that Doña Marisa and I were nearly connected to each other, but rather that Doña Marisa still pined for my papai, her first love, whereas he not for her, though she was not inclined to admit any of it. You see, my papai had come to love me, his love child, and Agnes Wharton, his true love. There, now, I have said it. But like all things clever or real or wise, no one else pays attention to them when their hearts and minds aren't open to receiving the truth or when, such as here, a small child uncovers the truth, and the truth of the truth is phoo-phoo'd by the all-knowing grown-ups.

My second truth, thinks I, though I am not inclined to admit it, is that I rather enjoyed cousining about with Pico. I wished to be a star, orbiting his bright star. Whenever he drew near, I gravitated towards him no matter how hard I tried not to. Yes, yes – I know what you are feeling. Shocking is it not? When we departed Rotterdam, I knew not what had happened to that rascal Pico. I knew not whether I would ever see him again, yet an inward feeling told me that I just might.

Near Nijmegen, an ancient frontier town, I espied a set of dark-haired, nut-brown people and a familiar assortment of painted wagons and old horses. As we drove by the gipsy encampment, I observed Pico 'a-grooming and a-grubbing' the gipsy duke's horse. My heart full, I almost cried out Pico's name. How wildly happy I was to see someone known to me after having travelled a hundred miles of dusty road in a strange country and feeling strange myself, for no one looked like me or spoke like me or thought like me. When the officials at Nijmegen gate stopped our carriage, demanding to inspect our passport and luggage, I jumped out of the basket seat where Josefina, the maid, lay sleeping, and I scurried to the gipsy encampment.

'Pico! Pico!' I waved at him in high spirits.

'Soofia-Eee?' Pico started at the sight of me. 'Wheer yer goin'?'

'The Land of Cuckoos.'

'Cuckoos?' Pico sighed. 'I canna goo wi' yer.'

The sudden appearance of the duke broke into our happy reunion. He swore in gipsy-talk – 'Boro Duvvel!' (Great God!) – and demanded that I pay him five sous for this bengel, this little blackguard, if I wished to buy him. I hastily dug into my waist-coat pocket, and I withdrew the five sous I had earned as a rope dancer. The duke, with raised brow, wondered how I, a wee foot-boy, had any money. 'Ja,' cried he, and with a wave of his hand, he dismissed his horse-keeper boy. Pico gave a whoop, and before you could say Pico Robinson, he seized his bundle of things, and the two of us ran off like hares to Nijmegen gate.

Inside our carriage Josefina fanned the sickly Doña Marisa, who pressed a handkerchief to her damp forehead. Señor Gonzalez, on seeing me dawdling near the carriage, let down the glass, and he ordered me into the basket seat again. 'We shall cross soon into the Rhineland,' warned he. *What luck,* I told myself. Now I would be rid of Josefina and her frightful temper, even if for a short while. The carriage jerked to a start, when Pico, who had been lurking behind a tree, scrambled into the basket seat. Once we had safely crossed the border, I learnt why Pico had gone off with the gipsies.

Pico recounted how the duke had captured him the day when he had been hiding behind one of the gipsy wagons – the day when Señor

Gonzalez had come to retrieve me after my rope dancing act. 'He accused me of being a chore, a thief,' said Pico. The duke, however, found nothing suspicious on Pico's person, and so he invited Pico to join him and his dog on a hunt for hedgehog. He captured two hedgehogs, each of which he wrapped in clay, and he placed them in the centre of the fire to cook them. When the meat was done, he broke the clay casings, now stuck with hedgehog bristles, and he showed Pico how to eat the white meat with his fingers.

'Gah!' I stuck out my tongue.

'It tastes chicken-y,' Pico assured me.

After Pico had supped on hedgehog, a gipsy fortune-teller read his palm and pronounced him kosko bokht – good luck – and thus, the gipsies welcomed this gadje, this foreigner, to live with them. He slept on straw that night and every night in the gipsy way. He ate rabbit stew with the potatoes that he had pilfered from the farmers' fields. He foraged for dead animals, having learnt that the gipsies preferred animals to have died by the hand of God and not by man. And once he had proved himself worthy, he minded the duke's horse – a great honour, indeed.

'I sold Waterloo teeth an' stuff an' I made a cart-load o' munny fer the duke,' bragged Pico. The day came, however, when his bokht or luck ended. He had become bored picking apples for a Dutch farmer, and so he began to sling stones at the apples hanging in a tree. The duke had to pay the angry farmer five sous for the spoilt apples.

'The duke wanted me to be gone.'

I nodded. 'He sold you for five sous.'

'Yer munny saved me,' Pico's voice quavered. I thought he would surely cry at that moment, so I did what I hoped would put him to rights again.

'Want you a stroopwafel?' I offered him my last stroopwafel that I had been saving.

'Yi, Hendrik,' Pico snatched the stroopwafel from me. 'Mmm… tastes chicken-y.'

We laughed into our hands and quietly so. But our mirth-making and chatting had attracted the attention of those sitting within.

At the next stage-house in Cleves, where the servants loaded our luggage onto a German post-wagen, Señor Gonzalez began to thrash the shrubbery with his bastón, his walking-stick. Having flushed his prey, Señor Gonzalez seized Pico by the lug, and the two of them began to tussle.

'Minha Senhora! Minha Senhora!' I banged on the door of the diligence with my fist, pleading for my lady's help.

'Voto a Dios!' thundered Señor Gonzalez. 'I shall take this boy to a foundling hospital in Cologne.'

'No, you shan't.' Doña Marisa's angry shout startled him, for she had alighted from the diligence. 'His fate is to be our foot-boy, at least for now.'

She had no sooner issued her command, than it began to drizzle. Señor Gonzalez hastened to hand his lady back into the diligence, he fearing for her wellbeing. 'Foot-boys! I wish for my foot-boys,' she demanded from within. With an impatient sigh, Señor Gonzalez ordered us into the conveyance, while the other servants – the valet and the maid – were made to sit on the box with the driver.

Doña Marisa fanned herself for a long while, her eyes intently fixed on me. 'Foot-boy, you remind me of a young girl I once knew.'

'Did she play a drum?'

Doña Marisa laughed. 'No, but she believed in the magic of the world.'

'Magic?' I sat on the edge of the seat, eager to hear more about this young girl who believed in magic.

'Ah, sí, a whimsical magic. There was once an industrious Gallego water carrier in Lisbon,' Doña Marisa began. 'He bought one small barrel, filling it up with water from a fountain. Balancing the barrel on his shoulder, he trudged up and down the steep streets of Lisbon every day, selling a cup of water here, a cup of water there, until he saved enough money to buy a second water barrel, a third barrel and then a fourth.

'This Gallego had married a lindissima named Jacinta, who came from a wealthy family, but she had fallen from grace, and together they raised one daughter, Marisa, and two sons, Gaspar and Gustavo.

The Gallego treated his daughter poorly, for the daughter was not of his blood. While his two sons sat idle, he ordered his daughter to fill up the barrels with water from the fountain and to drag a small cart from street to street, selling cups of water to the town-folk.'

'It isn't fair,' cried I.

'I shall challenge that old Gallego to a duel,' Señor Gonzalez shook his fist.

Doña Marisa tapped his arm with her fan to silence him. 'One day while Marisa's brothers lazed about the water fountain, taking snuff, they ordered her to check their heads for bugs.'

'I'm the champion of bug finders. Sister Matilde told me so,' bragged I.

'Pah!' Pico elbowed me, and I elbowed him, and soon our bout of elbowing turned into a monstrous row.

'Silencio!' Doña Marisa ordered us to behave. 'Now, Marisa set about to do their bidding, checking their heads for bugs, when a handsome officer from Inglaterra requested a cup of water. Ashamed of her dirty hands and her avid bug hunting, she blushed as she handed the officer a cup of water. "I thank you, water maiden," he winked at her. He mounted his Lusitano, and he rode away.'

'Humph. A British officer...' Señor Gonzalez muttered to himself.

Doña Marisa continued her tale. 'Marisa sat alone for a long while by the fountain, ruminating on the handsome officer's features – the darkness of his blue eyes, the crookedness of his grin – when, of a sudden, a fish landed in the fountain. Apre! The fish told her that he had swum a great distance by aqueduct and that he was ever so tired of swimming, and if she carried him in a pot of water to the river Tejo, he would place the officer under enchantment. Having done what the fish asked, she returned home where her father beat her for not having prepared their dinner.'

'He beat her?' I gasped, my eyes wide with fright.

Señor Gonzalez curled his lip. 'The old man is a dog. I shall tear him apart, limb by limb...'

Doña Marisa shushed her cortejo. 'Several months later, her father opened a caza de pasto where she worked as a tavern-maid. One evening, the officer strolled into this public-house where he drank many a cerveja, and just as the fish promised, the officer became spell-bound with this lovely maiden.'

'The magic fish kept his promise,' rejoiced I.

'Humph. A magic fish...' Señor Gonzalez muttered to himself.

Doña Marisa held up her hand to silence everyone. 'But in the morning, the enchantment was broken and the officer left her without a word, although he did leave her five réis. With a sad heart, she strolled down by the packet stairs leading to the Tejo, hoping to find the fish. Apre! The fish appeared, and he promised to place the officer under enchantment again.'

I clapped my hands. 'I knew the magic fish would come back.'

Doña Marisa cast an anxious look at me. 'A year and a half went by, and during that time, Marisa found herself with child, and she gave birth to a baby girl named Sofia. When she and the officer met for the third time, in the midst of a war, he became enchanted, indeed, and nothing could break the enchantment the officer felt when he held his own child. Alas, the officer mysteriously disappeared one day, and they knew not where he went and if he would ever return or if he was even alive.'

'Did Marisa ever find him? Please, please tell me more,' I bounced on the seat.

'What dost think?' Pico gaped at me in disbelief. 'Yer papa was lookin' fer you in Lisbon.'

I sat there thunderstruck. The British officer in the story was none other than my papai? I began to puzzle my wits together. 'The water girl, Marisa, loved the officer. But the officer loved the baby Sofia. And the baby Sofia was me, because the officer was my papai and Marisa was my...was my mamãe? Then papai looked for me. And he married Mrs Wharton, my mamãe in Scarborough.'

'That villano! I shall defend your honour, mi amor, and challenge this villain to a duel.' Señor Gonzalez sliced the air twice – 'whissshhh, whissshhh' – with an imaginary sword.

'Basta! Enough, all of you,' cried Doña Marisa, and she chided her cortejo for his love of duelling. She claimed she needed to rest, her story-telling having tired her. So close her eyes she did all melancholy-like.

I gazed at Doña Marisa, my heart thump-thumping, knowing now that she was my natural mother – the beautiful, the perfect Marisa Soares Belles of my dreams. Oh, how I wished to ask her more about my mysterious beginnings, the kind of questions I couldn't ask my papai, who, for some reason, became cross whenever I mentioned her. Soon, however, Doña Marisa fell asleep, and at the next stage-house, Señor Gonzalez banished us children to sit on the box with the driver. There was nothing for it then but to bide my time and not upset Doña Marisa, and perhaps, with any luck, she would tell me another story.

With the weather having turned warm, the horses plodded along, needing frequent rests. 'Dios mío!' muttered Señor Gonzalez. He claimed that the German post-wagens were the slowest carriages on earth. When he demanded that the driver go faster, the driver shouted 'Yaw! Yaw!' and flourished his whip, but the German horses ignored him and continued their slow pace. Doña Marisa uttered a thousand complaints about the heat and dust and slow horses, and I dared not go near her while Josefina attended to her.

The next day we reached a city called Cologne, a gloomy place with narrow and dirty streets winding their way on both sides of the Rhine. I observed many a sad-looking beggar at the convents and churches, where they lodged in the nooks of the convent walls. When I lived at the Convento do Desterro, I at least had a patch of straw to sleep on.

Doña Marisa grumbled about the stagnant air and the filth of Cologne. She declared this place disgusting and unhealthful, yet she wished to buy bottles of scent, something called eau de Cologne, which made no sense to me. Why would she want a bottle of scent that smelt as bad as Cologne?

'What a stinkin', rotten town,' complained Pico. The two of us sat again with the driver on the stink-box, which is what Pico dubbed it, because the odours that arose from the filthy streets and open sewers swirled round us, making us feel queasy.

'The town-folk are sad,' observed I.

'Yer canna be happy livin' in stink an' poverty,' reasoned he.

My heart sank to my toes, for most assuredly the Colognians did not belong to the race of moon-folk. The town-dwellers lived in a wretched state, their countenances sickly from having to breathe in the foul air. Having seen enough of this misery, Doña Marisa wished to push on. So hire a house-boat we did to take us up the Rhine. As our crew bent to their oars against the current, I summoned up my magical powers, telling Wind to help us get on, and I prayed to the angels to guide us and to protect us from crashing into rocks. Several times the current became too strong, however, and our house-boat had to be drawn by a horse or a small band of town-folk on the towing road alongside the bank of the river.

By and by, Doña Marisa's health improved, and she declared herself healed. She sat on deck of the house-boat holding court while Señor Gonzalez held her parasol. 'Holla!' She gave a friendly shout in German to the mariners who passed us going down the Rhine, and they being a reserved kind of people would silently tip their hat to her or simply stare at her, shocked by her brazenness. With Doña Marisa happy, Señor Gonzalez became happy, and the servants, in turn, became happy that their lady was happy.

'We daren't be happy unless our lady is happy first,' Pico drily observed to me.

Each night on the Rhine, our happy Señor Gonzalez got monstrously drunk from the fine German wine he bought, and he would howl like a dog at the bright white moon. 'Tonto!' his lady called him a fool. Pico and I would laugh into our hands until we were found out and scolded by Doña Marisa for not having gone to bed. She, having determined not to suffer another night at an inn with the happy Señor Gonzalez, declared we would lodge on the house-boat instead, it being secured at a landing-place. The following morning, while everyone still slept in their cabins, I sat on the after-deck with my drum, willing myself not to beat it. Bored,

bored, bored, I began to count the number of boats on the river, when…

Lo there, on the tow road! I espied an English gentleman with a crisp gait and commanding presence walking down river. Like a true officer, he gave a brusque wave to his driver, and just before he got into his carriage, I called out to him – 'Holla!' – but my voice drowned in emotion. I strapped on my drum, and I beat it in 4/4 time. P-rum p-duh p-rum p-dah, pa-da dum-dum da-dahhh. If he was my papai, then surely he would recognise the drum signal, for was not 'Tree on the Hill' our special song? I had no sooner beat eight measures, than Josefina stumbled on deck, heaping upon me a thousand curses.

'You no good penny,' her ferocious shout startled me. Wild with fury, she threatened to toss my drum into the river.

'Minha Senhora! Minha Senhora!' I shrieked in terror, as Josefina, who had gone mad, chased me round the deck.

'Silencio!' Doña Marisa commanded from her cabin, clearly annoyed. 'Josefina, come here and dress me.'

Josefina gifted me with the evil eye ere she disappeared into her mistress's cabin. Safe now from that bruxa, I searched for the carriage I had sighted on the tow road, but the carriage was long gone. I dared not tell anyone of the Englishman who resembled my papai, so I prayed to God instead. *Holla! God! Would you be so kind as to send down Sister Lisbet? I must needs speak with her.* And I waited and I waited. To my dismay, she, too, seemed to be long gone.

I sat on deck and wept, lost in my miserable thoughts and home-sickness. Then I remembered what my mamãe in Scarborough had mentioned about happiness, and if I truly wished for it again, I would be happy once more. Seized with inspiration, I beat my drum while I sang 'Tree on the Hill', ignoring the complaints and groans and curses below deck, and for a whole five minutes, I believed myself happy.

Later that day, we disembarked at Bingen, where Señor Gonzalez hired a carriage to convey us to a place called the Black Forest, or Schwarzwald. We spent many days on the road until we reached

Karlsruhe, and from there, we drove into the forest. Apre! To my surprise, the forest was not black but rather green, green, green, with fragrant pines and grassy dales. Could this green paradise be a moon world? I thought it just might be, for no one begged in the villages, the streams abounded with trout to eat and the forest-folk drank spa water in Wildbad for their health.

On our way to visit the mystical lake at Wildsee, we came upon a little peasant girl with red-stained lips, hands and feet, carrying an earthen jug of wild raspberries. She sold berries for two kreutzers to Señor Gonzalez, who wished to please his lady. The girl ran alongside us as our carriage drove off, and she tossed up some berries to me. What kindness there is in the Black Forest. As I waved good-bye to the girl, she scooped up some berries from her jug, and she crammed them into her mouth to eat.

We children were left to do as we wished in Wildsee while Señor Gonzalez and Doña Marisa strolled through the forest, romanticking themselves and feeding each other wild raspberries. 'Let us bathe,' suggested Pico, for it was unusually warm. We raced each other to the lake, whereupon we jumped into the cold water. There, immersed in our watery play-ground, I practised the tricks that my avô had taught me, such as swimming like a carp and turning somersaults like a dolphin. Near the bank of the lake I espied a slender man, deep in thought. I swam up to him, mermaid-style. The imp in me performed an aquatic somersault, splashing him with water. Once I came up for air, I burst into a fit of giggles.

The man gave a hearty laugh. 'You mischievous Undine.'
'Undine?'
'She is a water-spirit,' advised he in a broad German accent.
'A spirit? I can fly when I turn my mind to it,' boasted I.
'Fly, indeed! Do you have a name, little Undine?'
'When I'm a girl, I'm Sofia-Elisabete.' I spun round in the water. 'What's your name?'
'I am Friedrich, Baron de la Motte Fouqué.'
'Herr Fouqué, were you having deep thoughts?'

He gazed at me in astonishment. 'Why, yes. I was recalling my sad days in the army.'

'My papai is Colonel Fitzwilliam, and he gets deep thoughts under our Scots pine.'

'The Colonel experiences the deepest of thoughts under a pine?'

'Ay, when he hears his wind music.' I sank into the water and thereafter surfaced a few feet away. 'Ha! Ha!' laughed I, and I repeated my clever trick several times to divert my German friend. Later, while Pico and I baked in the sun to dry ourselves, I observed Herr Fouqué sitting under a pine, thinking his deep thoughts with his eyes half-closed, no doubt listening to the wind music.

I never did get a chance to speak again with Herr Fouqué, now that the Land of Cuckoos beckoned us, or rather, an impatient Doña Marisa, who wished to quit Wildsee. While we traversed the forest, she would order the driver to stop now and again, because satisfy her every whim she must, insisted she. 'Silencio!' she shook her fan at us. She leant out the open window, straining to hear the cuckoos. 'Goo-ko, goo-ko,' the birds warbled in the forest.

'Goo-ko,' Doña Marisa teased her cortejo.

'Goo-ko,' returned he, and he gave her a broad smile.

Pico shook his head, and he whispered to me, 'Them Spaniards act like half-wits.'

Near Hornberg, where we stopped for a small repast, Doña Marisa bought a peasant costume for me, complete with blue petticoat, red bodice, white cambric shirt and something called a bollenhut – gigantic egg-shaped red tufts of wool atop a straw hat. Pico convulsed with laughter at the sight of me in my bollenhut. Even the valet exclaimed, 'Dios mío!' and this from Enrico who never spoke a word to anyone, including to his master, Señor Gonzalez. Sometimes we forgot he existed, hence we called him El Fantasma – the ghost.

'Gah!' I stamped my feet – left, right, left, right – and I pitched the egg hat to the ground.

'You ungrateful, querulous child,' Doña Marisa raged at me. 'You daren't ruin my adventures in cuckoo-land.'

I stamped my foot again in reply.

'Apologise. Say goo-ko,' ordered she.

'Não. I hate the egg hat.'

'Goo-ko,' returned she in ill-humour, shaking her finger at me.

'Goooo-ko, goooo-ko, goooo-ko,' warbled I, but she sensed my mocking tone.

'Ay! Quita de ahí! Away with you!' cried she. And so I was banished from her presence for the whole of the day.

In Triberg, the next morning, I tramped behind Doña Marisa from thatched cottage to thatched cottage as she indulged in her latest fancy – cuckoo clocks – for the clock-makers all worked from their own cottages. She learnt from them that a famous clock-maker, a dwarf named Otto Faller, lived outside the village. So go there we did to his humble-looking abode where she bought two cuckoo clocks and a musical clock from him. I observed Señor Gonzalez speaking with Herr Faller and his wife and handing them money from his bolsa. Apparently, we children would lodge here, while Señor Gonzalez escorted Doña Marisa to see the sights and to enjoy the cuckoos before the birds flew south for the winter. When those two would return for us in Triberg, I knew not.

The clock-maker, Otto Faller, he being the same height as Pico, had married a regular-sized person, she being Elsa Faller. They had a regular-sized son named Hubert, who served in the army far away, and a regular-sized daughter named Mechtilde, who had married a man in Baden-Baden. Frau Faller, being a gentle soul, took pity on me, for I was made to wear the crushed bollenhut with lumpy eggs as punishment. 'Do not weep, child,' she soothed me. 'You needn't wear the bollenhut.' She bustled about to dress me in Triberg costume instead, complete with black skirt, red bodice, green apron and a chimney-pot straw hat – these things having once belonged to Mechtilde an age ago. Proud of my appearance, I believed myself a true Tribergite with my stylish straw hat.

It being noon-time, the dinner hour, Frau Faller beckoned us to the kitchen with its peculiar-looking round table and round chairs, all set lower to the ground for the clock-maker.

'Herr Faller, I'm glad you're a dwarf,' said I.

'Oh? Why is that?' asked he.

'I can see over the table on my own,' reasoned I.

Frau Faller smiled as she placed a large pot of potato soup in the centre of the table. She served us up black bread with butter, and cold milk that had been stored in a nearby stream to keep it fresh and sweet. Herr Faller led us in a short prayer, and when he had done, he dipped his spoon into the soup pot. He praised the soup, and he nodded to his wife, who dipped her spoon into the soup pot. She nodded to Pico who did the same, and then I took my turn at the soup pot. Round and round we went until I could no longer eat another spoonful. When the soup had disappeared, Herr Faller led us in a short prayer again.

'Children, go off and play. Do not go far. You must always be able to see our house,' Frau Faller led Pico and me out of doors. 'Farmer Dilger has a new horse.'

'Yes, go and see the horse,' urged Herr Faller. 'When I sound my horn three times, you must return, understand?'

Pico and I met up with three children from the Dilger farm, and the five of us gambolled in the dale, walking on logs, sliding down a straw-stack, chasing each other and thereafter racing to the hay loft located in the attic of their farm house. I asked to see their new horse, and to my surprise, I discovered that the stables and the barn stood next to the rooms used by the family. In this manner, the farmer's family and their animals lived in peace and warmth under the large, sloping straw roof of the farmhouse.

Paaah paaaa raaaah. Of a sudden, Herr Faller's horn blared three times. 'The horn,' cried Pico, and we raced back to the clock-maker's house. I asked Herr Faller if I could beat my drum, and he allowed me ten minutes with my drum but no more. I reached into my strap pocket for my drum sticks, but something felt odd. Ai de mim! Both of the drum sticks had been broken in two.

'Little Sofia,' Frau Faller pronounced my name in a broad German accent. 'Why do you weep?'

Her concern and kindness made me cry louder. I handed her my poor drum sticks, the drum sticks my papai had gifted me with.

The remembrance of the day, when papai had bought me my drum, made me miserable with home-sickness.

Pico started at the sight of my mangled drum sticks. 'That Josefina is a rum 'un.'

I choked on a sob. 'Jo...se...fina?'

'Do not worry, child.' Herr Faller examined the drum sticks, and using the various tools of his trade, he began to fashion new drum sticks using solid oak.

'My Otto is a genius. He can make anything,' Frau Faller assured me.

Like magic, the drum sticks slowly took shape in Herr Faller's hands. 'Everything is solvable once you put your heart and mind to it,' advised he.

Everything is solvable. Inspired by Herr Faller's maxim, I wiped the tears from my face with my apron. I determined then that if I wished my papai to find me and join us in our search for a moon world, I would need to beat a drum signal every afternoon – the secret drum signal that only he and I knew – using my magic drum sticks. In the loudest voice I could muster, I began to sing our special song.

Pico groaned when he recognised 'Tree on the Hill'. 'Canna yer sing summat else?'

After feeling cast off by Doña Marisa, I found myself in a loving home with the Fallers where the days passed with almost perfect happiness. Pico and I rose early, helped the Fallers with their work making clocks and plaiting straw, ate spätzle – an odd-looking maccaroni – and gambolled in the dale until the horn sounded.

In the evening, we sat before the kitchen hearth. Herr Faller would tell us a story – *The Elves and the Shoemaker* being my favourite – whereupon we children retired in a state of contentment on our straw mattress, a murmur of rushing water in the distance soothing us to sleep in the warmth of the Fallers' room. I dreamt once that the Fallers needed help in their clock-making business, and so two elves sneaked into their house late at night to finish the clocks for Herr Faller. To thank the elves, Frau Faller sewed little black breeches and jackets and red vests for them to wear.

On Sunday, we walked out with the Fallers to a gigantic waterfall, its seven cascades roaring and foaming in a wondrous rage, bringing to my mind Doña Marisa and her bad temper. Nearby stood calm pools with moss-covered rocks, the peacefulness of them reminding me of my patient and loving mamãe in Scarborough. A sudden weight upon my spirits made me gloomy. I knelt to dip my hand into the pool of calm water, staring at my sad reflection therein. Frau Faller called out to me in her gentle voice, and I wonder now if she had sensed my troubled soul.

'Little Sofia, come and plait straw with me.'

'Now?'

'Yes, it's always good to work.'

We followed another trail deep into the forest, plaiting straw as we walked. A bell of grace began to chime at the ancient church where the Fallers worshipped and where pilgrims came to pray to Maria in der Tanne – Mary in the Fir.

After Sunday service, while the parishioners gathered round to exchange greetings and news, I wandered down a shady path to an ancient fir tree, where I came upon a little peasant girl dressed in the peculiar fashion of long ago. She said her name was Barbara Franz, and once upon a time, she disobeyed her mother and took a parchment image of the Virgin of the Immaculate Conception that had fallen from one of the branches of the fir tree. Later, she became struck with an eye disease.

A dream came to her that she must return the image to the fir tree, and thus she and her parents set out to do just that. 'See it there?' She pointed to the parchment image on one of the lower branches. Her parents washed her eyes with water from the spring that bubbled from a rock near the fir tree, and a miracle occurred in that her eye healed and she didn't go blind.

'You must wash your hands in this spring,' Barbara Franz instructed me, 'and wash away the bitterness growing in your heart for Doña Marisa.'

I stamped my foot in protest. 'Why should I like her when she doesn't like me?'

'We must love one another,' advised she.

'Please tell me. Is this a moon world where everyone lives in peace and harmony?'

She shook her head. 'This is Triberg.'

'Ai de mim!' exclaimed I, my moon hopes crushed yet again. Hot tears began to form in my eyes.

'Listen to me,' urged she. 'You must attend Doña Marisa until she reaches her destination. When your heart is pure, only then will your papai find you.'

And so I knelt to wash my hands with the water from the bubbling spring, and I gave a thousand thank-you's to God for sending this Barbara Franz to speak with me. *Holla! God! I shall think of others besides myself.* My prayer done, and my mind resolved to go rightly in this world, I rose to thank my new friend, but the girl had gone, as had the spring and the image on the branch.

Chapter Eight

The Beau

MY FIRST BEAU, thinks I, was not a pretty moon boy, but rather, a Swiss named Denzler – a true manly man, just like my papai. I hear you cry, 'How could you wish for romantick adventure – you, the girl who always exclaimed "gah!" whenever she suspected her parents of romanticking themselves?' Well, I still say 'gah!' to them and all things romantick-y. Denzler and I shared a true friendship, a true affection, one that defied all gah-ness and silliness, unlike everyone else I observed when they romanticked each other.

In Triberg, the inevitable leave-taking of the Fallers and the Black Forest arrived sooner than I wished. But push on we must. Herr Faller chuckled at the sight of me, for I was dressed now as an English boy of quality in my nankeen breeches and red jacket. We shook hands, and he surprised me with a cuckoo clock of my very own. Que maravilha! What a wonder it was. When the hour struck, the trap-door at the top opened, and a little wooden drummer girl popped out.

'Ha! Ha!' I jumped with joy at having my very own cuckoo clock.

'God bless you, Sofia. God bless you, Pico. Be good.' Frau Faller wiped her eyes with her apron.

The glass having been let down in our carriage, Frau Faller kissed me and Pico one last time, and the sorrow of it pierced my heart and made me sob. I awaited Pico's unmerciful teasing, but now that I think on it, he never did call me a namby-pamby girl when I had wept. And that is how boys hide their own misery, thinks I; they become terribly quiet of a sudden.

As we drove down the dirt road past the Dilger Farm, the familiar paaah paaaa raaaah of Herr Faller's horn bid us a final farewell.

'The horn!' Pico grinned as he leant out of the window to wave his cap at the Fallers, now two specks in the distance.

'Ha, ha, you look like a cuckoo bird who popped out the trap-door,' teased I.

'Ha, ha, yer look like a blockhead.' He hit me on the crown of my head with his cap. And that is how boys become cheerful again, thinks I; they call you a blockhead and give you a rap on the head, while pretending to be disagreeable.

Several days later we crossed into a country they call die Schweiz, or Switzerland. In the town of Schaffhausen, Señor Gonzalez discovered that the northern shore of the Rhine here abounded with vineyards – an unexpected pleasure for him, to be sure. At midnight, the dog in him howled at the bright white moon in what had become his nightly ritual whenever he got monstrously drunk.

'Silencio!' cried Doña Marisa.

'Olé! Olé!' He stamped about, ignoring his lady's warning that dancing was forbidden in Schaffhausen.

The following day we travelled as far as Winterthur, a picturesque village surrounded by hilly pastures where fat sheep and horned cows grazed in a leisurely manner. Entranced, I thought it a waking dream, the lush pastures glowing green in my mind. Oh, how I wished to roll down a hillock to see if everything was real. Upon hearing my urgent pleas, Doña Marisa agreed to give us children exercise. 'Twenty minutes then,' said she.

Pico jumped out of the carriage first. With a whoop, I followed on his heels, and we gambolled and roistered in the pasture. Everything seemed so perfect, so pure in this fuzzy green paradise, until we came upon a cottage with its heap of stinking manure by the door, reminding us of the Dilger Farm in Triberg with its heaps of manure near the house. 'Pugh!' Pico wrinkled his nose. We raced back to where Doña Marisa awaited us by the carriage.

'How came you to be a swift runner?' asked she, brushing away bits of clover and trefoil from my hair.

I shrugged. 'My papai can run fast. He ran riot in London, where his papai never caught him...'

'Ay!' Doña Marisa frowned.

'...I heard him say so once,' revealed I with pride.

'Humph, ran riot...' muttered Señor Gonzalez from where he sat within, scribbling with his pencil in a small journal-book.

In Zürich, while Doña Marisa rested at our inn, we children accompanied Señor Gonzalez on a stroll. Pico counted fifty-four sails drifting on a shimmering blue-green lake, while I counted twenty peaks in the snow-topped alps that rose in the distance – twenty being the highest number I could count up to then. On our return, we passed by a hospital, where we came upon a curious sort of people lazing in the sun, one of whom was being fed by his mother. Señor Gonzalez recalled seeing similar-looking cretins in the mountains of Spain. He explained to us that these unfortunate souls were imbeciles, oftentimes deaf, and one could always tell a cretin by their enormous goitres, splay features and olive-tinted skin. On a sudden, one of the cretins uttered a shrill cry like that of a wild animal.

'Gad zookers,' Pico half-whispered in astonishment.

Señor Gonzalez shook his head. 'It is a cruel condition and without cure.'

I stood there and stared. How was it that a country with a charming landscape – its lakes that reflected the heavens, its majestic mountains that boasted seas of ice, its velvety green pastures that turned cow's milk into nectar – could also produce such shockingly deformed people? With mingled feelings of terror and pity, I wondered what could be done for these tragic souls. This place, this country, could not be a moon world, I thought to myself, because no one would suffer so in a perfect world.

At the inn, a cheerful Doña Marisa greeted us in her sitting room. 'Tengo hambre,' said she, rubbing her belly, and she requested that I fetch her something to eat called Emmental. I scampered away to the dining room where the staff at the inn gave me an unsightly cheese with holes in it. Ai de mim! What to do? Surely Doña Marisa would be angry with me if I brought her defective cheese. Struck with panic, I stuffed the holes the best I could with bits of apples and nuts and – oh yes – a wooden button that had been lying on the floor. Josefina, who stood like a sentry in the passage, gaped at the patched-up wedge of cheese I presented to her. 'Tonta!' cried she, tossing the button and other hole stuffings to me.

Later that night, when I told Pico of the cheese ridden with holes, he convulsed with laughter. That is when I learnt that Emmental comes with holes in it, though, I still couldn't understand why the Swiss took the trouble to carve out holes in their cheese and what exactly they did afterwards with the bits of cheese they carved out.

'Yer blockhead! The Swiss dunna carve out holes in the cheese.' Pico hit me with his feather pillow, for we had remained bedfellows ever since our sojourn in Triberg.

'But how do the holes get there?'

'Iviryone knows the elves sneak into the cottages at night an' make the holes,' exclaimed he.

'Why, the elves must be eating the bits of cheese they carve out,' reasoned I.

'The elves need summat to eat.'

'Cousin Pico, you are brilliant, thinks I.'

'Yi, yi. Now, go to sleep,' commanded he.

The next day Señor Gonzalez hired a guide by the name of Denzler, he being a youngish man, strong and trusty and well known to the trade. Denzler took us to the lake of Zug, a hugeous, emerald body of water eight miles long and filled with a million fish – pike, carp and a red trout called rolheli. I wandered to the end of the dock where I peered into the mysterious water. Oh, how I wished to be Undine and converse with the fishes. I removed my outer-clothes and shoes, and on the count of three, I dived into the dark blue-green-blue depths. Aieeee! The water was cold, cold, cold, and my teeth began to ch-ch-chatter.

'Foot-boy, where are you?' Doña Marisa looked round, having heard a big splash.

'Gad zookers! She's in the water,' Pico pointed to my head bobbing on the lake.

'It is too cold to swim,' advised Denzler as he and the others observed me being carried away by the current.

Doña Marisa blurted out, 'She is lost! She is lost!' Her agonizing shrieks carried across the water where some boatmen heard her wild cries of 'My child! My child!'

The boatmen rowed like madmen, for they expected a big reward to fish me out of the lake. Thereafter, the victorious boatman unloaded me on the dock, where I sat shivering while Señor Gonzalez paid him ten francs. At the sight of my blue lips, arms and feet, Doña Marisa uttered a cry, and she fainted away into the arms of Señor Gonzalez. Denzler, calm as can be, placed me on my belly on the warm dock. He rubbed me with his coat until I became a regular colour again.

'Denzler, I was as blue as the lake,' remarked I.

'Da wag – indeed.' Denzler wrapped me up in his coat. There, in his arms, I inhaled the singular scent of a Swiss man, who brought to mind a hodgepodge of green pastures and hay and milk and cheese and cherries, so different from that of my papai's earthy scent.

At our rooms in Hotel Ochsen, a frantic Doña Marisa bathed me in warm water, after which Denzler brought me warm goat's milk mixed with the juice of an herb called cheese clover to prevent any disease of the chest. When I refused to drink it, Doña Marisa shook her head. 'Tut, tut,' uttered she. And so I sipped the strange-tasting potion to please her.

I awoke later that night in Doña Marisa's snug bed, her arms wrapped round me, her sweet fragrance of blossoming myrtle tickling my senses. The light from a beeswax candle flickered on the perfect landscape of her face – the peak of her nose, the tiny fissures in her parted lips, the valleys of her sloping cheeks. Lo there! I beheld a faded, crescent moon on her left temple, and I wondered how the scar had got there.

At dawn of day I pretended to sleep while Doña Marisa complained to Señor Gonzalez about some curse that had returned and how it would do away with her near relations. 'Leidwerk! Witchcraft! That is what the innkeeper called it,' fretted she. Señor Gonzalez declared there was no leidwerk because I was still alive. 'They say misfortunes never come singly,' warned she. Señor Gonzalez sighed, for he claimed not to be a superstitious being. He kissed his lady's hand to bid her farewell, and he set off for a pleasant boat ride across the lake.

'I wish to ride in a boat with him,' declared I, standing up on the bed.

Doña Marisa felt my forehead for fever. 'You must stay in bed until it is safe for you to travel again.'

'It isn't fair.' I stamped my feet – left, right, left, right – but to no purpose. Tucked up in bed, I spent a cursed day there, drinking the horrid goat's milk with herbs and eating soggy rye-bread that had been soaked in the milk, while Señor Gonzalez and the others got to be explorers without me.

In the course of the evening, I paced to and fro, imprisoned in the room with Josefina, who had been told to sit up with me. When she slumped in her chair, fast asleep, I gave her the slip, for I was a naughty child. Having thrown my red capa over my night-dress, I wandered down to the water. Apre! A heaven-sent sunset unfolded at the lake of Zug – the sky ablaze in vivid oranges, reds and violets – and I gave a thousand thank-you's to God for it. I espied Doña Marisa and Señor Gonzalez strolling arm-in-arm near the dock and stealing a kiss or two.

'Ha! Ha! They are kissing.' I giggled at the ridiculous sight of those two romanticking themselves again.

'You, little one, ought to be in bed,' scolded Denzler, who, unbeknown to me, had followed me to the lake.

I spun round. 'Denzler? Please don't tell Doña Marisa.'

Denzler groaned. 'Kang – away with you now.'

'But Denzler...'

'Glik – at once,' ordered he, clapping his hands twice, and he cast a watchful eye as I scurried back to the hotel.

Having deemed it safe for me to travel, Doña Marisa announced we were for Küssnacht near the northern shore of the Lake of Lucerne. I learnt then that Denzler would guide Señor Gonzalez to the summit of the Righi, while the rest of us stayed at an inn. 'Please, Denzler, please let me go with you,' cried I in a burst of despair at being left behind again. But he pitied me not. And so I tugged at his sleeve, my eyes beaming with adoration, to be sure.

'Denzler, you're the handsomest man I know – well, other than my papai.'

'Jo?' Denzler seemed reserved as ever, yet I detected a slight twinkle in his eye.

'Truly, you are.' I gazed in earnest at his light brown hair and warm brown eyes. 'Denzler, will you not take me with you to Righi?'

'It is too arduous a climb for a young child, and besides, I expect flüderwetter – rainy weather – on the way.' Denzler eyed the grey clouds in the sky.

I hung my head in silence.

'When I return, I shall teach you the secret of jodeling. Jo?' Denzler held out his hand.

'Well and good,' said I, shaking his hand, for I had heard the Swiss children jodeling in the hills to entertain the tourists, who would give them a half-franc for a first-rate jodel. 'Will you also teach me how to shoot an arrow through an apple – an apple atop Pico's head?'

Denzler grunted, his Swiss pride undeniable. 'Wilhelm Tell, you cannot be. A jodeler, you can be.'

When the men returned two days later after having traipsed up the Righi to see the sun rise from the summit and to make a pilgrimage to the ancient chapel of Maria zum Schnee, or Mary in the Snow, Denzler kept his promise. He taught me the art of jodeling in the Swiss way – 'a-ho alli ho alli ho-u-u-u'. In the boat ride across the Lake of Lucerne, I drove my fellow passengers to distraction with my enthusiastic jodeling; at least that's what Señor Gonzalez said, and he paid me a franc to stop jodeling.

We disembarked near the foot of Mount Pilatus, where Denzler told us the legend of Pontius Pilate – the Roman Governor who had presided over the crucifixion of Jesus and who had later committed suicide – and how his body could not be laid to rest afterwards.

'Wherever they sank his body – the Tiber, the Rhône – it would wash ashore and wreak all sorts of havoc on the weather,' explained Denzler. 'His corpse then floated to the Lake of Geneva, and violent gales ensued, so the corpse was transferred to the Lake of Lucerne, here at Mount Pilatus. Some say Pilate's conscience troubled him for what he had done to Jesus, and that is why his soul wandered the earth until laid to rest in the dark waters of a lake.'

'Hateful man.' Doña Marisa no doubt referred to Pilate.

I shuddered with fear that Pontius Pilate's soul once wandered up on the mountain. Was the mountain still haunted? I kissed the cross on my necklace, the necklace that Sister Lisbet had given me an age ago, and I crossed myself and uttered a *Pater Noster* for double protection.

As our old carriages lumbered down the rock-hewn road, some children ran alongside us, selling bottles of milk and bouquets of eidelweiss and baskets of ripe, juicy pears. On the second day we arrived at our destination near the foot of the Bernese Alps, the plan being, said Señor Gonzalez, to journey through the Gemmi pass to reach the Canton of Valais on the other side. From there, we would go to someplace called Simplon.

Denzler agreed to guide us over the Gemmi pass but no further than Leukerbad. He mentioned that he had a cousin who lived near Leukerbad in a small village reachable by ladder and who could serve as guide to Simplon. Given that my time with Denzler would soon come to an end, I summoned up my courage to tell him what I had been hiding in my heart.

'Oh, hang it!' I stamped my foot.

'Hang it?'

'Denzler, I am in love with you,' pronounced I. 'Will you marry me?'

He started in surprise at my brazen proposal.

'I cannot,' replied he, his lips twitching as if he wanted to laugh.
'But why?' I became indignant.

'I am married already.'

'Oh.' Disappointed, I cast down my eyes. I shuffled about,
kicking a pebble or two lying near my foot. 'You could still be my
beau, my namorado, could you not?'

Denzler eyed my gloomy countenance. 'You, little one, remind
me of a legend I heard once about a charming little girl who lived in
the Jura mountains.'

'I do?' This bit of news cheered me that my hero Denzler
considered me charming. 'What did the little girl do?'

'Well, many, many years ago, a knight and his lady lived in a
castle high up on the Jura mountains. They had one child, a little girl
of four years, and...and, oh yes, a good jodeler she was.'

'Just like me.' I smiled.

Denzler nodded. 'The mother took her girl into the forest to
gather wood-flowers and wild strawberries and to jodel, when, of
a sudden, the girl's sharp cry echoed in the mountains. Struck with
panic, the mother rushed to the precipice, but her little girl was gone.
The mother hastened down the mountain path, her heart filled with
dread at what she would find there. At the foot of the mountain,
what do you think she discovered?'

'The girl had fallen and died?'

Denzler shook his head. 'The little girl was alive, and she ran
with joy towards her mother, jodeling in her sweet voice – a-ho alli
ho alli ho-u-u-u.'

I scratched my head. 'But how can that be?'

'According to the little girl, she was picking a beautiful flower
when she stumbled. As she fell over the precipice, a great noise drew
near her – a flapping of wings – and whatever it was, it grasped the
back of her coat, and it lowered her onto a patch of soft grass.'

'It must have been an angel,' cried I, my eyes wide with wonder.

A thunderous rumble broke into my thoughts. On the yonder
side of a mountain, a cloud of silver dust exploded into the sky.
Denzler shrugged. ʾTwas an avalanche, he explained to us. Doña

Marisa nervously fingered her rosary, having convinced herself that the avalanche was a bad omen, whereas Señor Gonzalez thought the avalanche the greatest spectacle on earth. 'Qué maravilla!' exclaimed he.

Early the next morning we mounted mules for the ride up to the summit, while porters carried our luggage. I, being the fortunate one, got to ride with Denzler at the front of our party, inhaling his manly Swiss scent and imagining him to be my beau. 'Trust your mules, because they are sure-footed,' Denzler advised us. I told him that I was an expert rider, having journeyed on the steep mountainside in Monchique many a time, and that I had no fear of heights. I patted our mule Choli. I whispered in the mule's ear that I trusted him and that he should trust me. 'Aw-ah-aw,' replied the mule, his ears tipping forward.

'Hü Choli,' cried Denzler.

'Hü Choli,' cried I. And away we went.

As our mules plodded up the path surrounded by pines and meadows covered in mist, the deep silence weighed on me such that I uttered hardly a word in the ascent except to speak with Choli – 'hüp hüp' – to make him go faster now and then. Riding with Denzler brought to mind the times I had ridden a donkey with my papai, whom I considered the best horseman in all of England. Ai de mim! I swallowed hard, not wanting to cry in front of Denzler – a namby-pamby girl I am not – but a deep melancholy set in, and I began to wonder where papai was now. Had he followed our trail to the Black Forest and to Switzerland?

'Hü-ü-ü-ü.' Denzler brought Choli to a stand.

Near the summit, where the land became bleak with grey cliffs, we stopped for refreshments at an old customs house, after which we walked and led our mules past the Daubensee, a small, lonesome lake filled with snow water and mud. Later, we prepared for the descent to Leukerbad on a treacherous, narrow path – Doña Marisa by litter, the porters by foot and the rest of us by mule. Señor Gonzalez wished me to go by litter, but Doña Marisa didn't trust me to sit still in one. *What luck,* I told myself. And so I got to ride again with Denzler.

We led the way on the steep, zig-zag path, inching our way down the precarious mountainside. I bravely peered down into the abyss, when I heard Josephina whimper. She heaped a thousand curses on her mule, who preferred to walk on the outer edge of the path, making her legs dangle over the precipice. 'Tonto!' she chided the mule. Filled with dread, she despaired that she would plunge two thousand feet and be smashed to atoms. 'Silencio!' shouted Señor Gonzalez, and he ordered that Josefina be blindfolded and placed in a litter. This, however, did not end her rant; for, after a minute or two, she cursed the litter carriers, the alps and Switzerland, in that order.

I caught Denzler's eye, and we shared an intent look, one that only true adventurers could understand, and I wondered if his fingers and toes tingled just like mine. But that excitement soon turned to terror. On a sudden, some rocks crashed down the mountainside. They tumbled over the precipice near us, and as they hurtled down into the chasm, the sharp echoes of the rocks being dashed to pieces filled me with fear and dread. Would we be swept away by an avalanche? Would I never see my beloved papai again? Startled, I held my breath when Denzler tightened his grip on me.

'Cuidado!' Doña Marisa warned us to be careful.

Just then, Choli, our trusty mule, stepped back to avoid another falling rock, when his hind foot stumbled over the edge. Doña Marisa screamed in terror, the echoes of her shriek ringing in our ears. Denzler had cautioned us never to meddle with a mule's instincts, but surely a little coaxing would not hurt, I thought to myself, given that Choli, with us upon him, seemed a few seconds from doom.

'Hü Choli!' I urged him.

Choli obeyed my command, and with a violent lurch, he mustered up his strength to pull himself upright, and in a matter of seconds we were on our way again. Doña Marisa cried a thousand tears of relief, claiming it was a miracle that Denzler and I had not perished before her eyes, this after I had prodded Choli. She, nevertheless, praised me for my presence of mind. I turned to face Denzler, whose broad grin betrayed his usual calm self.

'Denzler, did you hear the angel wings flapping?'

'Angel wings?'

'An angel helped push Choli back onto the path.'

Denzler gave a hearty laugh, it being the first time I recalled him having done so.

In Leukerbad, I passed a restful night, dreaming of my beau Denzler, the two of us riding Choli up and down the Emmental cheese wedges of the alps, and each time we came across a cheese hole, we would climb inside to listen to our jodels echo within. When morning arrived, I wished to tell Denzler of my alpine dream. Where could he be?

I sneaked into the men's bathing-house, hoping to surprise him. There, a dozen men dressed in long flannels sat stewing in the stinking hot spring water – what an odd sight it was – and near each of them floated a wooden table for their coffee-cup, newspaper and writing thing-em-bobs. One gentleman, who diligently scribbled in his journal, seemed familiar to me. I knelt to dip my hand into the spring water, and I sprinkled some drops onto his head.

He started in surprise. 'Undine?'

'Good morning, Herr Fouqué.' I held out my hand to shake his.

'What are you doing here in Leukerbad?' He gazed at me, wonderstruck.

'We're going to someplace called Simplon.'

'The Simplon pass?'

I shrugged.

'Do you know,' said he, 'I met a Colonel Fitzwilliam in Baden-Baden.'

I gasped, my heart thump-thumping, and I wished to know what I already knew. 'Is my papai looking for me?'

'He is, indeed. And then I met him by chance in Lucerne. I dare say he was destined for Geneva.'

'Ai de mim! Is he going the wrong way?' I frowned.

'It seems he is. Perchance I shall see him in Sion on my way to Geneva?'

'If you do, pray tell him to listen for my drum signal.'

Herr Fouqué knitted his brows. 'Drum signal?'

Before I could respond, Denzler called for me, his stern countenance making me giggle.

'I must go. My Denzler awaits me.'

'*Your* Denzler?' Herr Fouqué turned round to stare at the young Swiss man who stood with his arms folded.

'Ay. He is my beau.' I rose to leave. 'Good-bye, Herr Fouqué.'

'Hmm…a beau. Well, good-bye to you, Undine.'

Denzler introduced our party to his cousin who also went by Denzler. This Denzler No. 2 rarely spoke a word, and if you asked him a question, he would grunt – one grunt meaning yes, two grunts meaning no. I observed the two Denzlers sitting side by side, drinking their glasses of beer, having some kind of silent conversation, for they never uttered more than a few words or grunts. My Denzler, having caught me watching them, summoned me to his side to bid me good-bye.

'Denzler, now that you're my beau, will you not tell me your Christian name?'

Denzler considered this for a moment. 'You may call me Oskar.'

'Oskar?' I had never heard of the name before, and so I committed it to memory. 'Oskar…Oskar…'

'And what is your name, foot-boy?'

'You may call me Sofia-Elisabete,' said I with pride.

And that is how I met my first beau, a Swiss named Oskar Denzler. He told me he sorely missed his family and wished to return to Zürich, and so we shook hands and parted good friends – the best of friends. He strode up the steep Gemmi pass, sure-footed and confident. I strained my eyes to follow his ascent until he disappeared into the mist that clung to the face of the cliff and was gone for ever. I waited for the hot tears to fill my eyes, but for some reason, the tears never came. I stood there, as quiet and still as the alpine air, and then, finding myself lost and alone without my beau, I kicked some pebbles about.

Chapter Nine
The Three Curses

MY FIRST NEAR TRAGEDY, thinks I, on this long voyage to a moon world, was not when I nearly froze in the emerald waters of lake Zug, or when I nearly tumbled over a precipice in the Gemmi pass, or even when I nearly slipped into the wild torrent of the Saltina, although Doña Marisa, no doubt, would say I had been thrice cursed. You see, I believe 'twas when I nearly despaired of saving a friend from a life of poverty. And now that I think on it, I could persuade Doña Marisa to agree with me, at least on that point. In the stories Doña Marisa told me about her family, she, too, once suffered from poverty, and even though she somehow escaped a life of misery, she never forgot the desperation that comes from being poor. Doña Marisa, it turns out, possessed a compassionate heart, but only when she chose to lay claim to it. And so it is for us all.

With Denzler No. 2 acting as guide, we traversed the Canton of Valais – the 'Land of Goitres,' observed Señor Gonzalez, for many people here had goitres. Sometimes a goitre was the size of a cherry; other times, it grew as large as a peck loaf. 'Qué horrible,' whispered Doña Marisa, when a goitrous woman walked by us. Methinks the goitrous women took pride in their goitres. I heard one of them remark that Doña Marisa, being goitre-less, was goosenecked. It occurred to me then, as I felt my neck, that I was goosenecked, too.

The dusty road in the Valais led on for ever in my mind, and thus I became ever so restless and bored, bouncing on the seat or swinging my legs or leaning out the open window, although all I could see were marshy meadows. Finally, I espied something interesting – three small children riding astride an ancient mule.

'Holloah! Holloah!' I hailed them, leaning out the window.

'Siéntese!' Señor Gonzalez quickly pulled me back inside the carriage, for I had nearly fallen out.

Doña Marisa covered her mouth, horror-struck.

'She is safe,' he reassured her.

'She is cursed,' declared she. 'The witch has returned to harm my family.'

'The witch?' I gazed at her with curiosity.

'Once upon a time, there lived an ugly witch, a bruxa, in the French empire,' Doña Marisa began. 'She had deep-set grey eyes, a pale complexion, a curved nose and black greasy hair that she cut square over her ears, the rest of it being gathered in a long pigtail. One day she flew with the north-east wind – vuuuu vuuuu – to Portugal where she aimed to do evil to its people.'

'I can fly when I turn my mind to it,' boasted I.

Pico laughed. 'Liar.'

'But I can,' insisted I.

'Vuuuu vuuuu,' he teased me, and we began to elbow one another.

'Basta!' Señor Gonzalez's sharp reprimand quieted us.

Doña Marisa sighed, and she continued her story. 'The witch entered a caza de pasto, a public-house, in Lisbon where she requested a dish of bacalhau, a salted cod, but the proprietor, he being a prideful Gallego, refused to serve anyone French, while his two sons, Gaspar and Gustavo, mocked this dirty hag, this shabby creature. The witch gave them a penetrating stare, and though she stood a mere five feet high, her ire made her seem twice that height. A violent passion overtook her, and she railed against their ignorance, their abominable treatment of her. She cursed them three times in

French, and when she had done, she flew with a south-west wind –
hooom hooom – and return to Paris she did.'

'Hooom hooom,' Pico wiggled his fingers at me.

'What is a curse?' asked I, ignoring Pico.

'A curse is summoning the supernatural powers to bring about
harm to someone or something,' explained Señor Gonzalez.

'Doña Marisa, what happened next?' With cruel glee, Pico wished
to hear of doom and bloodshed, because he, just like the rest of us,
sensed that something bad was about to happen.

'Ere long Portugal prepared for an invasion by the French
Army,' recounted Doña Marisa. 'Gaspar and Gustavo served in the
Portuguese Army, but they perished in a fierce battle at Sobral. Heart-
broken at the loss of his sons, the Gallego contracted a mysterious
illness where he lay feverish in his bed, mumbling something about
a witch. Jacinta, who suspected that a bruxa had cursed her husband,
gathered a handful of réis that she had saved, and she hastened to
a dilapidated palace where lived the Barão de Catanea, a famous
curandeiro or healer from Brazil.'

I gasped. 'Did the witch kill the sons and make their papai sick?'

'That is what both the Gallego and his wife, Jacinta, believed,'
said Doña Marisa. 'Jacinta pleaded with the Barão to remove the
evil spirits from her home. He, having determined that the Gallego
suffered from the evil eye, burnt herbs and chanted to get rid of
these sinister spirits. He crushed a variety of medicinal roots and
herbs, and he prescribed a strong tea be brewed with them. Jacinta
did as she was told, but her husband, who refused to drink the tea,
succumbed to his illness the next day. Thereafter, Jacinta sank into
extreme poverty, and how she and her daughter and granddaughter
were to survive, she knew not.'

'The curse made everyone poor?' asked I.

'Sí,' replied she in a quiet tone. 'Tragically, half of my family
disappeared for ever.'

'But your papai beat you...'

'Nevertheless, he was the only papai I had,' returned she.

'You still had me and your mamãe,' I reminded her.

Doña Marisa bit her lip as she twirled the diamond ring on her finger, avoiding my stare of expectation.

'Please tell me another story, minha Senhora.'

'Perhaps, soon.' Her countenance wan, her eyes half-closed, she muttered to herself something about the witch's curse and my near tragedies at Zug and the Gemmi.

Oh, how I wished to ask her more about the curse and why the witch wanted to harm me. Was I cursed and really a 'no good penny' as Josefina would often remind me, and that's why bad things happened to me? I gazed at Doña Marisa's handsome features, wondering how she had become rich after being poor and why the witch hadn't cursed her. But I dared not bother her with my questions about the curse and be cast off again; besides, I had promised God that I would help Doña Marisa and think of her before I thought of myself.

At the foot of the Simplon pass stood a picturesque town called Brieg. One can always tell when one has reached Brieg, I suppose, what with three turnips topsy-turvy in the sky and always there to greet you. These big brown turnips or spires, I learnt, sat atop towers that called themselves Caspar, Melchior and Balthazar and protected Stockalper Palace. I thought of my avô and his turret at the hunting lodge, wondering why he had not named it anything, although he did have a bugbear to protect it. It seemed an age ago since I had last seen my avô, and I recalled our sad parting in the old wood.

Doña Marisa praised the beauty of Brieg, for the Rhône and the Saltina wound through it, and the surrounding countryside boasted lush meadows, fruit trees, white cottages, woods and thickets. Señor Gonzalez agreed with his lady's observations, remarking on the peacefulness and holiness of the town, that is, until the next day, when the blaring echoes of a shepherd's alphorn sounded at break of dawn.

Señor Gonzalez, who had fallen from his bed in shock, fired off a volley of oaths in Spanish as the cows, sheep and goats were herded into the town square, their bleats and bells creating a great noise. 'Spiegel! Falth! Lusti!' a shepherd called out to his beloved cows, one

by one. In the evening, the herds returned amidst the cries of the
shepherds. Then, in the morning, it began all over again with the
blare of a shepherd's alphorn, followed by a great noise of bleats and
bells, 'Spiegel! Falth! Lusti!' and Señor Gonzalez's never-ending oaths.

Here, in Brieg, we sat idle at the inn La Croix, waiting for
favourable weather in the Simplon pass, while Señor Gonzalez and
our guide arranged for horses to pull our two carriages. One morning
I walked out with Doña Marisa and Pico to the ancient chapel of
Saint Sebastian to pray for good weather, when we observed a young
girl afflicted with a goitre. 'Pobrecita,' uttered Doña Marisa. Her
hands trembling, Doña Marisa felt the gland at the centre of my
neck to see if a goitre grew there. Having found nothing lumpy, she
sighed with relief, as did I.

'No traveller passing through ever suffers from goitreism or
cretinism,' remarked a young Swiss girl wearing a brown frock made
of coarse cloth, a white apron and a Valais hat – a curiously shaped
little straw hat trimmed with green ribbon.

'Really and truly?' asked I, still fearful I would become goitre'd.

'Only people born in der Schweiz get it,' she assured me and
Doña Marisa.

Struck with awe by her big brown eyes and her nut-brown hair
dressed neatly in two long braids, I imagined her a shiny new doll.
'What's your name?'

'I am Emmerence Odet,' said she, and with the lady's permission,
she would tell us her story.

Enchanted by this pretty girl, Doña Marisa accepted her offer.

'I was born to two cloud-dwellers – a brave chamois-hunter and
his equally brave wife,' began the girl, proud of her heritage. 'In the
summer of my third year, we lived in an old chalet in the Bernese
Alps near Sion. One misty day, while in pursuit of a wily chamois,
my papi lost his footing on a precipice, and he fell five hundred feet.'

'Ay, Dios mío.' Doña Marisa pressed her fingers to her lips.

'Such are the perils of chamois-hunting,' remarked Emmerence
with a resigned air. 'My mami, who had heard his scream echoing in
the mountains, clambered up a crag where she was struck by a falling

rock. Five days later, the chamois-hunter Rochat found me hiding in the chalet, eating a raw potato. He took me to a convent in Sion.'

I tugged at Emmerence's apron. 'I lived in a convent where I slept on straw and ate watery soup.'

Emmerence expressed her surprise. 'Here, we survive on potatoes, milk and cheese. Herr Pfarrer Haas brought me to the Ursuline convent in Brieg where the nuns have schooled me in French, high German, Italian and English, although we speak Swiss-German to one another most of the time. I am a polyglot, which is what Herr Pfarrer says, because I can speak several languages with ease. I am now ten years of age, and I wish to be an explorer someday like Marie Paradis, a servant girl who climbed Mont Blanc.'

Pico gazed in earnest at Emmerence. 'But girls canna be explorers.'

'I'm an explorer,' declared I. 'I'm going to a moon.'

'Der mond? Oh, does not everyone wish to go to the moon?' Emmerence clasped her hands over her heart. Hearing a nun call for her, the charming girl bid us farewell. 'Uf widerluege.'

'Pobrecita,' lamented Doña Marisa. 'What dreams she has. Alas, she will be poor and live in Brieg for ever.'

The following day Pico announced he was of a mind to pray again for favourable weather, and he half-dragged me with him to Saint Sebastian. 'Hilfe! 'Hilfe!' a girl cried out for help. There, in Sebastian Square, two little boys pelted Emmerence with pebbles, taunting her with 'kretin! kretin!' Pico gave the miscreants a violent shove. 'Away! Yer villains,' thundered he. The rascals took to flight, for Pico stood much taller than them.

'Grüezi mitenand,' Emmerence greeted us, her dark brown eyes glistening with gratitude. 'How glad am I to see you both.'

'Grüezi. Why did they call you a cretin?'

She shrugged at me. 'The nuns say I have an old soul, whereas the children think me odd.'

'I dunna think yer odd.' Pico blushed to his eyes.

'Merci vielmal, Pico,' said she, her cheeks glowing.

I gaped at the two of them turning colours. Then I recalled how my papai did the same when he fell in love with my mamãe in

Scarborough and how he began to do strange things afterwards. *Gah!*
With an inward groan, I lagged my companions as they took three
turns in the cobble-stoned square, chatting about the North Sea and
packet-boats and gipsies and hedgehogs.

Enough, I told myself, and squeezing myself in between them, I
took ahold of my new friend's hand. 'Emmerence, do you wish to
skip?' She grinned at me and my childish impertinence. We skipped
merrily along, jodeling 'ho-u ho-u holli dulli hulli dulli ho-u-u-u',
and she taught me an old Swiss song about the coming of the spring.
Of a sudden, Pico nudged me at the elbow. 'Retreat!' warned he,
because, there, at the far end of the square, stood Señor Gonzalez,
scribbling in his small journal-book. And so we bid our friend a
hasty farewell.

'Your freckles have turned red,' observed I, as we scurried back
to the inn.

Pico seized me by the lug. 'Yer lug is turnin' red.'

'Yow!' I rubbed my sore ear.

The next day, once the pouring rain had stopped, Pico and I took
a ramble high up in the meadows when we heard Emmerence singing
the old Swiss song, the one about the coming of spring, the melting
snow, the blue sky and the return of the cuckoo. A first-rate jodeler
she was, her jodels so clear, so bright, so sweet in the still mountain air.

> *Der Ustig wott cho,*
> *Der Schnee zergeiht scho,*
> *Der Himmel isch blaue,*
> *Der Guger het g'schraue,*
> *Der Maye syg cho,*
> *A-ho alli ho alli ho-u ho-u ho ulli lui alli*
> *ho-u ho-u holli dulli hulli dulli ho-u.*

I jodeled in response to her, and she jodeled in return, and back
and forth we went with our jodels until at last we found each other
– she descending a steep mountain path. Pico turned gentleman,
offering to carry her basket, it being filled with fresh eggs. He declared

his wish to escort her back to town, his freckles turning bright red again. Ai de mim! I was surely in the midst of some romanticking going on, and so I linked arms with Emmerence, though, what good that did, when Pico still pestered us, sometimes overtaking us, other times flirting with her.

I gave up trying to separate those two. And lag them I did as we approached town. In the sulks, I shuffled over an old wooden bridge, its railings half-rotten with age. The recent rainfall had swollen the Saltina, and the roar of the wild torrent below made it difficult to think or even enjoy a good sulk. I kicked some pebbles into the raging river just because I could. And then I got the brilliant idea to kick the railing just because I could.

'Gah!' I slipped on a pile of manure, and I landed with a thud on my seat of honour. In an instant, I found myself sliding off the side of the bridge, my legs dangling over the frothing torrent. I grasped one of the rickety posts on the bridge and held on. I had no sooner pondered my terrifying predicament, than I felt myself dragged to safety by Emmerence, who had returned to look for me.

'Emmerence, you saved me, and we broke the curse,' rejoiced I, hugging my dear friend. 'The witch shan't ever get me now.'

'A curse?' Emmerence shot a confused glance at Pico, who had come running to join us on the bridge.

'A witch tried three times to harm me – first at Zug, then in the Gemmi pass, and here on the bridge – and each time she failed.' I gazed in earnest at my companions, but they thought I was crack-brained.

We sallied forth into town. I pledged to Emmerence that we would be the best of friends for ever and ever or at least a thousand years, seeing how I liked her hugeously, and that when I became a mamãe, I would name my first daughter Emmerence to honour her for saving me, and if I didn't have a daughter – well, now, I would name a donkey after her. Pico, with his cheeks aflamed, asked Emmerence to think on him whenever she chanced to see the sun and moon both hanging in the morning sky, and she shyly said she would. It was then that something strange occurred.

'The ground is moving.' I clung to Emmerence.

Emmerence patted my hand. 'Die Schweiz has hundreds of small earthquakes every year.'

From the open window above us, we heard Doña Marisa shriek as the inn swayed, and she blamed the witch who wanted us gone from Switzerland, so gone we would be on the morrow. This piece of news unsettled the three of us children, for we had become great friends.

Emmerence handed an egg to Pico. 'Farmer Müller claims his eggs will cure anything. Perhaps it will cure Doña Marisa's fears?'

Pico shook his head, and he returned the precious egg to her. 'Nothin' will cure her fears.'

Emmerence gave us a sad smile. 'I must return now to the convent. The good sisters await me and these magic eggs.'

'Não, não, não.' I clutched her apron, wishing her to stay with us.

'B'hüt euch Gott! God bless you!' cried she, her eyes bright and shiny. She choked on a sob or two, and in that miserable state, she scurried back to the convent, stopping once to turn round to wave at us and to give us a brave smile. When she disappeared, I covered my face with my hands to weep, while Pico turned strangely silent again.

That night I dreamt of Emmerence clambering up the Valais Alps, and when she tired, she rode a cloud in the shape of a mule that drifted by. Having reached the summit, she sat there alone, eating a sorry-looking shrivelled potato, and when she had done with her meagre dinner, she drank a handful of muddy snow water. Would she survive or perish as a cloud-dweller on her own? Alas, I would never know, what with Doña Marisa wishing to be quit of this country.

The weather now favourable, we set off for the Simplon pass. 'Twas an odd thing, though, that the shepherd didn't blare his alphorn as he usually did every morning. A murmur of tinkling cow bells in the distance greeted us instead.

'Where are the cows?' I rubbed my sleepy eyes.

'It would appear that Spiegel, Falth, Lusti and their compatriots have over-slept themselves.' With a smug grin, Señor Gonzalez glanced out the carriage window.

'Ay! What have you done?' Doña Marisa chided her cortejo.

Señor Gonzalez straightened his jacket. 'You see before you now the proud owner of an alphorn, having cozened it from the shepherd yesterday.'

As we neared Saint Sebastian, the tolling of the bells made a doleful sound, as if in mourning for poor Emmerence, whose destiny would be a life of poverty and loneliness here in Brieg. I puzzled my wits together, when I seized upon a brilliant idea to save Emmerence.

'Minha Senhora, may Emmerence be a guide and come with us to a moon? She's a pony-glot and speaks Italian…and French…and all sorts of things.'

Doña Marisa gave a start. 'The pretty orphan girl can speak Italian? Sí, sí – now I remember.'

'Mi amor,' pleaded Señor Gonzalez, 'we do not have the room, nor can we accommodate the extra weight in the servants' calash. It would not be safe to linger in the pass if one of our carriages broke down. She cannot come with us, and there's an end on it – no hay mas que decir.'

An anxious Doña Marisa fingered her rosary. She reminded me that something could still go wrong again in this 'cursed land and beyond', what with the banditti who roamed in the Simplon pass on the Italian side, eager to rob her of her precious orange diamond ring and her prized cuckoo clocks. I hung my head in sorrow and despair, knowing not how to persuade Doña Marisa to rescue Emmerence from her sad fate. I clasped my hands, and I prayed to God aloud.

'Grüezi! God! I thank you for sending Emmerence to me. If she hadn't saved me on the bridge, I would have fallen into the Saltina. So I humbly ask for your help to save her now from turning into a goitre or a cretin. We cannot take her with us to a moon. It cannot be helped. Truly! You see, our carriages are stuffed with people, and minha Senhora's cuckoo clocks, and bottles and bottles of Señor Gonzalez's wine, and the alphorn that he cozened from a shepherd, and, oh yes, his wheel of Emmental cheese that he hid in the boot, and there's an end on it. Amen.'

I had no sooner finished my prayer and crossed myself, than a miracle occurred. Que milagre! Pico resolved to foot it up the pass, and thus Emmerence could take his place in the carriage. Doña Marisa approved of this plan, and she scolded me for not telling her of my fall on the bridge and Emmerence's heroic act. She glanced with an arched brow at her cortejo as if challenging him to disobey her wishes.

'Humph. I am equal to the task,' declared Señor Gonzalez, who bemoaned that he would have to foot it as well so as not to be outdone by a mere boy. He leant out the window to rap the roof with his bastón, and he instructed the driver to turn the carriage round.

'Huzzah! Señor Gonzalez for ever.' I bounced in my seat in high spirits, my legs swinging when I chanced to kick him.

'Aieeee!' cried he. With a grimace, he gripped his sore knee.

On our entering Sebastian Square, a sweet-tone bell of grace began to chime, and the doors of the chapel swung open. With an eager eye, I watched the parishioners mount the few steps to the chapel, when I espied Emmerence standing at the entrance, her head bent as if in prayer. 'Emmerence,' shouted I, as I leant out the window of our carriage, wildly waving my cap. 'The moon! Come with us to a moon.' Emmerence started on seeing Doña Marisa speaking in earnest with Herr Pfarrer Haas, and she uttered a cry of wonder. As she ran towards us, I sensed the gladness and hope in her heart, and I knew then that we would be reunited with our friend, for God had ordained it so.

Chapter Ten

The Dancing Maja

MY FIRST BITTER HEART-ACHE, thinks I, began one bleak, rain-soaked day in the Simplon pass, the day I learnt why Doña Marisa had abandoned me as a bebê when we lived in Lisbon. She, who half-created me, had cared not whether I perished in a foundling hospital. She blamed Satan for making her do evil things in her past. Until then, I never truly thought much of evil, being a mere child at the time. I knew not the power of evil. I knew not how it can make you do things you know are wrong. I knew not how it can ruin you if you give it leave. But on that sad day in the Simplon pass, I came to know something of evil.

In Brieg, Señor Gonzalez hired a mule, claiming he could not foot it up the Simplon pass as promised because I had kicked him on the knee earlier that morning. I giggled into my hand, and when Emmerence wondered at my mirth, I explained how I had prayed to God to make Señor Gonzalez want to go rightly in this world. My new companion, on discovering that Pico had given up his place in the carriage for her, saluted him with 'merci vielmal' and waved her straw hat as we passed him on the covered bridge at the Saltina. She had never travelled through the Simplon pass before, and thus every bridge, every torrent, every cascade seemed vastly more interesting with her by my side, now that we would be girl explorers together.

At the first refuge or sheltering-house for travellers, shepherds and chamois-hunters along the Simplon pass, we came upon a Swiss girl of seven years of age, dressed in tattered clothes. This delicate girl had a sickly countenance like so many of the peasant-folk in the Valais. A shepherd's daughter, she had walked down the steep mountain-side by herself to sell pressed Alpine roses and leaves that she carried in a basket. Doña Marisa gave a franc to the girl. 'Merci vielmal,' whispered this tiny thing in a trembling voice. I wondered if she ever laughed or cried given that she seemed wholly without strength to do either.

'Pobrecita! What a sad fate she will have,' lamented Doña Marisa. When we departed the refuge, the sight of the diseased girl made Emmerence sob into her hand. She wiped her tears with her apron, and she thanked Doña Marisa again and again for taking her into her service. Doña Marisa handed her some pressed flowers and leaves. 'Keep these inside your Bible and never forget your homeland,' instructed she.

As we climbed up the dusty pass, Señor Gonzalez rode alongside our carriage to speak with Doña Marisa, he having found our guide Denzler No. 2 too quiet for his liking. He shouted to his lady over the rumble of the carriage that the Simplon pass was truly a noble road, similar to a carriageway with its posts or low walls. He thought the road most scenic, indeed, as it wound through hills covered with majestic pines.

'Qué maravilla!' exclaimed Señor Gonzalez. We had reached the gallery of the Ganther – a tunnel, which, according to our guide, had been dug by blasting through solid granite. On quitting the gallery, we crossed the lofty bridge of the Ganther, which is where I lost sight of Pico, he having fallen farther and farther behind on the road.

In Berisal we came across the third refuge with an inn and horses. I begged Señor Gonzalez to hire a mule for Pico, and he advised it would cost me nine francs. I dug into my pockets one by one, whereupon I handed him a total of eight francs he had paid me to stop jodeling whilst we travelled in Switzerland. Señor Gonzalez was all amazement that he had paid me that much money.

'You are a franc short, foot-boy,' noted he, jingling the coins in his hand.

I dug again into another pocket, and to my surprise, I pulled out something roundish, something I had put there an age ago during our stay in Zürich. With an impish grin, I handed a wooden button to him.

'A button does not a franc make,' insisted he.

'Señor Gonzalez?' I bit my lip.

'Sí? Well, out with it.'

I took a deep breath. 'A-ho alli ho alli ho-u ho-u ho ulli lui.'

He started at my loud jodel. 'Ay! I never want to hear a jodel again. How is it that a country of sublime beauty could have such a ridiculous jodel?'

I took another deep breath. 'A-ho alli ho alli ho-u ho-u ho ulli lui alli ho-u ho-u holli dulli hulli dulli ho-u.'

'Basta! Basta!' With alacrity, he paid me a franc to stop jodeling.

I examined the coin. With an air of triumph, I held out my hand. 'Ha! Ha! Here's the franc I owe you.'

Señor Gonzalez snatched the silver coin from me, and he began to grumble – something about being cozened by a mere child. When, finally, Pico trudged up to the third refuge, I told him that I had paid nine francs to hire a mule. 'Huzzah! Soofia-Eee for ever,' cheered he. And that is how I saved my cousin Pico for a second time, the first being when I had paid the gipsy duke to release him from service.

Thereafter, we passed through more tunnels – the Shalbert Gallery, the Gallery of the Glaciers – and, according to our guide, we had reached the highest point of the Simplon road. At dusk, we weary travellers entered a wild and lonely valley, where, in the hamlet of Simplon, we lodged at the Post-House and supped on fresh eggs and mountain trout and something called fritters, which turned out to be frogs legs. 'The fritters taste chicken-y,' declared Pico. But I wouldn't eat them, nor would I eat the eggs. Emmerence assured me the magic eggs could cure anything – disease, melancholy, fatigue. To please my companion, I ate a magic egg, but nothing of note happened to me once I did.

The next morning I wished for neatly-dressed braids, and so my companion braided my short hair and tied it with ribbon. She asked if I had any girl's clothes. To be sure, I quickly denied having any out of fear that Doña Marisa would make me wear the Black Forest costume with bright red bollenhut again. I told her that I, who had been hired as a foot-boy, preferred to dress in boy's clothes. My relationship with Doña Marisa confused her. I wonder now what she thought of our travelling party's foreign mix of manners and attitudes – British, Portuguese, Spanish – and how strange and shocking it must have been for a Swiss girl like her.

Our carriages ready, we began the descent on the pass. After we had quitted the shadowy gallery of Algaby, we traversed the dark and haunting valley of Gondo, where I imagined the restless and tortured soul of Pontius Pilate roaming in the barren landscape, drifting over the lofty rocks or hovering above the road carved on the granite. Señor Gonzalez must have sensed my dread, for he likened this gloomy place to the nether world of Dante's *Inferno.* When we crossed a sturdy bridge, below which in the abyss a whitish vapour rose from the raging and roaring torrent, I became convinced that Satan lived here, and I wondered if he knew this Signor Dante.

Strange grey clouds resembling whirligigs appeared overhead, and so we sought shelter in the ninth refuge, our party being the sole travellers at this lonely sheltering-house. While we waited for the rain to cease, an ancient shepherd, wild and hungry-looking, entered the refuge, asking if we had any food to give him. Doña Marisa handed him some bread and cheese, for which he grunted his thanks ere he vanished.

'Ay, poverty and hunger can make you desperate,' said she.

'I stole an onion once,' admitted I. 'Sister Matilde made me give it back.'

'Sometimes you can't take back what you have done,' returned she in a mournful tone.

This puzzled me. 'What do you mean?'

'Listen, and you will understand. There once lived a poor widow named Jacinta,' Doña Marisa began. 'Her sole occupations were to embroider shirts for a few réis while she cared for her grandchild. Her daughter sold roasted chestnuts in the Praça de Comércio, the Commercial Square, and often disappeared in the evenings. They barely made enough réis to survive, and they would go hungry when given the choice of eating sardinha for dinner or purchasing coal to heat their mean little abode during the winter.'

'But what was there to eat?' asked I.

'The trick is to drink down a great deal of water and then go to sleep so as not to think of food,' Doña Marisa revealed to me. 'One day, as Jacinta's daughter roasted her one thousandth chestnut, a fat friar dressed in a brown serge and black cowl and wearing sandals introduced himself as Brother Rustico. He asked her if she enjoyed dancing, to which she nodded in reply, and he convinced her that if she joined the sisterhood, she would never go hungry again.

'Brother Rustico conducted her to a convent surrounded by a high wall, its garden filled with exotic flowers, fountains, shady alcoves and sequestered walkways. There, in this veritable Eden, she partook of a banquet offered to novitiates like her. Later, she met with the Abbess, who would teach her how to dance the bolero, fandango and valza, how to speak proper English and Spanish and how to dress in maja costume, complete with a flounced basquiña, trimmed bodice with tassels, lace mantilla, embroidered jacket, snow-white silk stockings and silk slippers.'

I scratched my head. 'The nuns at the Convento do Desterro never danced.'

Señor Gonzalez uttered a loud groan, and I wondered why.

'My papai says I shall never dance the bolero.' I shuddered with fear when I recalled how angry he had become at the thought of me dancing the bolero.

'No te preocupes. Do not worry. I shall teach you the bolero.' Doña Marisa resumed her story. 'In the evenings, unbeknown to her mother, she joined the other nuns, these lindíssimas dressed as majas, to dance with noblemen, wealthy merchants and British officers. Her charms enchanted many a guest who wished to dance with her for ever, but the Abbess rejected each of the suitors. Until one day a Spanish nobleman named Don Rafael de la Riva y de León declared he would pay many a gold escudo for this lindissima. With the blessing of the Abbess, she danced away with Don Rafael, never to return to the convent.'

'Was Don Rafael in love?' wondered I.

'He believed himself in love.'

'Humph, in love...' Señor Gonzalez muttered to himself.

Doña Marisa continued. 'When Jacinta discovered the truth that her daughter had come under the protection of Don Rafael without being married to him, she bawled and beat her chest, and she made herself seriously ill. The day before she died, Jacinta gave her daughter an ancient key. She said it belonged to Don Luis de Luna, and she begged her daughter to find her real father in Cádiz before it was too late.'

'Don Luis?' I thought for a moment, before I remembered the story of the magic oranges. 'He tricked Jacinta, and he took the pretty orange diamonds.'

'Sí, and he gave Jacinta the ancient key,' said Doña Marisa. 'You have a good memory.'

'What was Don Luis like?'

Doña Marisa shrugged. 'Jacinta's daughter refused to see Don Luis. She scoffed at that idea of finding her real father when she had already set her heart on dancing the bolero with Don Rafael every night, wearing beautiful clothes, hiring her own servants and indulging in the best of food and drink.'

'Did Don Rafael like children?' I wondered out loud, but Doña Marisa glanced away, leaving me with an inward feeling of doom.

'The baby made too much noise and demanded her attention. Don Rafael told her that if she wanted his protection, she must make a bargain with him, to wit, she must take the baby to the Misericórdia, the foundling hospital in Lisbon.'

'What happened then?' I held my breath, my heart thump-thumping. I already knew the answer, but I wished for my own fairy tale to end happily.

'She made her choice,' said she in a low, tremulous voice. 'There, at the foundling hospital in the forenoon, she placed her bundled infant in the arms of a nun. She kissed her tiny daughter good-bye, and she began a new life with Don Rafael. And so that's what happened.'

'That's not how the story goes,' shouted I. My indignant outburst took Doña Marisa and everyone by surprise. I knew how the nuns had found me, and like any child who recalls particular details of a story, especially one involving herself, a sense of outrage occurs when a story-teller changes the story.

'Ay! What a temper you have,' exclaimed she.

'You put me in the roda during the night,' I accused her. 'Sister Matilde said so.'

'Well, I *might* have done. It does not signify.' Her evasiveness put her in the fidgets.

Señor Gonzalez's groan of disbelief only heightened my own disquietude. It seemed to me that a mamãe should not give up her own child. Had she not been all I had in the world after my avó, my grandmother, died? This touched me to the quick, and the insides of my belly began to burn from the red-hot heat of a thousand buried suspicions and hurts. A sudden ferocity overcame me. I imagined myself under a spell in which I had been turned into an angry lion – rrraaaawwrr! – clawing my paws in the air and making a great deal of noise with my snaps and snarls.

'Silencio!' Doña Marisa chided me, grasping my arms. 'I came back for you, did I not?'

I struggled to be free of her. 'Tell the truth.'

'You must tell her, now that you've started this,' admonished Señor Gonzalez.

'Then listen.' Doña Marisa trembled. 'Sí, I did a terrible thing. I put you in the roda at night, and I left you there with a note. I must have…I might have rung the bell to alert the nuns.'

'Sister Matilde found me in the morning. She said I was half-frozen.' My heart sank to my toes. What I had inwardly suspected and wished not to be true had indeed been true, namely, Doña Marisa had not wanted me, and she got rid of me in a most cruel and reckless manner.

Doña Marisa's eyes turned shiny. 'I was young and foolish at the time, and I was lured by the temptation of wealth and its evil charms – the devil saw to it.'

'Tonta!' cried I. A bitterness filled my heart, and I wept.

'It seems…it seems I have much to atone for,' her voice quavered.

'Indeed, but better to do it in this life,' muttered Señor Gonzalez.

Doña Marisa searched her cortejo's face, and when he cast down his eyes, she raised her hand to her left temple as if she wished to rub away her crescent-shaped scar there.

When my papai had first told me of the erstwhile Marisa Soares Belles and how she had abandoned me at a convent when I was a bebê, I began to dream of her. I had formed a definite image of her in my mind, for no doubt she was a lindissima who tripped about with castanets in her hands because she loved to dance the bolero every night. I imagined her the most beautiful, the most perfect creature in the world, which is why papai had been placed under enchantment.

But I hid my curiosity about her, along with my suspicions and doubts as to why she did not want me, deep in my heart where they remained safe from my papai, and oh yes, from myself. Now that I knew why she had abandoned me and how Satan had befriended her, I discovered that she had not always been kind, not always been loving, and I wondered yet again how the tiny crescent-shaped scar on her left temple got there, a suspicion of which I locked inside of my heart.

Señor Gonzalez, who took pity on me, went searching for me after I had fled the refuge. There, out of doors, the rain had stopped, and the sun ever and anon peeked behind the dreary grey clouds. Señor Gonzalez removed his capa, and he wrapped me up in it to keep me warm.

'Each of us is a contradiction, and Doña Marisa is no exception,' posited he. 'Do you know what I mean by that?'

'Não,' replied I, reverting to Portuguese to comfort myself.

'We each of us contain conflicting qualities.'

This confused me. 'Não entendo.'

'Take yourself, for example. You appear to be an artless and charming girl, yet you can be cunning and mischievous. You appear to be a dainty little thing, yet you enjoy being a daring girl, dancing on a tight rope and diving into a cold lake.'

'Sim?' I wrinkled my forehead.

He pointed to the road. 'Look round us at the Simplon pass. Napoleon built this noble road, this remarkable feat of engineering, yet he could be cruel and destroy villages and the people who lived there.'

'O diabo!'

'The devil he can be,' Señor Gonzalez nodded. 'Now, let us think on Doña Marisa. She can be a noble woman, yet she can be childish. She can be caring and generous, yet she can be selfish and unkind. One cannot reconcile – make sense of – these contradictions. They just are.'

I struggled to make sense of what could not be made sense of, but my wee brain could not grasp this thing called contradictions. I remained in ill-humour, refusing to speak to Doña Marisa at first, and when I deigned to speak to her, I did so in Portuguese – sim for yes, não for no, &c. It seemed that whenever I spoke in Portuguese, it irked her, and I wonder now if she wished to forget her past life of poverty in Lisbon – a life that had once included me.

A hint of suspicion tugged at my heart as to whether my papai had wished to forget me and the war as well. I had lived for three years at the Convento do Desterro, and yet papai never came for me during that time. He blamed the war for having separated us. He searched for me in Lisbon at one point, while the war still waged, but what of the years before then? Had he forgotten me during that time? Could it be that neither of my parents had wanted me when I was a bebê?

Doña Marisa requested that I join her in the calash, just the two of us, as our party continued on the descent to Domo d'Ossola. I sank into the seat next to her, where I sat brooding, my eyes cast down.

Doña Marisa patted my hand. 'Minha Sofinha, why must you be stubborn this way, speaking in Portuguese? Hmm?'

I snatched my hand away from hers. Only Sister Matilde had called me by the tender endearment of Sofinha, a name that had made me, a lonely orphan, feel loved and wanted.

'Me chamo Sofia-Elisabete,' said I, and I folded my arms to make my point.

'I named you Sofia, and Sofia you shall always be.'

'Não,' I shook my head. 'Me chamo Sofia-Elisabete.'

Doña Marisa sighed. 'Listen, you were much safer at the convent than with me. Don Rafael was a bad man with a bad temper, and I came to live in terror of him. I worried that he would do you harm. I sent Josefina to the convent to deliver a note, in which I urged the nuns to take you somewhere far away. I gave them a generous donation. And I gave them your real name. Do you understand why I did that? I wished that I might find you again someday.'

'Mentirosa!' I called her a liar, and I said a mamãe should love her child and not send the child away.

'Eu amo-te, minha Sofinha,' she half-whispered in Portuguese as she smoothed my hair.

I drew back upon hearing that she loved me, and I sensed she wished that I loved her. How was it that she could both love me and abandon me? I shook my finger at her, lecturing her that a child needs her mamãe and that a mamãe protects her child; at least that's what my mamãe in Scarborough had told me. She, Aggie Fitzwilliam, had once declared that she would have walked a thousand miles and crossed a thousand bridges if it would have saved her own son, because nothing could be stronger than a mamãe's love.

Doña Marisa coloured. 'Ay! Perhaps you should return to this... this ancient mamãe in Scarborough who enjoys scampering about in the countryside.'

Angered by her mocking and superior tone, I told her that I loved my mamãe in Scarborough – the best mamãe in the world. Doña Marisa's cheeks turned crimson, and she chided me for being a most ungrateful, unkind child. Our strained conversation, having

turned into angry shouts and taunts, was overheard by everyone —
our travelling companions, the driver, the servants, the guide, the
peasants passing by. Even the two mules for our calash flattened their
ears, and they half-whinnied, half-brayed as only mules can do.

A grim-faced Señor Gonzalez approached us, no doubt disturbed
by this latest quarrel, and he signalled the driver to stop. Doña
Marisa alighted from the calash, whereupon she tossed up her head,
and angrily so, ere she stalked off in a sullen mood. I sat alone in a
miserable state, until Emmerence got into the calash to comfort me
and to wipe the tears from my cheeks.

'Have you ever prayed a novena?' asked she in a gentle tone. I
shook my head. In times of difficulty she would make a novena — a
daily, devotional prayer for nine days. She believed it would help me,
and so she uttered a simple prayer to the Holy Ghost to guide me on
the path of love, mercy and forgiveness.

> *Oh, Holy Ghost,*
> *Bend my stubborn heart,*
> *Melt my frozen heart,*
> *Sweet'n my bitter heart,*
> *And guide me, for I have lost my way.*

I repeated the prayer after her, but half-an-hour later, I confess
that my heart froze with bitterness once more, and the sacred words
had been forgotten. Oh, how I fervently wished to see my papai
again, to be at home again with him and to speak with him in my
lingua matriz, my mother-tongue, as we often did and with such
ease. But no thanks to Doña Marisa's recent revelations of how she
had abandoned me, my embittered heart was far from pure; ergo,
it would be a long time before papai would find me now, and how
could I forgive her for that?

Chapter Eleven

Majo Girl

MY FIRST BOLERO, thinks I, was when I leapt so high that, with my outstretched hand, I could have thumped a crescent moon to make it sway to and fro. Dancing is a salve to the soul, they say, because it can heal almost anything – sorrow, melancholy, illness. I can swear to the truth of it, having suffered heartbreak in the Simplon pass when I learnt why Doña Marisa had abandoned me as a bebê. But little did I know then how dancing would help heal the breach between Doña Marisa and me.

We entered the valley of Ossola on a colossal bridge that connected two mountains, the river Doveria flowing below. 'Qué magnifico!' cried Señor Gonzalez, and he declared the two arches of the bridge at Crevola divine. In the town of Domo d'Ossola he found us lodgings at Hôtel d'Espagne, where he observed that we must be in Italia now, for the great Spanish Hotel had stone floors, painted ceilings and the filthiest of rooms and necessaries. Not understanding his meaning, I wondered why a Spanish hotel had been built here. Señor Gonzalez described how the medieval town of Domo d'Ossola, with its ancient loggias, arcades, ornamented arches, balconies and fortified walls, had once been ruled by Spain for two centuries.

A signora with eyes as black as olives and a red silk handkerchief tied round her head, beckoned us to the sala, the dining room. 'Sedetevi, per favore,' she motioned to the chairs, and she hastened to serve Señor Gonzalez and herself a goodly amount of red wine. 'Alla salute!' She toasted to his health, and he to hers. With a broad grin, she served us up generous portions of vermicelli soup. I sank into my chair, poking at the skinny worms floating in my bowl of minestra. Oh, how I missed my old friend Mr Maccaroni, whom I had not eaten up in months.

'Mangiamo!' the signora urged, setting down a gigantic platter of steaming maccaroni tossed up with cheese and olive oil. 'Maccaroni! Maccaroni!' cried I, my belly grumbling, my attention riveted by the mound of maccaroni before me. But Pico got to it first. To my surprise, he turned gentleman, and he served us up a heap of maccaroni. 'Mangiamo,' insisted he.

Emmerence stared at her plate, not knowing how to eat what was for her a strange dish. At a table near us, I observed an Italian merchant using his hands to twist and pull the maccaroni, which he crammed into his mouth. Intrigued by his style of eating, I tossed my fork and did the same. And that is how I learnt to eat this doughy and cheesey goodness in the Italian way.

In the course of the evening, after we children had gone to bed, the haunting blare of an alphorn – and one poorly played – disturbed our dreams. The mournful eeriness of it, though, far from lulling me back to sleep, kept me now entirely awake. I trampled over Pico to reach the window where I beheld the tranquillity of the vale during the moonlight hour.

Bwwaaarrrhhhmmm.

Emmerence yawned into her hand. 'Is that Señor Gonzalez's alphorn?'

'I'd rather he howl at the moon when he's drunk,' grumbled Pico, covering his head with a pillow.

'Um bêbado!' I called Señor Gonzalez a drunkard.

No thanks to his drunken, mid-night rambling, Señor Gonzalez set about half-asleep the next morning to hire two gendarmes to protect us, or should I say, Doña Marisa's jewels and cuckoo clocks, from the banditti who roamed in the hills. These two gendarmes, being Italian, rather enjoyed slapping each other on the face and calling each other a fool (sciocco!) or a rogue (mariolo!), and after a half-an-hour of bandying insults, they would kiss and embrace each other like the greatest of friends. 'Tontos,' muttered Doña Marisa. We set off then with our buffoons and a sluggish Señor Gonzalez, who armed himself with a brace of pistols and his sword.

To my surprise, the countryside abounded with goitrous cretins lazing in the groves, and I felt a thousand sorrows that the people of Italia should also suffer from this horrendous disease. Could not some magic eggs cure them? Alas, we had eaten them up in Simplon, and there were no more to be had. Doña Marisa had seen the cretins as well, and she fingered the centre of her neck, still anxious that she would find a lump there. To please her lady, Emmerence examined my neck, prodding it for lumps. She declared me lump-less and healthy. Doña Marisa gave me a tentative smile, but I turned away in a pout. I felt my heart harden and a chill in the air.

We crossed a handsome bridge over the Toce, when suddenly Señor Gonzalez slumped onto his mule, the dustman having come for him. And so our men tossed him in our carriage where his snores vibrated like the music of an alphorn. 'Tonto!' cried Doña Marisa. Vexed with her cortejo, she removed a small enamel box from her reticule, and she began to cover her face with a heavy layer of white dust. When she had done, she smeared a scarlet-coloured jelly onto her lips, making herself ghoulish, indeed.

'Emmerence, you must speak Italian and tell the banditti that I'm a witch and that I shall eat them up if they don't less us pass unharmed. Entiendes? Do you understand?'

Emmerence gulped. 'Yes, Doña Marisa.'

'Ánimo! Courage! Let us hope that the banditti are fools, just like our gendarmes and Señor Gonzalez,' said she.

'Não vás,' I begged Doña Marisa not to leave me, surprising us both with my outpouring of concern. A sense of terror overcame me as I recalled the stories our innkeeper had told us of the banditti

attacking innocent travellers. Why, just a sennight ago, the banditti
had murdered an English gentleman in a gun fight when the latter
refused to give up his gold Napoleons, which he had hidden in a
secret drawer. And a month before that, the banditti had stolen away
the wife of an Italian nobleman, but the nobleman refused to pay the
ransom because he never did like his wife that much. Unfortunately
for him, his spiteful wife resolved to take to the mountains – andare
in campagna – which meant she turned bandit, and with the aid of
the banditti, she seized her husband's carriage, robbing him of his
valuables, money and the outer-clothes that he wore, and thereafter
ordered the bandits to drag him in the mud.

Just then, we heard two shots in the air, and a band of masked
banditti, who had come riding down the hills, surrounded us. They
began to lay hold of our men as prisoners, punishing them with
blows and kicks, and all this time Señor Gonzalez snored on, for
nothing would waken him now. Doña Marisa covered herself with her
black mantilla, whereupon she alighted from the carriage, grasping
Señor Gonzalez's sword. The bandits murmured disgusting words of
pleasure at the alluring Signora in their midst, and they commenced
to fight over who would get her. Tearing away the handkerchief from
his face, the bandit chief, the one whom they called capo-brigante,
advanced towards her with a sinister eye. My heart filled with dread
that this blackguard would harm Doña Marisa.

'Attenzione!' warned Emmerence in Italian. 'Lei una strega.'

'Uah! Uah!' laughed the bandit chief, his two front teeth black with
rot. He drew a small dagger from his belt, and he pointed it at them.

'Tengo hambre,' screeched Doña Marisa in Spanish. 'Ahora te como!'

'Ho fame,' interpreted Emmerence. 'Adesso ti mangio!'

With a fierce attitude, Doña Marisa flung her mantilla aside to
reveal the wild fright she had become, her scarlet lip jelly having
smeared onto her teeth. She spun round – to the left, then to the
right – brandishing her sword and bursting into demonic cackles.
Believing her to be the spectre of a witch, the bandit chief started
back with terror, for a coward he really was. 'Alla speranza di Dio!'
He begged for God's help, grasping the medals and relics he wore

round his neck. He thereafter vaulted his horse with alacrity. 'Andiamo!' he ordered his fellow bandits to make haste, and they, being struck into a panic, rode off with him in a frenzy, disappearing into a swirl of dust.

Safe now from these marauders, I heaved sobs of relief in rhythm with Señor Gonzalez's tranquil snores. 'Tonto!' I slapped him on his cheek in the Italian way, but he slept on in a peaceful dream. Emmerence returned within, convinced that a miracle had saved us from the bandits. Pico, however, turned glum as he rode past us, grumbling that our brief clash with the banditti had sorely disappointed him after hearing the tales of wild bandits.

A brave Doña Marisa rode a mule until we reached Ornavasso, 'the better to guard our carriages', said she, and I have no doubt her gruesome face scared off many a witless bandit. 'She is a heroine,' declared Emmerence when some barefooted peasants dropped to their knees on the road and crossed themselves, much to Doña Marisa's pleasure and amusement. So that is how the legend of Donna Marisa senza paura – Doña Marisa the fearless – spread throughout the land.

Afterwards, in Ornavasso, no matter how many times I tried to persuade Señor Gonzalez that Doña Marisa had turned herself into a bruxa while he had been sleeping, he refused to believe his beloved lady had turned into a hideous hag. And although I was all amazement at Doña Marisa's derring-do, I wondered why she had lacked the courage to choose me over the evil Don Rafael and why she hadn't cast a spell over him when he had hurt her. My thoughts in a tangle, I began to brood again, muttering to myself in Portuguese.

Señor Gonzalez dismissed the two dunderheads he had hired to protect us from the banditti, and he thereafter made arrangements with some boatmen to take us and our prized possessions down the Toce to Lago Maggiore, where our carriages would meet us in the town of Baveno. Emmerence, having never been inside a boat before, was wild to ride in one. She squealed with delight whenever the sprays of water drenched us or a fish swam alongside us.

The friendly fishes brought to mind the day my papai and I had befriended two dolphins when we had journeyed by coble to Filey Bay. With a secretive smile, I began to jodel in Portuguese a tune that would surely make papai laugh: oh-lah pa-pai ah-deh-oosh. My ode to papai must have vexed Doña Marisa. She demanded that I speak English again or else she wouldn't take me to the palaces on the Borromean Islands.

'Nunca,' I refused to speak English ever again.

She glared at me. 'Ay! Josefina will mind you while we visit the islands.'

Ora essa! Well, I never! I spent the next day locked inside my gloomy bedchamber at our inn, the Croix de Malthe, while my companions got to visit noble palaces and rich gardens on Isola Bella and Isola Madre. 'I shan't feel sorry for myself. I shan't,' I muttered to myself as I stamped to and fro in the room.

I imagined myself a princess yearning for her best beloved papai, but my evil mamãe had locked me away in a tower. I leant out the window with a tragic air, breathing in the sharp scents of forest-trees, olive-trees and vineyards. Sadly, my brave papai never came to rescue me. And when my gaoler, Josefina, brought me some sustenance – a wretched piece of crust and worm-filled soup – I knew that the minestra had been poisoned, yet I ate it anyway. Don't you know – a pining princess has to maintain her strength to do all her pining?

But my pining turned into childish resentment, and my resentment turned into childish revenge. I had no sooner thought of a brilliant and devious means of escape, than everyone had returned from their jaunt to the islands. When my gaoler released me from the tower, I bounded to the lake where I set about to kick some pebbles. Señor Gonzalez chanced upon me; at least that's what he wanted me to believe, because I had seen him lurking behind a tree.

As we strolled the shore of the lake, Señor Gonzalez said he would tip me the wink. I shrugged at him, and so he explained he would reveal a secret to help me. He said that while Doña Marisa could be stubborn now and then, her temper improved after she had time to ponder things. He believed that she and I were similar in that we both could be stubborn, and it reminded him of a joke he had heard once about two strong-minded politicians.

'What do you get when you cross a stubborn mule with another stubborn mule?' asked he.

'Uma mula estúpida,' replied I in Portuguese.

'A stupid mule? No, no, no. When you cross a stubborn mule with another stubborn mule, you get nothing – nothing at all. A mule cannot be crossed with another mule. So therein lies the joke.'

I shrugged at him.

Señor Gonzalez sighed. 'When two stubborn people, just like two stubborn mules, come together, nothing is ever resolved, and as the story goes, what begins ill comes to a bad end. Do you see my point?'

'Agora sim, Señor Gonzalez.' My response of 'to be sure' seemed to satisfy him.

The sun having set, we gathered on the balcony at the inn to listen to a musician who roved the street below, strumming a mandolino. Señor Gonzalez encouraged me with a slight nod, and thus I approached Doña Marisa. She, wondering what we were about, scowled at us with a suspicious eye. Speaking in Portuguese, I scolded her, telling her that she was a stubborn mule (como uma mula!), and if she was monstrous cross towards a stubborn mule like me, well, believe you me, she would end up with nothing (nada!) and it would be very bad for her (muito mal!) – oh, and Señor Gonzalez had tipped me the wink about this. Doña Marisa gasped at my impertinence. She turned to her cortejo, narrowing her eyes at him.

Señor Gonzalez raised his hands in submission. 'Ay! That was not my point. She has misconstrued my meaning.'

'Humph,' returned she.

Pico snickered at me. 'I dunna know what yer said, but yer both in the suds now.'

The next morning Emmerence took me to the ancient Church of Santi Gervasio and Protasio where I said my novena. When I had done, she asked me if I was truly sorry and wished to stop quarrelling with Doña Marisa, given my outburst yesterday. 'Agora sim,' I half-assured her and myself. Her eyes widened in astonishment at my

coolness, and thus I hung my head, ashamed of having lied inside
God's house. I held my breath, waiting for an avalanche to crash into
the chapel, but God had spared me this time.

'Look over there,' whispered Emmerence, nudging me on the
arm. A sad woman, her head bent low and covered with a black
mantilla, prayed with her rosary in hand. It took me a moment or
two to recognise Doña Marisa, who sat there alone as frozen as a
marble statue. With the feeling of a true penitent, I resolved to wash
my hands in a magic spring, and if there wasn't a spring here, then
a magic lake just might do. Emmerence and I sallied forth to Lago
Maggiore, where I knelt to cleanse my hands in the cold, blue water,
and I prayed to God to help me wash away the bitterness in my heart
and to let my heart be pure. *By the bye, God, please help me find the
moon world, for surely it will cure Doña Marisa's sadness.*

The time had come to get on, yet Señor Gonzalez still refused to
believe my tale about the banditti on the road. 'Es imposible!' said
he, but I detected a twinkle in his eye. He, having heard enough of
my cries and angry pleas, hired two private boats that conveyed us
and our carriages to Sesto, at which point our guide quitted us to
return to the Valais. From there we continued our journey by the
great military road to Milan.

Señor Gonzalez joked with Doña Marisa that Milan is a city where
the wealthy Italian matrons and their cicisbei or escorts frequented
the shops during the day and La Scala in the evening where they sat
in their boxes gossiping or playing at cards. Given that he travelled
as Doña Marisa's escort, Señor Gonzalez believed the two of them
would be most welcomed here. We set off then to see the sights,
including the white marble palace of the Milan Cathedral, when
something singular happened.

'Arre, burriquito, arre!' I kicked my heels into Señor Gonzalez's
sides.

'Aieeee! That hurt,' Señor Gonzalez chided me, for he had become
my beast of burden as we climbed up the staircase of the cathedral.
There, perched on his back, I inhaled the singular scent of a Spanish

man, who brought to mind a hodgepodge of tobacco and red wine and oranges and figs.

The difficult climb of more than five hundred steps had tired Doña Marisa, and so I kept her company while the others roamed the rooftop of the cathedral, the better for them to view the spirals, carvings and sculpture. Near us stood a finely dressed Englishman sketching one of the fretted spires. His handsome profile suddenly being revealed to us, Doña Marisa gasped, and she spun round, holding her belly. With alacrity, she draped herself with her black mantilla, her head bent as if in deep prayer. When the light-haired gentleman with the noble mien passed by us, he slowed his step to stare at her for a moment or two, and then he went on his way. I believed he was as baffled as I about Doña Marisa's belly, which seemed a bit swollen to me.

'Doña Marisa, did you eat too much maccaroni?' I stared at her roundish belly.

She grinned at me, pleased I had spoken in English. 'Sí, I ate too much maccaroni,' she patted her belly.

'Jesus likes maccaroni, thinks I. He told me so at The Last Supper when I dreamt of it last night.'

'The Last Supper?' Doña Marisa wrinkled her forehead. 'Ah, sí, the fresco we saw at the convent yesterday.'

'Jesus said unto me, "I hunger." So I served him up a dish of maccaroni. And then he told me to serve up a dish of maccaroni to the poor. "Verily I say unto you, you ate up all of the maccaroni," complained I to Jesus.'

Doña Marisa smiled into her hand. 'What did Jesus do?'

'Like magic, dish after dish of maccaroni appeared, and so I fed the poor. Methinks it was a miracle.' I nodded to her.

On the ninth day of my novena, I met with Doña Marisa in her sitting room, where we exchanged pleasant buongiorno's. 'Sofia-Elisabete, I wish to find la luna,' said she, and my heart warmed at her use of my true, chosen name. Having recalled her promise about la luna, I shared her wish to find a real moon world because none of the places we had journeyed to – what with everyone fighting, begging or walking about with sad faces or goitres – resembled the society of the moon-folk in the least.

Doña Marisa revealed that ere long we would be nearing la luna, and we would know it when we reached the sea, but it would be difficult to find la luna. If we prayed hard enough and puzzled our wits together, we might succeed, and succeed we must. Would I help her find la luna? I nodded, and feeling most knightly, I knelt on bended knee and pledged my loyalty to Doña Marisa in her quest to find la luna, the chivalry of which diverted her.

'I have a surprise for you, my little knight, and I hope I have done right this time. Did you know that here, in Italia, it's considered fashionable and diverting for the ladies to dress as men when they attend the theatre?' Doña Marisa winked at me. 'Well, now, you can dress as a real Spanish majo, just like Señor Gonzalez. We majos and majas in Spain are a proud, defiant people, and that is why we wear our national costume.'

With great pride, she displayed a brown capa, soft brimmed hat, untanned shoes with green silk strings, white leather knee breeches, a red silk sash, a short waist-coat and a velvet jacket covered with rich embroidery, silver buttons, spangles and ribbons, all made for a tiny child like me. My eyes became round as saucers.

'How do you say the clothes are beautiful?'

'Say, "qué preciosas".'

'Qué preciosas!' I fingered the delicate embroidery on the jacket. 'Doña Marisa, please teach me the bolero?'

'Sí, I promised you that I would. Many children in Spain dance the bolero.' Doña Marisa smiled broadly, her eyes as bright as spangles. 'The bolero is an elegant, sprightly dance, and the steps should be performed with, as the dance instructors say, violencia – violence.'

Doña Marisa, she being a proficient in all things bolerología, taught me the art of the bolero, theatrical-style. When, in the beginning, I became annoyed at my clumsy self for turning the wrong way, she stressed the importance of doing a bolero well, but that it made no sense to attempt the bolero if one's heart was not in it.

She corrected my posture, the frame of my arms, the movement of my hands and the position of my heels, toes and legs. She taught me how to do leaps, crosses, turns, beaten steps, sliding steps, advance and retreat steps and something called mata la araña or killing the spider where a glissade ends with one foot extended in a point.

One day she demonstrated a paseo – a graceful walk – and we promenaded together round the room several times. Another day she taught me a bien parado, she preferring a sudden stop with her arms raised in a graceful attitude and her left foot suspended in the air. I, however, preferred a defiant pose with my hands on my hips, my head held erect and my body tilted slightly backwards.

But my favourite part of learning the bolero was snapping the castanets. The right hand held the castañuela hembra or female castanet with its higher, subtle pitch, while the left hand held the castañuela macho or male castanet to create a deeper, heavier sound. Sometimes I snapped both castanets together; other times each of my castanets got a single beat. And then there was the rapid fire of beats to produce a trill.

'Olé!' cried I, rapidly rolling my four fingertips on the female castanet, followed by one quick snap on the male castanet.

Doña Marisa sobbed into her hand for several seconds.

I spun round to stare at her. 'Why are you crying?'

'Oh, hija de mi alma. You are the daughter of my soul, for you possess the spirit of a true bolero dancer.'

'Truly? Am I good enough to dance the bolero with you?'

'Sí, I shall take you tomorrow evening to meet the Marchesa Castiglione.' Doña Marisa caressed my face. 'Such rhythm. Such gracefulness. You astonish me when you're a…'

'A hoyden? My papai court-martials me when I do hoydenish things.' I wondered if he would court-martial me for having learnt the bolero against his wishes.

'A court-martial?' She wrinkled her brow.

'My papai sits behind his desk, scowling at me. He says I'm a bad soldier. He sentences me to fatigue duty or a good flogging with the cat o' nine tails, or he sends my drum to gaol.'

'A flogging? Ay! Dios mío.'

'Oh, but he never flogs me. My mamãe told him that if he did, she would use the cat on him.'

She gave me a wan smile when I mentioned my mamãe in Scarborough. 'Hmm. Perhaps I shall like this Mrs Fitzwilliam.' And, having said that, her countenance brightened somewhat.

The following day I rehearsed the bolero again and again as if seized by witchcraft until Doña Marisa cried out 'Basta!' and she ordered me to rest. At dusk, she made me bathe in warm water scented with the essence of orange blossoms. Once that unpleasant task had been completed, because I disliked sitting still in a tub of water, I stood in front of the looking-glass, proud of my majo costume and the green ribbons woven into my short hair.

'Che bella bambina. How pretty you are.' Emmerence embraced me, and she wished me luck. In the carriage ride to Casa Castiglione, Doña Marisa fussed over me, applying rose-coloured salve to my lips. 'All this to dance the bolero for Milanese society,' grumbled Señor Gonzalez, reaching for his castanets. Together we practised snapping our castanets, he having taught me the secret of playing them with a majo attitude.

At Casa Castiglione, Doña Marisa introduced me to the friendly Colonel Thomas Fitzgerald, he being the escort of the ancient lady known as the Marchesa Castiglione. Doña Marisa whispered to me that the two lovers had been separated by war, and twenty-five years later, they had reunited. 'Qué romantica!' she pressed her hand to her heart. *Gah!* How silly she looked.

To be sure, the ever devoted and besotted colonel showered a thousand attentions on his lady, the Marchesa. When he had done romanticking her, he led Señor Gonzalez to a salon where the people known as the literati engaged in a heated discussion about something boring called politics. Left on our own, Doña Marisa and I drifted to another salon turned into a dancing room, where three couples danced a waltz.

'Ah, the lovely and fiery Doña Marisa. We meet again.' A handsome Englishman kissed Doña Marisa's hand. I recognised him as the light-haired gentleman we had seen atop the cathedral roof – I was sure of it.

'Lord Scapeton,' uttered Doña Marisa with a clenched jaw.

'Does little Rafael know you're mixing with gli italiani now?'

Doña Marisa gasped. 'You mock Don Rafael, and this after he gave you what you really wanted.'

Ignoring her complaint, he turned to scrutinise me. 'Well, well, who is your cicisbeo now? Ha! The Spanish keep getting shorter and shorter. I dare say this one is a nano, a dwarf. You, elf-boy, are not fit to hold a candle to me.'

'This bella bambina is my daughter,' Doña Marisa spoke with pride.

Lord Scapeton gave a contemptuous laugh at my boyish attire. 'Do you have a name bambino?'

'Go on. Speak your name,' Doña Marisa urged me.

I did as I was told. 'I am Sofia-Elisabete Fitzwilliam.'

He gaped at me. 'Imposter! Who are you, really?'

'My papai is Colonel Fitzwilliam, and my avô is Lord Matlock,' declared I, with a proud spirit.

'What nonsense,' retorted he.

Something of his countenance and bearing struck me at first sight – something familiar to me. Was it his sharp, beak-like nose? The grumpy tone of his voice? Likewise, Lord Scapeton, having become keenly uncomfortable, must have detected something disturbing in my phiz.

'What are you doing here?' He towered over me, casting me a menacing eye, but I stood my ground.

'We are dancing the bolero for the Marchesa,' boasted I.

'*You* dance the bolero?'

I nodded. 'Doña Marisa taught me, just like the nuns at the convent taught her.'

Lord Scapeton sneered at Doña Marisa. 'O, ho! And now, finally, it comes out. The noble Doña Marisa once belonged to *that* kind of sisterhood, plying her trade.'

With an arched brow, a defiant Doña Marisa placed a protective hand atop her maccaroni-filled belly, and this, for whatever reason, raised his ire. His eyes flamed up like red-hot coals. And that is when he whispered something to her, as if he had spat on her. It must have been a low word because Doña Marisa looked as if she would explode into a thousand angry pieces. So I did what any child would do to defend her mamãe – I kicked this scoundrel in his shin.

'Olha maroto!'

'You loathsome brat,' thundered he. 'You're as crazy as your boorish father.'

So I did what any child would do to defend her papai – I kicked this villain in his other shin. 'Yow!' He grimaced in pain. Just then, the guitarists began to play up, on a signal given for the next dance – the bolero. I grasped Doña Marisa's trembling hands out of fear she would slap this blackguard and she would thereafter be sent to gaol or be hurled down to Signor Dante's nether world.

'Minha Senhora, would you do me the honour to dance the bolero with me?' asked I in the polite manner in which Señor Gonzalez had taught me.

'Con muito gusto,' returned she in Portuguese, reminding me of my homeland far away.

'Sì, sì. Donna Marisa, you and your daughter must honour us with a performance of the bolero,' urged the Marchesa, who, along with her guests, had been enjoying this piece of choice entertainment. La nobiltà milanese whispered amongst themselves about the cicisbeo inglese, he being spiantato, which I later learnt from Emmerence meant that the former escort of Doña Marisa was a cast-off, a penniless person. This made no sense to me. Lord Scapeton, with his rich clothes, gold signet ring and perfectly dressed hair, certainly didn't look penniless.

Ignoring the whispers and stares, I summoned up my majo attitude to lead Doña Marisa in a graceful paseo. We concluded our promenade at the centre of the dancing room, where we stood facing each other, six feet apart. Mirroring one another using opposite feet, we each extended a foot and a curved arm, and we commenced to dance to the sprightly tune. Oh, how we dazzled the dancing gods with our graceful leaps and quick, firm steps – such violencia – and the rattling of our castanets that marked the rhythm.

In the heat of our dancing duel, Doña Marisa and I exchanged an arched look, our own story being acted out on this stage – she challenging me, I responding to her in kind – reflecting our oft times fiery relationship. Then Doña Marisa sought me, her lips curved into a smile, and we came together nobly and gracefully, but quicker than a thought, she abandoned me, and thus we separated in anger, turning away from each other.

We came together once more to make things right, bursting into a sequence of rapid footwork, our beaten steps in rhythm with the staccato trills of our castanets – ta-ria-ria-pi. The hoyden in me relished this finale and the clashes of our castanets, and I longed for this joy and mirth to last for ever. But all things must end, and with an abrupt stop, we froze with a grand flourish, our arms raised in a triumphant attitude, our left feet suspended in the air. 'Olé!' cried the guitarists. 'Bien parado!' cheered Señor Gonzalez. A large crowd had gathered round to watch us, but I hardly noticed them now, for Doña Marisa and I had danced com coração e alma, with heart and soul, and with each beaten step, we had moved closer together.

Chapter Twelve

La Luna

MY FIRST ROSOLIO DROPS, thinks I, became my fond acquaintances on this journey to a moon world. But like all sugary sweets, they proved in the end to be fickle friends; at least that's what I've come to believe. They tempted you with their sweet aroma and bright colours, and when you gobbled them up, they gave you ten seconds of happiness before they forsook you, vanishing without a trace. And if you ate too much of them, they would make your belly hurt or rot your teeth or make you fat like the Prince of Wales. Can anything sweet be faithful and wholesome?

In the wake of our triumphant performance at Casa Castiglione, Doña Marisa and I created a sensation as a dancing duo. From casa to casa, we performed our brilliant bolero, and after our fifth such performance, Doña Marisa exclaimed, 'Basta! We must leave this place to find la luna.' A fit of packing ensued, and once the servants had fastened our travelling-trunks and what not onto the carriages, we set off for our destination, it being some place near the sea. On the second day of our journey, as we traversed the Apennines, I begged Doña Marisa to tell us about la luna.

'What is la luna like? Are the moon-folk good there?'

She considered my questions for a moment. 'I have no doubt la luna is a magical place.'

'A magic place?' My toes and fingers began to tingle.

'Very much so. Listen, and I shall tell you how I came to know about it. Once upon a time,' Doña Marisa began, 'a maja dancer rose from obscurity, and after she had given up her infant daughter, she married a Spanish nobleman and that is how she became a Doña. Some days she suffered greatly from her husband's violent temper, other days she loathed his cruelty to others, yet it was the only life she knew, and she swore she would never be poor again, roasting chestnuts and begging for food. She and Don Rafael had removed to Seville, to his ancestral home, and after one season, he became disenchanted with her, and she with him.'

'He's a bad man.' I thought again of her scarred temple.

'True, but he was wealthy and titled. In Spain, one must marry such a man to be free,' she revealed to me. 'You see, it is customary for a Doña, being a married woman, to choose a cortejo, an escort, and thus she needn't see her husband that much.'

This confused me as to why a husband and wife didn't want to see each other, and when I glanced at Emmerence, she seemed just as puzzled as me.

'One day,' continued Doña Marisa, 'a handsome nobleman, he being an avid art collector from Inglaterra, wandered to Seville to view the paintings by Velázquez, Zurbarán and Murillo. This English nobleman, known to all as Lord Scapeton, came under the Doña's spell, and he consented to be her cortejo, escorting her in town, serving her chocolate, whispering sweet words into her ear and paying her a thousand attentions.'

I gaped at her, nearly falling from the seat. 'Lord Scapeton, the ogre? I kicked him good and hard.'

'You kicked him? When?' Señor Gonzalez was all astonishment. 'Why was I not told of this?'

Doña Marisa shushed him. 'The Doña and her English cortejo became inseparable. Together they sojourned in Cádiz, to find the Doña's real father, Don Luis de Luna, who, to their surprise, was a prosperous Genoese merchant. He had obtained naturalisation and the status of hidalgo in Spain, and thus the Spanish pronounced his surname de Luna instead of di Luna.

'When the Doña claimed to be his natural daughter, Don Luis cast a sceptical eye upon her, for he was a childless man. She showed him the ancient key that had once belonged to her mother – the key that Don Luis had given her mother an age ago when the two of them had been lovers. Startled at first, he gathered his wits, and he pronounced that if she could find Villa La Luna – a hidden villa in a place near the sea in Liguria – and if the key opened the door to his villa, then he would acknowledge her as his natural daughter.'

My eyes became round as saucers. 'Where is the key?'

With great care, she removed a necklace that she wore underneath her clothes. She dangled the chain, attached to which hung an ornate iron key with la luna, the full moon, at one end. My fingers tingling, I cupped the key in my hands, to feel the weight of it, the magic of it. Señor Gonzalez pointed to the handle of the ring, which he called the bow. The middle part he called the stem, and the bottom part he called the wards, which reminded me of the teeth on a rake.

'On their return to Seville,' continued Doña Marisa, in a low voice, 'the Doña's cortejo became drunk from a flask of red wine, and he revealed to her that his younger brother had fathered a child with a "low creature" in Portugal during the war and had brought the child to live with him and his wife in the town of Scarborough.'

I wrinkled my brow. 'Scarbro'? That's my home.'

Doña Marisa nodded, and she resumed her story. 'No thanks to his brother's foolery, he said, everyone in Inglaterra knew of this illegitimate child and her origins. He grumbled that the Portuguese mother of the child was not of their rank; for, had she been, a good match could have been made for the child, and his family would have benefitted from the alliance.'

I stared blankly at her, wondering what this meant.

'Do not you understand?' Doña Marisa grasped my hand. 'Lord Scapeton is your papai's brother. I had no idea until then. Believe me, when I say, no two brothers could be more dissimilar.'

Thunderstruck, I cast down my eyes, recalling Lord Scapeton's cold contempt for me. 'My papai says I'm his love child and his creature.'

'You are my creature, too,' Doña Marisa assured me, squeezing my hand.

'Lord Scapeton and Colonel Fitzwilliam are brothers? What insanity is this?' Señor Gonzalez uttered a ferocious growl. 'What happened to this English cortejo?'

'He disappeared one day with the south-west wind,' recalled she. 'Upon learning the identity of the child, the Doña suffered a shock, and when she dared to whisper the name of her child – the child whom she had believed lost to her for ever – it broke the spell that had bound the cortejo to her. Without so much as a proper leave-taking, he forsook her once he had obtained his true heart's desire – a rare copy of Goya's controversial *Los Caprichos* that Don Rafael had kept hidden behind a false wall in his library and had finally agreed to sell to him.'

'Ay! What a tragedy to give up those rare prints.' Señor Gonzalez bemoaned the loss of what he referred to as Goya's critical eye of Spanish society.

I puzzled my wits together. 'Lord Scapeton tricked everyone?'

Doña Marisa paused for a moment to rub her maccaroni-filled belly. 'He cared not a whit for his lady,' admitted she. 'The Doña served as a means for him to get close to Don Rafael. With a celerity that astounded many, the Doña chose a new cortejo among her many admirers, he being a kind and honourable Spaniard named Sábado Gonzalez, who agreed to escort her to Inglaterra, although he nor anyone else knew at the time of her secret plan to find her long lost daughter. How intractable she was of her desire to see Inglaterra, so much so that Don Rafael gave her a small chest containing many gold escudos in exchange for leaving him in peace. "Begone for ever," thundered he. She set out in the world then, determined that she, with her daughter by her side, would find Villa La Luna.'

Señor Gonzalez grasped her hand to kiss it. 'Mi amor, I shall help you find this Villa La Luna.'

'What if we can't find it?' worried I.

Doña Marisa wiped a tear or two from her eyes. 'We must find it. I cannot return to Spain because of the bargain I struck with Don Rafael. He gave me the money for the journey on the condition that I begone for ever.' Soon the story-teller in Doña Marisa turned melancholy after relating her sad history to us, and she thereafter dozed with her head resting on her cortejo's shoulder.

At the summit of the Bocchetta pass, where we espied a dazzling city far off in the distance, I swore I could taste the salty air. 'The sea!' enthused I, rousing Doña Marisa from her deep slumber. It occurred to me then that I hadn't seen the sea since our departure from Rotterdam. Emmerence, having never seen the sea before, wondered if it ended at the horizon, until Pico explained to her that no one ever reaches the horizon – it runs away from you – and, once out on the high seas, you're surrounded by this wily horizon, which is why some folks get lost and end up captured by pirates or blown overboard by a French man-o'-war.

I had a better theory. 'God made the sea touch the sky where He lives. He likes to dip His toes into the cold water to refresh Himself.'

'Dip his toes into the water like a dandy? Yer nincompoop,' exclaimed Pico. 'When God wishes to refresh Himself, He makes it rain. Once He soaps up, He stands underneath a rain cloud an' makes it shower. That's why the next mornin', the air smells fresh an' clean.'

'God doesn't bathe much in the summer,' observed I, recalling the dry summer days in Portugal.

Pico slapped his forehead in exasperation. 'That's why God makes flowers bloom in the summer. All the heavy perfume in the air masks His manly odour.'

'But you said God isn't a dandy,' protested I.

Señor Gonzalez scoffed at us. 'Qué absurdo! What nonsense! God does not smell. And He's not a dandy. He's a true majo who wears a capa flung over His left shoulder.' Señor Gonzalez muttered that he would go distracted, and if he had his way, children would be sent up to the moon until they could speak sense.

Thereafter, we descended into the heights of San Pietro d'Arena near the entrance of Genoa – the native city of Don Luis de Luna.

'Genova, la superba, ti saluto,' Señor Gonzalez greeted the city in the Italian way.

'Genoa, the proud,' his lady agreed.

'Mira! There's the ancient light-house, La Lanterna, at the entrance to the harbour.'

She viewed the busy harbour with her spyglass. 'There must be a thousand boats and vessels floating on the water.'

'Oh, how the marble palazzos glow. Such wealth. Such brilliance.'

'I wonder which palazzo is ours?' she teased him.

It seemed to me, though, as if Genoa had been enchanted into a state of drowsiness. Did Napoleon, he being a stregone or sorcerer, cast a spell on the Genoese long ago to trick them and render them powerless? From our lofty position here on the heights, the life below reminded me of tiny insects, creeping along inch by inch, and the lateen sails, like triangular ghosts, drifted in the harbour and beyond, as if bored and listless from finding nothing much to haunt on the water.

Señor Gonzalez had praised Genoa. But a seasoned traveller I had become, at least I thought so, and a city from afar often presents a vision of magnificence, filling you with the highest of moon hopes and expectations. Then, more often than not, you end up having the great misfortune to journey inside such a city, where the poverty and misery and rot press up against your carriage window, stirring up many an unpleasant sensation in your weary traveller's soul.

Sure enough, as our carriages conveyed us through the crooked, stinking lanes of Genoa with its tumble-down tenements, I suffered yet another keen disappointment, because a moon this was not. Oh, if the maids in Rotterdam could scrub these streets clean. The lanes here were so narrow that the tall houses, each painted a different colour and covered with dirt, seemed to lean towards each other, leaving just a sliver of blue sky above. My spirits low, I closed my eyes to feel a prayer. *Ti saluto! God! Please do not hide Villa La Luna in one of these miserable lanes.*

I pressed my nose to the glass, observing the streets teeming with endless activity. The Genoese gathered amidst the twists and turns of the vicoli or alleys, chit chatting in high spirits. Señor Gonzalez drily remarked that conversazione seemed to be the favourite form of amusement here. We drove by a knot of men playing a noisy, rapid game with their fingers, shouting bets and arguing and hurling insults at each other. Having my own fingers and knowing how to count fingers, I wished to learn the game, and so Señor Gonzalez promised to teach us this thing known as Mora. For a moment, I convinced myself that life here wasn't as bad as I had imagined it would be, until we came across the churches and convents, where hundreds of friars, monks and priests swarmed in the squares, some of these religious men carried in sedan chairs with utmost ceremony to avoid the stenches and squalor and dirty people.

As if he could read my gloomy thoughts, Señor Gonzalez ordered the driver to advance towards the centre of the city, to Pietro Romanengo fu Stefano. He had heard of this confectioner's shop, and he believed it would be just the thing to cure what ailed me. We stopped in front of an elegant shop with tall glass windows and two cherubs poised above the entrance to greet patrons. There, inside this sweet-smelling shop, stood many a French-designed glass case displaying brightly-coloured candies, or rather 'sugary gewgaws', which was how Señor Gonzalez referred to them.

A wealthy signora dressed in the French fashion and attended by her escort, swept forward to buy boxes and boxes of candies, fixing her eyes, ever and anon, at us children and Señor Gonzalez. 'She assumes I'm their father,' he whispered to Doña Marisa. This confused me until the escort handed his lady into a carriage where two young children awaited them, and I overheard the shop-keeper's remark that the signora had seven children fathered by her cicisbeo. 'Seven!' Señor Gonzalez drew back in horror, and he fumbled with his bolsa to buy sugar-coated fichi or figs for his lady and a box of rosolio drops for us children.

'Genova, la superba,' mumbled he, as he sucked on a rosolio drop.

I licked my lips in anticipation.

'Niños?' He cupped his ear.

The three of us giggled. 'La superba.'

'Bueno. And now for your reward.' He placed a rosolio drop onto each of our tongues, where the tasty sugar pebbles burst into a flavoured liquid – violet for Emmerence, mint for Pico and rose for me.

We set off next for Albaro, a suburb of Genoa, where, with our letter of introduction from Marchesa Castiglione, we would stay as her guests at Villa Leone. Señor Gonzalez claimed that our bolero dance had intrigued the Marchesa, who had taken a liking to Doña Marisa, thereby saving us many a franc. Did not we look forward to being served cioccolato every morning? I bounced with eagerness at the mention of chocolate, because cioccolato italiano was like no other chocolate on earth, and I hadn't savoured it since we quit Milan. Pico declared it a cup of tasty mud, as did Emmerence, who pondered whether Jesus would drink it. When I told her that Jesus ate maccaroni – he having told me so in my dream – she laughed good naturedly when I insisted that he did.

'What are you writing, Señor Gonzalez?' inquired I.

He scribbled something in a small journal-book that he always carried with him. 'Hmm? Oh, I'm just imagining how an object without a mouth could eat maccaroni.' Lost in his thoughts, he turned to gaze out the window, as if something on the street would reveal the answer to him.

As I've said before, I'm of the opinion that grown-ups often don't make any sense, and when they do utter nonsense, it's best to ignore them. So when we reached the grand Villa Leone, and he and Doña Marisa broke out into silly raptures with the elaborate frontage of carved lions, the captivating loggia, the number of glazed windows, &c., I gave an inward shrug. Those sorts of things did not signify to me. We children had come under the spell of a rather large frog that chirped in the fountain. Señor Gonzalez bemoaned that here, surrounded by wealth and beauty, the sole thing we cared for was a silly frog and whether it would eat maccaroni.

'Señor Gonzalez, may we give froggy a rosolio drop?' I held out my hand.

'Absolutely not,' Señor Gonzalez guarded his box of sugary gewgaws.

'If he croaks "la superba", may he have one?' pleaded I.

'Humph. If your frog can talk, then I am emperor.' He struck a mock pose, raising an imaginary sceptre.

I pointed to one of his boots. 'Señor Gonzalez, what's that thing on your foot?'

'Ay! Scorpion!' Of a sudden he turned into a wild man, swinging his arms and kicking his legs high in the air, while the odd little creature dashed off to safety, snapping its pincers. Once Señor Gonzalez had regained his breath and manly composure, he flung his brown capa over his left shoulder, and he hastened to join his lady. She, having watched this spectacle with undisguised mirth, awaited him near the balustraded flight of steps.

Inside Villa Leone, the two of them broke out into raptures with the marble floors, the double staircase, the tapestries, the frescoes, the ornate furniture and the chandeliers, their duelling cries of 'look here' and 'look there' in each salon making my head spin like a teetotum. I imagined that a king and queen must live in this palace and that they mustn't have any children, because no child would be allowed to sneak and play at bowls inside any of the long passages, or press his greasy fingers on the highly-polished furniture when the butler wasn't attending to him, or throw his pease out the window while the grown-ups amused themselves in one of the salons.

Each day at our lavish abode, where we supped on omelette, potage au macaroni and crème au chocolat, Doña Marisa would puzzle her wits together to find Villa La Luna. Some days she and Señor Gonzalez journeyed eastward on the coast; other days they journeyed westward. While they were from home, we children sometimes received a visitor named Padre Pozzi, he having formed an acquaintance with Emmerence during his sojourns in Brieg. The padre and Emmerence would converse in Italian and discuss the history of Genoa while Pico and I sat under a fig tree, playing a noisy game of Mora or throwing mounds of fig leaves at each other.

Whenever Doña Marisa complained of head-ache, Señor Gonzalez would take us children to Genoa. One time he took us to a puppet theatre where the marionettes performed a comedic ballet that turned into a bizarre riot where the puppets hit each other with sticks. 'Qué ridiculoso!' exclaimed Señor Gonzalez. Another time he bought bright red Genoese caps for Pico and me, and a mezzaro or white veil for Emmerence. But if there was one thing Señor Gonzalez dearly loved to do in Genoa, it was to drive through the stench of the city to reach the Strada Nuova and Strada Balbi – the streets of palazzos – where he goggled at 'the extravaganza', and thereafter to visit the Annunziata, a church made of pure gold inside.

One day, when the winds presented favourable, he hired a small felucca, an open boat with two lateen sails and six rowers and steered by an able mariner. Here, afloat in the noble harbour, we sailed by small boats called gondolas and many a picturesque felucca, some of the larger open boats having three lateen sails and twelve rowers.

'La superba,' Señor Gonzalez saluted Genoa. 'See how the marble amphitheatre of palazzos rises from the sea, surrounded on high by a dozen hills the colour of crème au chocolat and dotted with white country-houses?'

'La superba,' we obedient pupils agreed with him.

'Otra vez,' commanded Señor Gonzalez. 'Again, but with feeling.'

'La superba!' We waved our hands high above our heads.

'Bueno. And now for your reward.' Señor Gonzalez placed a rosolio drop on each of our tongues.

I closed my eyes, eager for the sugar pebble to explode on my tongue in a burst of flavour. 'Mmm, I got lemon this time.'

Bom! Bom! Bom! The brass-cannons situated on the jetty saluted an important personage. Having espied three royal carriages, Señor Gonzalez announced that the Queen of Sardinia had arrived to join the King and that the Queen's suite was en route to the Palazzo Doria. Our Genoese boatmen spat into the sea on hearing this piece of news, and I wondered why. Señor Gonzalez explained that Genoa had once been the capital of an independent republic for eight centuries until Napoleon vanquished it, and now that Napoleon had been vanquished, Genoa belonged to the Kingdom of Sardinia.

I wrinkled my forehead. 'Is that why they speak Genoese and not Italian?'

Both Señor Gonzalez and the mariner laughed as if at a good joke, and I prided myself on being clever even though I had no idea why I was so. But I dared not ask them about it. Papai always said there's nothing worse than spoiling a good joke afterwards by trying to explain it.

We disembarked at the landing-wharf near a galley filled with a gang of slaves chained at the ankles. With mingled feelings of compassion and terror, I gaped at the sweaty, ragged men. Señor Gonzalez learnt that they were criminals, and he asked us, did not it instil a fear of being punished likewise for committing a crime? I nodded in reply. 'Libertas,' said he. 'One must never take freedom for granted.'

Further down the pier I observed children a few years older than myself wearing a tin medal of Infant Asylum round their necks and embarking on a voyage to a destination unknown. Some of the shoe-less children stared at me as if they knew I had been a foundling. Once you are a foundling, you are always a member of the foundling club, thinks I, because the taint and sorrow of it always seems to follow you – to remind you of it – even if your papai is of noble blood.

Upon our return to Villa Leone, we found Doña Marisa reclined on a chaise longue, weeping into her handkerchief. How glum she looked. Alone in the villa with no one to speak to, she had been struck with sudden doubt. She feared we would never find Villa La Luna and we would be homeless, for ever to roam the continent like gipsies. Señor Gonzalez grasped her hand to kiss it, and he begged her to repeat what Don Luis had told her.

Doña Marisa became thoughtful. 'Don Luis said it was "a hidden villa in a place near the sea". Those were his exact words.'

'Ay! What a conundrum,' lamented he.

'A riddle? Almost every village here in Liguria is "near" the sea. We shall never solve it.' Doña Marisa sobbed into her handkerchief.

'A place near the sea...' repeated Emmerence. 'Padre Pozzi knows the history of many a village here.'

As quick as can be, we got into the carriage, our destination being the Santa Maria del Prato to speak with Padre Pozzi. He disappeared for several minutes, when he returned carrying a large, ancient book, its binding crackling with age. For the next fifteen minutes, we waited patiently while he turned the musty pages until he found something of interest. He mentioned there was a small fishing village about four miles distant to the east called Nervi, the name of which might come from a Celtic phrase, for the Celts once settled there before the Romans. 'Guarda!' cried he, pointing to a drawing of the Nerviese coat of arms with its motto 'near av inn' or 'place near the sea'.

Doña Marisa hung her head, confessing to the padre that she had overlooked Nervi, not thinking it of consequence, or rather, not befitting her station. Now humbled, she thanked the padre, and she begged for God's forgiveness. The padre told us that Nervi is known for its excellent air, lofty views, rich gardens and groves, and temperate weather all the year round. It serves as a place to heal, he believed, and several wealthy families have built villas there – Grimaldi, Gropallo, Saluzzo, Gnecco. Near Villa Bonera, the noble Ponte Romano provides passage over a torrent. Once, as a young man, when he had suffered from doubt, he walked across this ancient arched bridge, and when he reached the other side, he obtained clarity of mind.

In Nervi the next day, all this sleepy fishing village offered as far as I could see, besides the small harbour, were the ruins of a castle and hay tower, and several villas half-hidden in the green mountain sides. But on closer inspection, I espied lemon groves, orange groves and olive trees scattered throughout the peaceful hamlet. And near the wild cliffs, the views of the sea abounded. Doña Marisa appeared half-anxious, half-determined as she searched the hills with her spyglass.

'I don't care if it's a mud hut,' declared Doña Marisa. 'We shall be happy at Villa La Luna.'

Señor Gonzalez examined the large, ancient key on her necklace. 'Mi amor, it must be a very large mud hut.'

This made her laugh, and it was then that I knew without a doubt that Señor Gonzalez truly and sincerely loved her and that he would live in a mud hut if it pleased his lady. The two of them linked arms, and they strolled off. For the first time, their romanticking didn't bother me.

Having found the Ponte Romano – the one that had helped a young and confused Padre Pozzi – we determined to cross this ancient Roman bridge. While Doña Marisa and Señor Gonzalez stood atop the highest point of the arched bridge, speaking in whispered tones, we children descended to the other side where a young italiano and his donkey cart approached us. He was a handsome italiano with nut-brown skin and curly raven hair, and he whistled a sprightly tune.

'Buongiorno,' I waved my red cap at him.

He touched his cap. 'Buongiorno.'

'Sì?' I pointed to the donkey.

He nodded, and thus I petted the gentle beast. I nudged Emmerence with my foot, giving her the broadest of hints.

'Come ti chiami?' inquired she.

'Luca,' said he with a blush.

'Ask where he's going?' I half-whispered to Emmerence.

'Dove andate?'

'Villa La Luna.'

Emmerence and I shared a look of amazement, whereupon we became nearly wild with excitement. Our burst of loud squeals startled poor Luca, who wobbled about as if his legs had turned to maccaroni. Emmerence gleaned from our shy friend that he was the gardener, the ortolana, at Villa La Luna, and he would guide us there; otherwise, we would never find it – so well hidden it was. Pico rushed back to the bridge, shouting 'La Luna! We found La Luna!'

Doña Marisa cried out in wonder ere she fell into a half-swoon. 'Help me, Pico,' ordered Señor Gonzalez. Pico fanned Doña Marisa with his cap, while Señor Gonzalez placed a small phial under her nose, giving her a whiff of orange-blossom scent to revive her. 'I'm quite recovered,' protested she, when Señor Gonzalez carried her down the bridge. But I thought she looked as pale as an orange blossom.

Worried that Doña Marisa could not walk far, Señor Gonzalez placed his brown capa inside the donkey cart for his lady. There, situated amongst pots of flowers and baskets of fresh vegetables and grey kittens with yellow eyes, Doña Marisa reclined inside the cart in a most noble fashion, shading herself with a parasol. She laughed at herself, saying, 'Is it not befitting that I'm being conveyed to Villa La Luna in a donkey cart? It serves me right for thinking so highly of myself. Andiamo!'

Luca led us in a long march west, after which he turned seaward. He approached a thick grove of dark cypress trees, where a dirt path wound through it until it ended at an unadorned iron gate. Señor Gonzalez handed his lady out of the cart, and he escorted her into a small park of sorts. Luca, who served as cicerone, pointed out pine trees, olive trees, oleanders, myrtles, and in the distance, a bowling-green and a magic orange grove protected from the strong winds. An Italian garden came into view, and Luca, with great pride, drew our attention to the rows of potted lemon trees, low box hedges, flower beds and octagonal fountain depicting all sorts of moons – crescent moon, half-moon, gibbous moon and full moon. He swept his arm upwards to the villa at the end of the gravelled path.

The villa was anything but a mud hut. The colour of it reminded me of a pale lemon, while the shutters were a peculiar green – something that Señor Gonzalez referred to as Veronese green – but now weathered with age. On the ground floor stood the entrance with an arched wooden door. Above it, the first floor boasted several arches, which Señor Gonzalez described as an open loggia with a view of the sea. And above the loggia, on the second floor, a row of round windows brought to mind full moons.

But the most fascinating feature of the villa, at least for me, was the lofty tower that rose in the centre, as if it had burst through the roof. I imagined myself in the evenings sitting high up in this fortress, where I would reach out to the starry heavens and rearrange the stars to my liking, and once I had done creating new constellations, I would curl up to sleep, safe in my celestial dream.

Doña Marisa pressed her hands to her face. 'I must be dreaming,' murmured she, staring at the grand vision before her.

I nodded like a wise man. 'It's a waking dream.'

'How do you know what that is?'

I shrugged at her. 'My papai has them often.'

Doña Marisa and I advanced towards the wooden door, her hand trembling in mine. She kissed the ancient moon key, and with a deep breath, she inserted the key into the lock. This key, being rather large, required both of her hands to turn it, so turn it she did two-handed with alacrity. Click. Click. The door opened, creaking on its hinges, and we stepped inside as silent as thieves. There, in the spacious entrance-hall, she knelt to embrace me with happiness and relief, the tears sparkling on her cheeks like tiny diamond stars. She spoke to me in a quiet, confidential tone.

'There are those who say you and I are low creatures, but mind you, we are descended from a titled Spaniard, Don Luis de Luna, he being a native Genoese.'

I wrinkled my brow. 'Is Emmerence a low creature? What of Luca?'

This gave her pause. 'The truth is, we are all equal before God.'

Thereafter, our companions joined us inside, and Doña Marisa and Señor Gonzalez broke out into raptures with the fine frescoes, the lofty ceilings, the great staircase, the niches with statues, &c. Doña Marisa found the bell-pull, and within seconds, a robust housekeeper appeared. She bowed to us, introducing herself as Ninetta, the housekeeper and cook for Villa La Luna. To Doña Marisa's surprise, Don Luis had written to Ninetta several months ago, instructing her to ready the villa for her new mistress, Doña Marisa, and so she had done. 'He must've recognised the key when I showed it to him,' murmured Doña Marisa. Ninetta left us then to prepare a small repast for us.

Of a sudden, Doña Marisa clutched at her belly.

'Ay, I've felt it move,' marvelled she.

'Is your maccaroni swimming in there?' wondered I.

With a broad grin, she patted my cheek. 'I'm having a baby, and you will have a new brother or sister.'

I goggled at her swollen belly. 'Truly?'

'Indeed,' confirmed she.

'Will you put it in the roda?' I frowned at the thought of my baby brother or sister eating meagre soup every day, sleeping on a patch of straw and begging for alms.

This shocked her. 'I shan't go near a foundling turnbox wheel again.'

'Do you promise?'

'Sí, I promise,' said she in a clear and quiet voice.

She placed my hand on her belly, and I felt something mysterious move therein. Had I ever lived inside of her belly? I certainly didn't remember having done so. And that is how I discovered the best thing in the world would happen and by far much better than a moon, namely, I would have a new brother or sister. That night I dreamt of a tender-hearted boy, a sweet boy, with golden hair, rosy cheeks and clear blue eyes as pretty as rosolio drops, the two of us sitting under an orange-tree arm in arm, feeding each other sugary gewgaws. I kissed my little brother, and I tickled him on his belly. 'Ha! Ha!' giggled he, my half of a brother. Thereafter, I dressed him in my majo costume, and he leapt high in the air, crying 'Olé!' He possessed the spirit of a true bolero dancer, because he was the brother of my soul.

Chapter Thirteen

The Lion and the Savage

MY FIRST BIG LIE, thinks I, was the one I kept telling myself that the perfect world of a moon existed. On this journey, I had discovered that we lie because we refuse to own the truth. We lie to make ourselves feel better. We lie because we don't think we'll be caught, and so forth and so be it – there are a thousand reasons to lie, it seems to me.

When I think on it now, of the sizes and shapes and appearances of lies, I imagine a sea filled with fishes of all sorts. Some are pretty colours and fanciful, others are ugly and vicious, and then there are the skittish ones, which dart about, not wishing to do any real harm. Sometimes a small fish is gobbled up by a big fish, such as when a small lie turns into a bigger lie. Sometimes a fish is hooked or caught in a lie. Sometimes a net catches a boatload of fish, and all the little lies come to the surface to be revealed. Sometimes a cunning fish eludes capture and it becomes emperor of the sea, until one day it is vanquished, and its lies and deceptions sink to the bottom of the sea, where there is nought but the murky truth; at least that's what my papai said.

At Villa La Luna the days passed by with almost perfect happiness, the main thing wanting here being a reunion with my papai, my mamãe Aggie and my puggy. After Ninetta prepared us children our noon-day meal of minestra or polenta, I would beat my drum in the garden, hoping that papai would recognise 'Tree on the Hill' and find our hidden villa near the sea. One such afternoon Señor Gonzalez followed me to the garden, and he asked me why I always played the same drum beating. I told him that it was a special one that I must needs play every day.

He paused to examine my drum. 'I wonder, does your drum ever talk to you?'

I considered this for a moment. 'It says rat-a-tat-tat tap-too.'

This made him laugh for some reason.

'Señor Gonzalez, do you like being a cortejo?'

'I beg your pardon,' he tugged at his jacket. 'I am not just a cortejo. Have you ever heard of the book, *Adventures of a Wheel of Cheese?* No? Well, what about, *The Life and Times of a Hairless Hare?* No?'

I shrugged at him.

Señor Gonzalez groaned with disbelief. 'Well, I wrote them for children but under a lady's name, of course.'

I scratched my head. 'Why would you do that?'

'Why? Because I, being a manly man, don't want my good name associated with books where a wheel of cheese speaks to people, as does the hairless hare.'

I squinted at him. 'But cheese and hares can't talk.'

'Indeed, that's why the books are droll and written by the drollest of drolls, Madame de Coccinelle, otherwise known in England as Lady Le Buggo. I am now writing a book titled *The Magic Drum's Grand Tour.* The drum, which has eyes, ears and a mouth painted on it, befriends little boys and girls wherever it goes on the continent.'

To be sure, I was wholly bewildered. 'Do you like children?'

'Ay, Dios mío!' He waved me off as if to dismiss the thought. 'The crying, the whining, the jodeling – I can do without them.'

This gave me pause. 'Señor Gonzalez? Methinks you're a contradishin.'

'A ha!' He smiled broadly. 'You do understand what a contradiction is.'

In the course of the evening, as we sat in the loggia watching the sun set, Señor Gonzalez got monstrously drunk, calling himself a 'big lying bug' and bemoaning that he could never publish anything of significance now. Doña Marisa pulled the bell with alacrity, and she requested that Ninetta take us children to our rooms. That night, as we slept, I heard the mournful blare of an alphorn in my dreams. Bwwaaarrrhhhmmm. I opened my eyes, wondering what Señor Gonzalez was about. I sneaked up to the tower where I could watch him in his tipsy state, tottering to and fro in the park, with his alphorn slung over his shoulder. By the light of the moon, I observed instead a white triangular ghost sailing atop the orange-trees. I rubbed my sleepy eyes, convinced that it had been real.

A young child I might have been in those days, but I knew enough of the world to realise that I lived amongst pairs of people in this ark near the sea: Doña Marisa and Señor Gonzalez being one; Pico and Emmerence being the other. One day, when everyone had paired off – the grown-ups strolling near the cliffs, and Pico and Emmerence playing at Mora – I felt it most keenly. I pondered whether Oskar Denzler, my Swiss beau, pined for me as much as I pined for him, because an inward feeling told me he just might not. To cheer myself, I determined to go courting. I wore my stylish majo breeches with red silk sash, white cambric shirt and bright red Genoese cap set jauntily to one side. From the tower, I espied my prey: Luca, the shy and handsome gardener. I rushed out of doors, barelegged and barefooted in the Genoese way, intent on making him mine.

'Luca! Oh, Luca!'

Luca touched his cap and grinned at me. 'Scì?'

'Luca, I have come to flirt with you in the Genoese way.'

Luca shrugged, because he didn't understand English.

'Amô! I am in love with you,' I clasped my tiny hands over my heart in a grand gesture of devotion.

He cast a worried side-glance at the orange grove. 'No, no, no,' he shielded himself with one hand as if I had the plague.

'Scì, scì, scì,' I pressed my suit. 'Luca, will you be my beau?'

I had no sooner made my proposal, than Luca hastened down the foot path, pushing his ancient wheelbarrow at great speed.

'Oh, hang it!' I pitched my red cap onto the ground. As if in concert with my dismal mood, the sun hid behind a heavy bank of clouds, and a ghostly gloom descended on earth.

'Have you forsaken me already?' A hoarse, strangled voice called out to me.

Confused, I spun round. I peered into the darkness of the orange grove, where a shadowy figure sat on his haunches, fanning himself with his hat.

'Are you a g-g-ghost?' I trembled, believing him to be the spirit who haunted the grove.

'Humph. Not yet I am,' replied he in a gruff voice.

I froze with fear, imagining he might be a stregone, one who could disguise himself in any form, whether it be man, beast or otherwise.

'Come here,' urged he in a sorrowful tone, beckoning me with his hat, 'and be quick about it.'

My curiosity heightened, I advanced, but then an inward voice urged caution, and thus I retreated. How long this mysterious stranger had been watching me I knew not. I looked round for the best route of escape, having determined to run for it, and so I did.

'Must you run away and crush my heart into a million pieces again?' he shouted after me, his voice breaking.

I came to an abrupt halt, my heart thump-thumping. 'Papai?'

'O, ho! *Now* you remember me,' said he in a half-joking, half-serious manner. 'Vem cá. Come here, you silly gooseberry.'

Could it really be him, my best beloved papai? Had I truly forgotten the sound of his voice? As if God had sensed my bewilderment, the sun escaped its dark prison and illuminated the orange grove for me. Now, on bended knee, with his riding-coat slung over one arm, papai eyed me curiously. With a loud yelp of recognition, I bounded into the grove to where he awaited me, and like a wildly happy puppy-dog, I threw myself into his solid embrace.

Be it said we wept a thousand tears. Oh, how I chided him for taking a monstrous long time to find me. Did not he hear my drum beatings for our special song to guide him along the way? He nodded in reply, my words of reproach having overpowered him, until finally he uttered the magic phrase 'Tree on the Hill', and he explained that Luca had let him inside the gate. There, smothered at my papai's breast, I inhaled his manly perfume, that familiar scent of cloves and cinnamon and heavy dew and bark and musty earth.

I pinched my nose. 'Papai, you smell.'

'I dare say I have not bathed since you ran away several months ago,' joked he with tears in his eyes. 'I have traipsed through five – no, six – countries on the continent searching for you, and I would traipse through a thousand more.'

Feeling guilty for the trouble I had caused him, I fidgeted with a button on his waist-coat. 'I was searching for one of the moons. I looked and I looked. But I couldn't find it – the one that Domingo Gonsales flew to with his gansas.'

'*One* of the moons?'

I nodded. 'The moons wear all sorts of colours – orange, grey, blue...'

Papai pressed a finger to my lips. 'The earth has one moon, and that is all.'

'Truly?' I gaped at him.

'One moon. One earth. One sun.'

My heart sank to my toes on hearing this piece of bad news.

Papai sighed. 'Now, why would you want to go to the moon?'

I fidgeted anew with a button on his waist-coat. 'To help you.'

'To help me?'

'On the moon, everyone is happy, and no one ever gets sick.'

Papai gave a soft groan, and he stilled my hand. 'My dear child, there is no utopia, no perfect world. The bishop who wrote of Domingo Gonsales' travels was only dreaming of such a place on the moon.'

Ai de mim! There it was – the shocking truth, the finality of which I had to accept. The story of the moon and the moon men and moon children had all been a big lie. And somewhere along my journey, I had refused to own it whenever I came across misery, poverty, disease or hatred. Oh, how cruel was my disappointment after having deceived myself. My spirits sank with grief and despair at ever finding a cure for papai's illness, what with my moon hopes being dashed to pieces.

Papai traced the circle of a full moon on my palm. 'Do not you understand?'

I gazed into his dark, watery-blue eyes. 'But I don't want you to get sick again. I don't want…you…to make…mamãe sad,' I choked with sobs.

'Nor take away your drum?'

I nodded, wiping my face with my sleeve. When, after a few minutes, I had calmed myself, he spoke again.

'Most days, I am the happiest man on earth, and thus I am amiable and all that is good and noble. Then there are days I am the unhappiest man on earth, overcome with misery and doubts, and thus I say or do terrible things that I come to regret later.'

I considered this for a moment or two, and with a serious tone, I declared, 'Papai, methinks you're a contradishin.'

My pronouncement made him start, but then he turned over in his mind what I had said. Grave as a judge, he placed me on his lap. There, under the orange-tree, we sat in perfect quietude, he kissing my forehead with great tenderness.

I knew not how long we had sat there, when I heard Doña Marisa calling for me. 'Sofia-Elisabete! Where are you? It's time for maccaroni.' I urged papai to join us before the maccaroni disappeared. With a slight grimace, he put on his riding-coat and hat. Together we walked hand in hand down the gravelled walk – he with a heavy step, whereas I with a light step, now that I made up a proud pair with my papai.

'Doña Marisa! Doña Marisa! My papai has come at last.' I romped towards her in celebration, and she, with her shiny eyes, drew me into a tight hug, caressing the crown of my head.

'Well, well, the British lion has found our den,' Señor Gonzalez struck a defiant pose with his hands on his hips. He turned to whisper something to his lady.

'Colonel Fitzwilliam, you are come,' said she with a frowning brow. 'Welcome to Villa La Luna.'

Never one to feel intimidated by a cool welcome, papai grasped her outstretched hand to kiss it. 'Doña Marisa, you're just as handsome as the time I had met you in Lisbon and we danced the valza, and oh yes, you lied to me then, sending me to the wrong convent to find Sofia-Elisabete. I wonder why?'

'I know you'll never believe me, but I did it to save us all from harm,' replied she.

Papai scowled at her when, out of the corner of his eye, he detected Pico slipping away. 'Pico? Pico Robinson! My boy, when I get through with you, you shan't walk for three days,' thundered he.

'Please, Colonel...' Pico pleaded for his life.

'Go and get me a stick. Make haste, boy.'

Surely papai was joking. An awkward silence followed, when Doña Marisa cleared her voice to introduce papai to Señor Gonzalez, her cortejo, and Emmerence Odet, her interpreter and my companion. Papai grunted at both of them.

It was then that Pico shuffled back from the orange grove. He handed a small branch to papai, who scoffed at it and snapped it over his thigh, breaking it in two.

'Go and get a bigger one. I promised your father that if I found you, I would give you twenty thumps on your backside.'

Struck with horror, I clung to papai's leg. 'Run, Pico, run!'

'Yer canna save me this time, Soofia-Eee.' Pico's shoulders slumped.

'I shall run away then,' threatened I.

Papai humphed. 'Well, if you must, you must, but I shan't traipse through any more countries searching for you.' He shook me off, and I fell on my seat of honour.

I gasped at his lie. 'But you said that you would.'

'O fie! I'm too weary now.'

Doña Marisa interrupted our quarrel, demanding that papai put an end to his nonsense. She, being the grown-up, claimed full responsibility for deceiving Pico and me into running away with her to la luna. Surprised by her confession, papai gaped at her, as did I. He gave up, for the moment, but he threatened to punish Pico in some other fashion once he thought of something good involving muck, and much of it; otherwise, papai could never face his brother Tom again for having shunned his manly duty.

'Ay!' exclaimed Doña Marisa. Having heard enough of his 'manly gibberish', she beckoned everyone upstairs to the loggia where a festive table had been set for our mid-day meal.

Having sensed my papai's ire, I grasped his hand to drag him upstairs to the loggia, because once he ate the magic maccaroni, his humour would improve – I was sure of it. We sat at table, where papai scowled at Doña Marisa, until I nudged him to serve me 'a heap of tasty maccaroni, please'. With undisguised glee, I took hold of some maccaroni on my plate, twisting and pulling it. Then came my best trick. Holding the strands of maccaroni high above my head, I leant back and opened my mouth wide to devour the doughy, cheesey goodness. 'Ha! Ha!' laughed I, proud of my achievement.

Papai gaped at me. 'Gad zookers! You've turned into a savage, eating maccaroni like an Indian sword swallower.' With a huff, papai scissored up my maccaroni with his knife and fork. He scolded me for being a hoyden, saying I could never mingle with polite society again eating that way. His mouth half-opened, he was about to tell me something else, when he noticed Señor Gonzalez scribbling in a small journal-book, and the oddity of it made him forget what he had wished to say. Vexed, papai told me to have at it again, but this time with a fork, which he placed in my hand. I frowned at my mangled maccaroni, for it never did taste the same after that.

On a sudden, papai turned gentleman, helping Doña Marisa to more wine. 'I thank you no,' replied she, patting her belly. Papai gaped at her roundish belly, he having not noticed it before. He turned to Señor Gonzalez with a questioning look, but that man held up his hands and shrugged at him.

Papai fumbled with the decanter, nearly spilling its contents. 'I thought my brother was funning me about it. I met up with Scapeton in Milan.'

I had no idea why the grown-ups looked at one another in a peculiar way. 'I kicked him good and hard,' boasted I.

'Ha! You *are* my daughter.' Papai turned to grin at me.

'That's what he said. He told me you're a bore. I don't think you're boring. I think you're the most jolly-ish papai in the world.' Papai must've liked that compliment because he chucked me under the chin.

Doña Marisa invited the 'most jolly-ish papai' to lodge with us at Villa La Luna, and he said he would because the wrong sort of persons hung about the inn in the village, eating maccaroni with their hands and going barefooted. Papai winked at me, and he placed me on his lap, calling me the right sort. I picked up a strand of maccaroni from his plate, and I stuffed it into his mouth as his reward.

'Mmm...lemon, olive oil and cheese.'

'Ninetta makes everything taste good in her magic kitchen,' said I with pride.

Papai gave me a greasy gooseberry kiss on my cheek, and I erupted into giggles. He was about to do it again when he noticed Señor Gonzalez scribbling away at a furious rate. When Señor Gonzalez glanced up to spy on us, papai fixed him with a questioning stare.

Later, that afternoon, I crept into my papai's room where his man, MacTavish, assisted him with his bath. Doña Marisa had complained of papai's manly odour, and thus she had ordered Ninetta to prepare hot water for papai.

'Viva! MacTavish,' I greeted my old friend.

'Aweel, aweel, are ye done trampin' aboot?'

'Ay.' The two of us exchanged broad smiles.

At the dinner hour, I came upon papai at the top of the stairs. He gaped at my majo costume but gathered his wits to compliment me. 'You seem, ah, very spangly this evening,' observed he. When he noticed my coloured lips, he wiped off the rose lip salve with his pocket-handkerchief, telling me that I was too young to wear such a thing and that I was already rosy and pretty without it. He bent down to kiss my forehead, and in that moment, I glowed inward and outward from my papai's attentions. Hand in hand, we descended the great staircase to join the others in the dining-room.

After supper I entertained everyone with a solo bolero dance while Doña Marisa and Señor Gonzalez snapped their castanets to mark the rhythm. I began with the paseo, the promenade, and when I came to a stop in the centre of the room, I extended a foot and a curved arm. Soon, I became lost in the joy of the dance, with its graceful leaps and quick, firm steps, and rattling of castanets – ta-ria-ria-pi. At the end, when I froze in a defiant pose with my hands on my hips, my body tilted slightly backwards, Señor Gonzalez cheered me with 'Bien parado!'

From where he sat, papai held out his arms to receive me, and I sensed the trace of trouble on his face. I hung my head, ready to be court-martialled for dancing the bolero against his wishes.

'You are astonishingly good but too young to be dancing with… with…' stammered he.

'Violencia?'

'Yes, violencia.' He tapped my nose. 'You must promise me to dance the bolero only for family and never in public again.'

'Oh yes, papai.' Relieved, I stood on my toes to kiss him good-night.

Snug in bed, I dreamt of marionettes dancing a sprightly bolero, when they began to shout 'Olé! Olé!', sounding very much like Señor Gonzalez. I cried out, 'No-no-no', but I couldn't save my fanciful dream. My marionettes had been dashed to atoms. Emmerence, having grown used to Señor Gonzalez's drunken bouts, slept through it all, while I, a restless soul, got out of bed. I shuffled into my papai's room. Just then, Doña Marisa's musical clock struck eleven o'clock as I crawled into papai's bed.

'The devil take those cuckoo clocks,' thundered he. 'I'm murdering cuckoos tomorrow.'

Five minutes later, the eerie blare of Señor Gonzalez's alphorn sounded not once, but thrice. The man must have drunk a goodly amount of red wine in the course of the evening. Bwwaaarrrhhhmmm.

'What the deuce was that?' Papai bolted upright in bed.

'Alphorn,' murmured I. 'Señor Gonzalez plays it when he's drunk.'

'That crazy Spaniard…Sofia-Elisabete, what are you doing here?'

'Please, papai. I missed you terribly.'

Papai groaned. 'Vem cá. Come here.'

And so I did, and he kissed me good-night.

Papai had discovered hidden small lakes in the heights above Nervi while he had traipsed in the mountains searching for me. He hired a mule to carry the two of us up a steep path, and when he located the trail that he had marked a few days ago, he led me deep into the woods. 'Lo there!' He pointed to small pools of bubbling blue-green water surrounded by hugeous slabs of rock. After watering the mule, he tied it to a tree.

We followed the banks of the various water pools until we found a picturesque one with a waterfall. 'It's magic water,' I half-whispered, wonderstruck. Papai determined the best place for us to do flying boulders, given the number of rocks lying on the bottom of the pool, after which I practised the swimming tricks that my avô had taught me. It seemed an age ago since I had swum in Wildsee, where I had met my friend Herr Fouqué.

'Herr Fouqué called me Undine.'

'Oh yes, our good friend Baron de La Motte Fouqué.' Papai grinned. 'Did you know he's a popular writer? He wrote *Undine*, a beautiful fairy tale, and I had him sign a copy for you.'

'Señor Gonzalez is a writer.'

'Indeed?' Papai eyed me with disbelief. 'What has he written?'

'He wrote of a wheel of cheese and a hairless hare, and he made them talk.'

Papai laughed. 'I shall purchase these books and have him sign them.'

'Oh, but you shan't find them under his manly name.' I shook my head.

'Why ever not?'

'Lady Le Buggo and Madame de Coccinelle wrote them.'

Papai convulsed with laughter, slapping the surface of the water with his hands as if I had told a good joke. He drifted to the bank where he clambered up a slab of rock, declaring it the perfect thing. 'Vem cá. Come here.' He beckoned me to the rock, and he lifted me onto it. There, atop our slab, papai stretched out in the sun to warm himself. He patted the hard surface next to him, and so I joined him, stretching myself out. When he placed his hands behind his head, I did likewise, which amused him.

'Papai, did you fight Napoleon?' My question surprised him.

'I did, indeed.'

'Was he a bad emperor?'

'He was the master of lies, and he used the power of lies to control everyone and everything in his empire. Thankfully, he is no longer emperor.'

'If he's no longer emperor, where do the lies go?'

Papai paused to think. 'They mix with the truth, where it shall take a long time to untangle them, if it can be done.'

This intrigued me, and I wondered if my own lies mixed with the truth such that I could no longer recognise the truth or even the lie.

Papai turned his head towards mine. 'Listen, my girl. It's time for us to return home. We must get on before the snowfall makes the roads impassable.'

This troubled me. 'I want us to stay here for ever at Villa La Luna.'

'Do not you miss your avô and your mamãe?' He gave me a curious look. 'They wish you to come home. They miss you terribly.'

'Can they not come here instead?'

'Your avô has many responsibilities in England, as does your mamãe. Many lives depend on them.'

'I have sponsabillies here,' insisted I. 'I'm a foot-boy for Doña Marisa.'

'Indeed? What does a foot-boy do?'

'I fan her. I run errands. I fetch her food. I dance the bolero with her.'

Papai humphed. 'You cannot always want to be a foot-boy. Life is not all mirth and play. The time has come to return home.'

Hot tears tumbled down my cheeks. How could I give up Doña Marisa and Señor Gonzalez and Emmerence and my way of life at Villa La Luna? I turned away to weep. Papai patted my back, calling me his dear little girl whom he could not live without, and begging me to think of my mamãe Aggie and my pug Tin-Key, both of whom were heart-broken and miserable without me, but his pleas made me sob louder. Why, oh, why could they not come here to live with me?

'Come – let's get on,' papai sat up.

I shook my head. When I refused to leave the rock, he carried me down against my will. 'Não, não, não,' protested I. Slung over my papai's shoulder, I kicked and I kicked. Oh, why did I ever think these small lakes were magical when they made me feel wretched? They must be hidden lakes of sorrows, and thus I dubbed them for ever in my memory.

To my amazement, papai didn't mention our leave-taking that evening. But to be safe, I hid in the orange grove the next morning, climbing into one of the trees. I had been on the look-out for a long while, when I needed desperately to relieve myself. I was about to climb down, when I heard familiar voices, and to my great horror, papai and Doña Marisa stood underneath my tree, romanticking each other; for, papai had been placed under enchantment.

'Must your cortejo play his alphorn every night?' complained papai.

Doña Marisa sighed. 'He is worried that I'm still in love with you. That's why he gets drunk in the evening.'

'Well, are you, Marisa?' Papai gave her a lopsided grin.

'I shan't deny that my heart warms whenever I think of the handsome British officer who loved me first and is the father of my child. But you – you never truly loved me, did you?' Doña Marisa cast down her eyes.

Papai leant forward to kiss her tenderly on the cheek. I covered my mouth with my hands to stifle a squeal.

With a broad grin, Doña Marisa cupped his face with her hands. 'Qué milagro! What a miracle! The spell is broken, because at the moment, all I can think of is my Sábado and what he's thinking of and hoping he thinks of me.'

Papai returned her smile, and he held out his arm. Once the two erstwhile lovers strolled away, I pulled down my majo breeches to water the orange-tree. Oh, relief at last. My business done, I climbed down part of the way and thereafter dropped to the ground.

'Ai!' cried I in surprise, when papai seized me by the scruff of my neck.

'I don't know which is worse,' he chided me, '– you being a savage and watering the tree from on high, or you being an eavesdropper and listening to a private conversation.'

'Olha maroto! I shall tell mamãe that you kissed Doña Marisa.' I shook my finger at him.

'O, ho! Threatening a superior officer, indeed. Prepare to be court-martialled, soldier. I'm confiscating your maccaroni today.' He turned me round for a forced march back to the villa.

That evening, papai announced to everyone that he and I would leave Villa La Luna three days hence, as would Pico, who would be delivered up to his parents in Edwinstowe. Doña Marisa burst into tears. 'I knew how it would be. You have come to take away my daughter,' cried she. Doña Marisa begged papai to let me live with her. She was my true mamãe, she argued, and a mother and daughter should never be separated.

With a stern look, papai ordered us children to retire for the night, and we would talk more of this on the morrow. My anxiety heightened, I half-heartedly kissed papai and Doña Marisa good-night. Emmerence put me to bed, and when I knew for certain that she had fallen asleep, I gave her the slip, because I had more important things to do than sleep tonight. Having crept down to the doorway of the drawing room, I observed my papai and Doña Marisa argue; for, papai's enchantment had been broken.

'I thank you for sending me a tress of her hair.' Papai glowered at her.

'You are most welcome,' replied Doña Marisa.

'How dare you cut off her hair. I am of separate minds on whether to punish you for stealing away my daughter,' thundered papai.

'Hmm. I wondered when you would become angry at what I had done. But you, sir,' Doña Marisa shook her finger at him, 'have never apologised for what you had done – deserting us in Lisbon all those years ago.'

'I shan't argue about that now.' Papai folded his arms.

Doña Marisa tossed up her chin. 'Listen, I am her mother, and she belongs with me. My daughter has a prodigious imagination and a natural curiosity of the world, and here at Villa La Luna, she will be brought up in a liberal manner, with the freedom to explore...'

'Freedom? Why, she has turned into a little savage.' Papai scoffed at her. 'You live with a man who is not your husband. You are with child by a man who is not your husband. And now you're wealthy and titled, yet you're the same as you always were.'

Doña Marisa rose in defiance. 'You condemn me and my Spanish customs, yet your English customs are no better – a mistress here, a mistress there, a love child here, there, everywhere. I know you "ran riot" in London at one time, and thus you were no better than I was at that young age,' retorted she.

Papai bit his lip and turned away.

'A ha! Your countenance belies you, and I begin to think you've done something unspeakable in your past.'

'Whatever I have done or not done is between me and God.' Papai grimaced. 'But it does not change anything. Sofia-Elisabete will return home with me where she will learn to behave like a proper young lady and where she will receive the best education.'

'Ay, Dios mío!' Doña Marisa stamped her foot. She railed at him in a blend of Spanish and English, in which she proposed that I should choose where I wanted to live.

I covered my ears, not wanting to hear another word. Looking round and finding no one in the passage, I ran up the stairs of the tower, away from the all-knowing grown-ups. Safe now in my fortress and consoled by the starry night sky, I curled up with my imaginary pug-puppy, and I recited in my head a bed-time story – the one I knew by heart because it was my own story...

There once lived a tiny girl named Sofia-Elisabete in the mountains near Monchique, Portugal. A foundling she was for more than three years until she set out in the world guided by her guardian angel, Sister Lisbet, to find her papai, he being a colonel in the British Army. One day they found each other in York, and thereafter they lived as father and daughter for the whole world to see.

She, however, learnt that she was a love child – a child born out of wedlock – and that her mother had abandoned her at a convent in Lisbon. This troubled her, but she hid her curiosity about her real mother deep in her heart. Thereafter, her papai married a lovely and kind lady named Aggie, whom Sofia-Elisabete called mamãe, and the three of them lived happily in the town of Scarborough.

Until one day when her papai started to gad about with the evil Mr O. P. Umm, who made him melancholy and turned him into an ogre. Sofia-Elisabete ran away, having been placed under enchantment by a beautiful Spanish maja named Doña Marisa who promised to take her to la luna – the perfect world in a moon – a place where no one ever gets sick or sad and where there is no hunger or hatred. In the beginning, she earnestly believed her papai would come and get her, because those are the rules, you know, when your papai loves you and you run away from home, and besides, this moon would cure her papai and he would never be ill again.

And so her extraordinary adventure began, travelling hundreds and hundreds of miles from England to Rotterdam, Cologne, the Black Forest, Zürich, Brieg, Milan and Genoa, as she searched for the perfect world in a moon, but where instead she came across misery, poverty, disease and hatred. She persisted in this quest for a perfect moon world, refusing to accept the truth of her observations. She never did find it, because it turned out to be a fanciful world, a dazzling lie.

But along the way she discovered her real mother, Doña Marisa, and the reason her mother had abandoned her. Her heart filled with bitterness as she struggled to understand and accept her mother's love and abandonment. Then, once her heart became pure, she became reunited with her papai, this after months of separation, but the consequence of it all was she would have to choose one parent and abandon the other.

She, the lonely orphan turned lucky child, had become an unfortunate child again, this time to be wrenched apart from those whom she loved. If she chose to live at Villa La Luna, she would undoubtedly pine for Scarborough, and if she chose Scarborough, she would pine likewise for everyone and everything at Villa La Luna. Her story didn't end perfectly ever after, and she has come to believe that endings never turn out the way we really want them to.

Chapter Fourteen

The Changeling

MY FIRST AND LAST STREET-FIGHT, thinks I, was a monstrous set-to that nearly began a riot. Struck with dismay by my boisterous behaviour, papai wondered what had become of his sweet little girl – the one he bought chocolate for, the one who wished to be a nun someday. Papai became convinced that the fairies, having stolen away his true child, determined to leave a wild and unruly one in my place. I, the fairy child, had nothing in common with the real Sofia-Elisabete, said he, what with my boyish clothes, shorn hair, insolent manner and black eye. With his sad countenance, his eyelids crinkling, papai gave me a mournful look. 'I went to sleep one day under my pine tree, and I awoke several months later, the father of a completely different child,' lamented he. When I asked him where the fairies had taken me, he eyed me with suspicion, insisting I knew full well where I had gone.

'Mamãe Marisa! Mamãe Marisa!' I scurried to the entrance of Villa La Luna where Doña Marisa sobbed into a handkerchief. 'I forgot something.'

Doña Marisa suffered from shock to see me, for I had already bid everyone a long and tearful adeus. 'Minha Sofia-Elisabete? What did you forget?'

'I forgot to…I wished to…' My hums and haas diverted her.

'Hmm?'

'I forgot to give you a proper good-bye. A bênção minha mamãe.' I kissed her hand to bless her, which made her sob again.

Doña Marisa held out her arms, and the two of us embraced, she kissing my cheeks one after another, when I heard papai cough in the distance, no doubt upset by my dawdling. I took one last look at Villa La Luna, committing it to memory. 'Uf widerluege,' cried Emmerence as she and Señor Gonzalez waved good-bye from the loggia. And so I bid my good friends adeus for the hundredth time, waving my cap at them. With the heaviest of hearts, I turned a right-about-face, the hot tears tumbling down my cheeks, and I ran back to where papai awaited me.

I hear you cry, 'Why did you choose to return to England with your papai?' What happened was this. That night in the tower, when I had escaped from the all-knowing grown-ups, I had the great fortune of speaking with Sister Lisbet. I scolded her for having ignored me of late, but she explained that she served as guardian angel for many an orphaned child, and she had been ever so busy these past few months finding homes for them. 'I suppose so,' mumbled I, betraying my grudging heart.

We puzzled our wits together to solve my dilemma. Should I live with papai or Doña Marisa? We gazed into the starry heaven to locate the two brightest stars, and having found them, we tugged at the stars to bring them closer. Papai had two stars orbiting him, they being me and my mamãe Aggie, whereas Doña Marisa had four stars orbiting her, they being me, Señor Gonzalez, Emmerence and my unborn half of a brother.

Papai's star flickered, while Doña Marisa's star remained bright and strong. 'Papai is ill, thinks I.' Worried, I thought it best to stay with papai. But then Doña Marisa's star flickered, and it must have done so when she grieved for me. What to do? Sister Lisbet wrapped me up in her red capa, and together we flew towards a bright white moon – higher and higher and higher. She pointed to the earth below, all blues and browns and white swirls on one side and darkness on the other side, and as the earth spun like a teetotum, the light side moved into darkness, to be ruled by the moon and stars, while the dark side moved into lightness, to be ruled by the sun.

'Night and day, night and day, the two halves of the earth take turns being warmed by the sun.' Sister Lisbet inclined her head towards me, when she began to fade.

'Wait!' called I, but she had gone. I closed my eyes, praying for the answer, when I found myself snug in bed.

I shook Emmerence awake to tell her of my dream. She, thoughtful and sensible as always, reasoned that my parents should both raise me, taking turns to do so.

'It takes a year for the earth to revolve the sun,' noted she.

'Isso! Exactly!' cried I.

A miracle occurred when my papai reluctantly agreed to my crazy plan, as he called it, although he proposed a longer period instead – three years in Scarborough, followed by two years in Nervi, and round and round I would go, each parent taking a turn to raise me. 'How would we know if it could really work if we didn't ever try?' pleaded Doña Marisa with tears in her eyes.

I thought the whole thing brilliant, until I began to pack my things, and the unsettling thought of quitting Villa La Luna for three years put me in ill-humour. Papai ordered me to travel very light, and so there was nothing for it but to leave all of my playthings and treasures behind, including my prized drum, the cuckoo clock that Herr Faller had made for me and the clogs shaped like little canoes that the twins Niesje and Kaatje had gifted me with. I wept and stamped my feet – left, right, left, right – over the loss of my drum, but papai stood firm with his arms folded.

It was no secret that papai disapproved of my boyish attire, and thus he demanded that I dress in girl's clothes for our journey home. But I had only one such thing in my possession, namely, the blue petticoat with red bodice and white cambric shirt from the Black Forest. What to do? A ha! I knew how to act. On the morning of our departure, I dressed in my foreign costume with bright red bollenhut, knowing it would vex my papai, and to be sure it did.

'Heaven and earth! What are you wearing on your head?' Papai gaped at the gigantic red tufts of wool on my straw hat.

'It's a Black Forest hat. What say you of it?'

'I say, you shall leave that ridiculous costume here,' ordered he.

'But papai, I wish to…'

'Permission denied. No child of mine shall be seen in public looking like a looby.'

'Yes, papai,' I hung my head to hide my impish grin.

Dressed now as an English boy of quality, I ran into the orange grove to bid adeus to my favourite orange-tree. But a most disturbing sight awaited me there – the sight of Pico and Emmerence romanticking each other. *Gah!* Curious as ever, though, I hid behind a tree to listen to them. Pico asked her to think on him whenever she chanced to see a crescent moon in a starry night sky, and she said she would. He vowed that when he became a first-rate seaman, he would come back for her. Together they would be sea gipsies, roaming the high seas, battling pirates and duelling with those plaguy Americans.

'Ai!' cried I in surprise, when papai seized me by the scruff of my neck.

'Eavesdropping again?' papai chided me.

'Shush, papai. I heard Pico say…' whispered I.

'There's nothing worse than a busy body, tattler or backbiter,' admonished he.

I scratched my head. 'Which one am I?'

Papai groaned as he steered me away with one hand atop my head, and so I never did get to say good-bye to my favourite orange-tree.

We journeyed through the land of Napoleon, the country called France, in two cabriolets – papai and I in one, MacTavish and Pico in the other. The French postillions wore gigantic jack-boots, and each morning we gathered round to watch the spectacle of them being hoisted into their boots. 'En route! Hi!' They cracked their long whips – crac-crac – making the horses squeal, and away we went. Sometimes on the great road we would pass barns on wheels, these straw-thatched diligences conveying people and their dogs from one town to another. I wished to ride in a barn, but papai dismissed that idea, because he had been ever so busy 'murdering fleas' last night at our inn, and he imagined a passenger in a diligence would suffer likewise from flea-hunting.

I wrinkled my nose. 'Papai, I stink like a horse.'

'Well, now, you bathed three days ago. I dare say you're good for another sennight.' He winked at me.

I scratched my flea bites. 'Papai, I itch.'

'Vem cá. Come here.' Papai applied salve to my arm.

Feeling wretched and filthy, I counted the days until my next bath – yes, I, who disliked bathing. But when you're travelling on the road and covered with white dust and stinking like a dirty horse, you begin to pine for a warm bath scented with the essence of orange-blossoms. The sweet memory of my mamãe Marisa bathing me on our last evening together made me melancholy of a sudden. She had tugged at my hair to help my hair grow. A habit with me now, I reached up to my hair to give it a good tug, when I noticed papai eyeing me with curiosity. Struck with horror, he grasped my head to search it for bugs, and having found none, he kissed the crown of my head with relief.

One rainy day in the town of Avignon, papai burst into our room at the inn, worked up to a pitch of great excitement. With a waggish grin, he waved something in his hand. Apparently, at the bookseller's shop, he bought two books written in French by a certain Madame de Coccinelle, or Señor Gonzalez as we know him. Papai beckoned me to sit on his lap, while he read out loud a few choice passages from *Adventures of a Wheel of Cheese* in his bad French, but each time he convulsed with laughter and couldn't finish. I pleaded with him to read it to me in English, and so he did.

''Twas a cold and windy day,' papai began, 'when the wheel of cheese rolled into the town of Marseilles, but it stank as bad as a fusty old piece of cheese, and no one would get near it. The only person who befriended it happened to be the gruff proprietor of a cheese-shop. "How much for a slice of you?" the cheesemonger demanded to know. "I beg your pardon," cried an indignant wheel of cheese in its muffled voice. "I'll give you four sous," offered the man. The wheel of cheese scoffed at him, mumbling "How ridiculous!" as it rolled out of the shop, whereupon the cheesemonger set his dog on it, and the dog, with a growl and snap, growl and snap, chased it out of town. "Aieeee!" howled the wheel of cheese as it bounced down the bumps on the roadside.'

'How droll,' declared papai.

'I like the wheel of cheese.'

Papai was all wonderment. 'Indeed?'

I nodded. 'I want the wheel of cheese to be happy and not be eaten up by anyone.'

'Humph. A stinking wheel of cheese sketched as a hero?'

'All good heroes smell.' I kissed his forehead. 'Papai, I stink as bad as a wheel of cheese.'

'Listen, my girl. We're on a long march to Calais that will take us three more weeks. When I led my soldiers on a long, forced march, and we travelled on foot, we were lucky if we even got a pail of cold water at the end of it.'

I buried my head into papai's chest, miserable at the thought of just a pail of water at the end of three long weeks. Several days later, my misery increased ten-fold when we came upon Vienne. On the approach to this ancient town, it presented agreeable and charming, but once we neared the centre of it, the dirt and filth and untidy homes and beggary made me wonder if Napoleon had cast a spell of deep gloom on the town-folk.

We stopped at a wretched inn, where we ate coarse food and thereafter slept on lumpy beds. That night, papai cried out in his sleep – 'Riflemen! Riflemen!' – the first of many nightmares he suffered on our journey home. I patted his head until he calmed, after which he turned on his side and wept quietly into his pillow. When I asked him at day break what he had dreamt of, he mentioned the war, something gruesome he had seen near Fuentes de Oñoro, a town on the border of Spain and Portugal, and he would say no more.

'Papai, did Napoleon cast a spell on you to give you bad dreams?'

'Humph. You might say that,' he rubbed his forehead with worry.

My eyes became round as saucers. 'Will he put a curse on me?'

'He cannot do you harm,' papai assured me.

Papai and MacTavish exchanged a knowing look. They began to draw the charges of their double-barrelled pistols and load them afresh, something they did each morning as was their habit. Nevertheless, I feared that Napoleon meant to do us harm, and I blamed the evil emperor for cursing my papai. The curse of the emperor! My ire heightened just thinking of what the emperor had done to papai. No wonder papai suffered from melancholy and gadded about with Mr O. P. Umm.

Grieving for my papai and his troubled heart, I followed him silently to the filthy dining room where we ate sour bread with butter and drank sweetened tea served up by a sulky landlady. Oh, how I missed the magic oranges at Villa La Luna and how Señor Gonzalez would tease me at breakfast that an orange is gold in the morning, silver at noon, and lead at night. But I dared not bother my poor papai by asking for an orange here in this God-forsaken place.

Later that day we arrived in Lyons where papai spoke to some of the town-folk, who blamed the English for letting Napoleon escape from Elba. They said the English didn't like the terms of peace and wished to stir up another war, and so that's what happened. Papai also heard violent arguments between those who liked the king, Louis XVIII, and those who liked Napoleon. 'Buonaparte is still very popular with some of the French people,' warned papai. I shuddered with fear at the thought, and I remained on my guard for the evil emperor.

The next morning, as we prepared to depart Lyons, we observed some French soldiers carrying a wounded soldier, the bright red blood staining his uniform. Papai learnt that a duel had been fought with another soldier, their weapons being swords. With a grimace, papai told us the duellists had fought over something ridiculous, such as a hasty word or a minor insult, and this unfortunate soul, now covered in blood, was not one-and-twenty. I clasped my hands in prayer as the poor soldier sank into the repose of death.

Upon our arrival in Dijon, the town-folk's devotion for Napoleon had seized them with great fervour, for many of the shops sold images of Napoleon on plates, cups and candle-holders. 'Vive l'Empereur!' the shop-keepers would cry to passers-by. Even some of the workmen carried spades and hammers with the image of Napoleon on their tools in trade. At our inn, a framed picture of Napoleon adorned each room, the better for this stregone, this sorcerer, to spy on us. Later, when we supped, papai complained that he would suffer from indigestion, because every time he ate a forkful of food, the image of Napoleon on the plate would stare back at him.

The next morning, having finished my meagre breakfast of cold tea and sour bread, I was seized with a real fit of the fidgets, and so papai ordered Pico and me to visit the Necessary House and to be done with it as soon as we could. Believe you me, no one wants to linger there. When we had done, Pico and I amused ourselves with a bout of fisticuffs, he teaching me how to deliver a sharp blow with a manly spirit. 'Yer a strong girl,' acknowledged Pico, cradling his left arm where I had rapped him with my fist. Two crabbed-looking boys gathered nearby to observe us, the older one chewing on a straw. The rascals staged a mock fight, acting foolish and dandyish and leaving no doubt of their dislike of us foreigners.

'Rosbif!' The older boy spat out his straw.

'Frogs!' retorted Pico.

'Rosbif!' The younger boy gave us an ugly gesture of his hand.

Not knowing what his gesture meant, I turned myself into a lion and roared – rrraaaawwrr! – and I clawed my hands in the air. My snaps and snarls, for whatever reason, upset this hot-headed boy, and quicker than a thought, he attacked me, pumping his fists into my sides.

'Aieeee! Aieeee!' yelped I in pain.

'Defend yerself,' urged Pico.

And so I did. I rallied with a mighty roar that shook the heavens. Taking good aim, I gave a punishing hit to my foe, who thereafter tumbled onto the ground.

'Well done, Soofia-Eee!' Pico cheered me on.

Some of the town ruffians gathered round in search of entertainment, their clamour attracting a wide crowd as my foe and

I returned hit for hit. Of a sudden, someone lifted me up, tucking me under his arm, while I wriggled and kicked. 'Manso! Be still!' ordered papai. MacTavish, meanwhile, had seized Pico by the lug. 'Yow!' cried Pico, as he struggled to free himself.

We hastened to our cabriolets, an ugly crowd at our heels. 'En route! Hi!' The postillions crac-crac'd their whips, the horses squealed and our cabriolets rumbled off, departing Dijon in a cloud of white dust.

We had no sooner got away, than someone behind us fired a pistol – poomb. 'Duck down,' papai ordered me. So obey him I did, curled up on the seat, my heart thump-thumping with fear that Napoleon would attack us. I goggled my eyes at papai, who turned round to fire off a warning shot with his double-barrelled pistol, the loud report ringing in my ears. On seeing me quake from head to toe with fright, papai assured me that this had stopped the angry mob from pursuing us; nevertheless, he remained on his guard for what seemed a long while, instructing me to be quiet.

When papai finally deemed us safe, he gathered me into his arms, where I clung to him until he had calmed my fast-beating heart. He examined my injuries from the fight with the French boy, wiping the blood from my nose and thereafter cleaning my face with the liquor in his flask. Shaking his head slightly, he fingered the tears in my clothes to determine if they could be mended by MacTavish, but there was nothing for it, I would need to wear the other set of clothes I had brought with me. Papai cupped my face with his hands.

'Where, oh, where did my little girl go?' his voice trembled with sadness.

I frowned. 'Go? Nowhere, papai.'

'Changeling!' he accused me. 'I want the real Sofia-Elisabete returned to me.'

'I am Sofia-Elisabete,' declared I.

'Impossible! My sweet little girl would never have engaged in fisticuffs with a ragged urchin.'

'But papai, he called me rosbif.'

Papai groaned. 'Do you even know what that is?'

I shrugged.

'It means roast beef.'

'Roast beef?' My eyes widened.

'It's just a word that the French soldiers use for the English.'

'Just a word?'

Papai gave me a stern look. 'The next time you and Pico take a freak to fight the French on French soil over a stupid word – well, you've got to restrain yourselves.'

I scratched my head, wondering how I could restrain myself when threatened by a rude, hot-headed French boy.

Papai tried again. 'My dear child, you cannot follow up on every mad freak that comes into your head. It can be dangerous. Do you understand?'

I hung my head in disgrace, wondering why I got into a bout over English roast beef and French frogs. I recalled the surly look on the boy's face and that of Pico's. Ai! The evil Napoleon must have cast a spell on us, making us hate each other, when we neither of us were truly roast beef or frogs. But if one believes in a lie, it becomes one's truth, thinks I.

In Langres, papai took me to a kindly French doctor, who dressed my wounds. The doctor said my red, swollen eye would turn black for a fortnight before the bruise would fade. He suggested a good inn for us, and there, I bathed in warm water. The landlady, on seeing my wounds and bruises, scowled at papai, and no matter how hard papai tried to convince her otherwise in his bad French, she was sure he had beat me.

'She believes I gave my own daughter a good drubbing,' he muttered to himself in disbelief.

'Papai, I'm ready for you.'

Papai picked up the clothes that MacTavish had set on a chair, when he realised that it was my majo costume.

'Where are your foot-boy clothes?' he demanded to know.

I shrugged. 'Those are my clothes.'

Papai grunted. 'Did not you pack your livery?'

'You said I cannot be a foot-boy for ever. I wish to be a majo now.'

And that is why for the remainder of our journey through France, I wore a spangly majo costume. I don't know what the town-folk wondered at first – me, the majo girl, or me, the pugilist with a black eye. Pico thought it grand to have a black eye, it being a badge of distinction for having defended good old England, and he envied all of the attention I received. But the best thing of all to him was the spectacle of the French women giving the evil eye to my papai; for, they assumed that he, being an English brute, had beat me. Pico said the ridiculousness of it somehow reminded him of the bizarre comedy we had seen once at the puppet theatre where the puppets rioted and beat each other with sticks.

Having deemed me fit for travel, papai announced we would quit Langres on the morrow. That night, papai shouted in his sleep. 'Frogs! Frogs!' He swung his arm round and round as if he brandished a sword. I seized the glass of water set on the small table near the bed, and I poured the cold water on papai's face. 'Pfft,' sputtered he. With a moan, he rubbed his face, and then he fell silent, but I knew he laid there awake and troubled. That morning, I kissed his hand, and I greeted him with a blessing.

'A bênção meu papai.'

Papai chucked me under the chin. 'Oh, how I missed your blessing each morning and night.'

'What did you dream of?'

Papai became thoughtful. 'I dreamt I was battling the enemy during the war.'

'Did they call you rosbif?'

He fingered my black eye, lightly tracing its purplish edges. 'I do believe they did.' And he half-smiled at me, wearing those sad, crinkling eyes of his.

Near Troyes we entered a kind of 'desolate nether world', which was how papai described it. All that remained of the village were roof-less houses and black-burnt beams. The ragged villagers peeped at us from behind the ruins, their sickly countenances and hopeless despair piercing my heart. 'Cossacks set fire to their village during the war,' explained papai, 'and they believe the Cossacks will return.

They know not or refuse to accept that the war has ended.' I kissed the cross on my necklace, and I said a prayer for these poor souls.

That night, papai screamed 'Retreat! Retreat!' in his dreams. He pointed his finger as if he brandished a pistol, firing at the enemy. This time I knew how to act, thanks to the memory of when my mamãe Marisa had swooned on the bridge in Nervi. She had gifted me with a phial of orange-blossom scent to remember her always. I placed this phial under papai's nose, and sure enough, it brought him out of his fitful dream. He lay awake troubled, no doubt reliving what must have been a terrifying battle during the war, and so I clung to him until he began to breathe easy and he patted my hand.

Papai determined we would quit the countryside and take the great road to Paris, and from there, to Calais. MacTavish heartily agreed, because in every village we passed, the 'withered crones' sat in front of their houses peeling onions, and if he had to see one more fright, one more ugly onion-peeler, he would turn into a madman. With a secretive smile to papai, MacTavish declared he would march to Paris and vanquish anyone who stood in his way of true love and a good-looking woman. 'Vive l'Amour!' his eyes beamed with excitement.

I tugged at papai's coat. 'I don't want to go. The emperor scares me.'

'You needn't worry,' papai patted my head. 'Buonaparte is exiled on St. Helena.'

'I wish for my own pistol then.' An image of myself wielding a gun to protect my papai somehow appealed to me in an exciting kind of way, for I was keen to be an excellent markswoman like my mamãe Aggie.

'Silly gooseberry,' cried papai. 'What you wish for is a pretty frock. Your dear papai shall purchase you one. You shall wear the very height of Parisian fashion.'

I stamped my feet – left, right, left, right. 'I don't want to be tall. I want to be a majo for ever.'

'When we reach Paris, your majo days are done,' papai shook his finger at me.

And that is why I blamed that evil Napoleon for making me dress as a girl again, because if he hadn't cast a spell on me to turn me into an ogress who fought with her fists, I could have been a majo for ever. In Paris, papai dragged me to a dressmaker, a Madame de Montreux, where I suffered through three fittings to turn me into a little angel dressed in white, albeit an angel with a black eye and an impudent manner.

On my last day of majo-ness, whilst we waited for my clothes to be done, Madame de Montreux suggested with a wink that papai visit the menagerie to view the heavenly creatures. There, in the Jardin des Plantes, Parisian ladies dressed in white gowns and elaborate bonnets promenaded with their coxcombical poodles, who were beribboned and perfumed like their mistresses. Some of these stylish ladies strolled together arm in arm, tittering and fluttering round papai, who, being the perfect gentleman, gave them a tip of his hat and greeted them with a jolly 'bonjour, bonjour, bonjour!'

'Mon Dieu,' papai murmured to himself when he observed one of these heavenly creatures lifting her gown to reveal her white-stockinged ankles.

I tugged at his sleeve. 'Papai, I want to go to chapel.'

'Now? Are you not enjoying the menagerie?'

'There are no wild animals here,' complained I.

This diverted papai, who led me to Notre Dame, near which some squalid children begged for alms, but the passers-by, including the ladies and gentlemen dressed in the height of fashion, ignored them. Papai struck up a conversation with a British officer to determine the news of the day, while I pondered how I could help these poor, starving children. What to do? I, Sofia-Elisabete, must beg for alms again. Isso! Exactly!

I dropped my majo hat onto the ground to collect the coins, whereupon I promenaded round it twice in a graceful paseo. I positioned myself, extending a foot and a curved arm, and with a snap of my castanets – ta-ria-ria-pi – I danced a solo bolero. Soon, I attracted a wide crowd, and when I ended my bolero with a sudden stop, a bien parado, the sous rained down on me. I gave out the coins to the poor children. 'Merci!' they each cried, and they ran away.

'Olé!' papai cheered me.

I cast down my eyes, preparing myself for a court-martial. But to my surprise, papai knelt to kiss me on my forehead.

'I'm proud of you, and I know your mamãe would be as well.'

I tilted my head to the side. 'Which mamãe? Mamãe Marisa or mamãe Aggie?'

'Why, both of them would be proud. You're the luckiest girl in the world to have two mamães.' Papai wiped his eyes with his pocket-handkerchief.

'Papai, is that why you're crying?'

'O, filha da minha alma,' he called me the daughter of his soul. 'I'm happy and relieved that the fairies have returned my Sofia-Elisabete to me.'

I opened my mouth to protest that I hadn't gone anywhere, when papai declared I could remain a majo if I promised to wear my white muslin frock with blue silk sash and matching bonnet in Scarborough. 'Would not your mamãe Aggie wish to see you in stylish Parisian dress?' I pondered his question. I believed my mamãe Aggie would rather see me in my stylish majo costume, but I dared not voice my opinion. 'Huzzah! Papai for ever,' cheered I, content for now in my majo-ness.

We didn't stay longer than three days in Paris, which suited me. The din of the city never ceased from day break to mid-night, and thus I hardly slept, whereas papai snored soundly despite the screeches and shouts and neighs and squeals and rumblings of carriages and pealing of bells. He, who could not sleep in the quiet of the countryside with the mournful blare of an alphorn now and then, found it the most natural thing in the world to be lulled to sleep by constant, loud noise. And I wonder now if those noises drowned out the nightmares swirling round in his head?

On the road to Calais I observed women with faces as brown as leather ploughing the fields, old peasants wearing cocked hats and a genteel-looking woman with a bright white cap and gold earrings riding astride a horse, just like a man. Ragged urchins accosted us at each town, some of them selling cakes, but papai would not buy any cakes for me. 'Hola, ho!' our postillion cried out whenever we drove by a drunken man tottering down the roadside.

Several days later we reached our destination at Calais, where we sat idle at Hotel de Bourbon, waiting for favourable winds to carry us across the water to Dover. Boredom having set in, Pico and I played at Mora, the noise of which drove papai and the other lodgers to distraction. Another day we amused ourselves by following a servant from room to room as he skated round with a small brush fastened to each foot to clean the boards, that is, until he locked us inside the brush closet, for he had gone quite distracted with our endless questions about his skating habits.

At noon, we supped on soup and bouilli, a kind of meat and vegetable stew, and on meagre days, when no meat was to be had, we supped on fish or omelette with fried beans or sallad. I hadn't savoured a dish of maccaroni in many weeks. In the afternoon, we drank boiled tea sweetened with coarse sugar and mixed with a goodly amount of boiled milk. Oh, how I missed my cioccolato italiano. I have since come to the conclusion that meagre food makes you cross, because the English travellers here argued endlessly over the hotel charges, and they complained of the number of toadstools sprouting in their rooms – either that or the disagreeable smell of aniseed from the French brown soap used by the hotel.

One evening, I eavesdropped on the landlord and papai while they drank a glass of capillaire, a 'disgusting syrup', which is what I heard my papai mutter once. 'Très bon, très bon,' papai lied to please his host. This landlord, Monsieur Rignolle, who went by the name of Lapin for some reason, bragged that he had many a lover and thus 'many a bâtard'.

'How many children do you have?' asked papai.

'I make twenty-seven of them,' returned Lapin with cool indifference.

'Twenty-seven?' papai's voice squeaked.

Lapin shrugged. 'I send them to foundling hospital.' He yawned just then, as if his children meant nothing more to him than, say, a cart-load of vegetables or legumes.

An image entered my mind of the despicable Lapin with his twenty-seven chickpeas, each of the chickpeas having a tiny, sweet face, and he tossed them one after another into the foundling turnbox wheel. A dark cloud of troubled thoughts passed over me, and before I could stop myself, I turned into an ogress, ready to pounce on this rogue.

'Olha maroto!' scolded I from the doorway.

Papai scowled at me and my clenched fists. 'Miss Changeling? Pray ask Sofia-Elisabete to return at once. Now go and do my bidding,' said he in a harsh tone.

Papai's censure stung me to the quick. I took to my heels, running out of doors, to search for myself, but no matter where I looked, I could not be found. Distressed at the thought of losing papai's good opinion, I trudged back to the inn where he awaited me in ill-humour.

'Well, now, have you returned to your senses?' His brow darkened.

I hung my head. 'I can't find me.'

'Are you certain you've looked everywhere?'

I nodded. 'I've looked high and low.'

'O fie!' papai growled out, casting me a severe look.

'Papai,' I inched closer to him so as to fidget with a button on his coat. 'I know why mamãe Marisa left me in the roda when I was a bebê.'

This piece of news unsettled him, and his countenance softened. 'Indeed?'

'She said she did a bad thing.'

'To be sure she did.'

A hint of suspicion tugged at my heart again – that dim feeling of doubt and hurt that lives inside of you, taking shape without your knowing it or wanting to know about it. I peered into his dark blue eyes, whereupon I blurted out, 'Papai, did you forget me?'

This home question deeply affected him, and he swallowed hard.

'I never forgot you.' Papai drew me to his breast. 'I wasn't man enough at first to come and look for you. I was a lost soul. Will you forgive my weakness?'

I knew papai spoke the truth, because Sister Lisbet had once described him as 'so very lost'. And that is why I grasped his hand now to kiss it. 'A bênção meu papai.'

Mid-morning the next day, the pilot of the *Princess Augusta* sent word that we would up anchor in half-an-hour. The whole hotel was in confusion as we lodgers bustled about to pack our things. After papai had settled our bill with the landlord, we hied to the dock, my papai carrying me and our portmanteau and hat-box. Pico lagged on the pier until papai ordered, 'Come, lad, quick march.' It hadn't occurred to me that Pico dreaded going home to Edwinstowe where a day of reckoning with his father could no longer be put off. MacTavish grasped Pico by the scruff of the neck to prevent his escape, and when they came on deck, he tied down Pico until we were safely out at sea.

'Gad zookers,' complained Pico. 'I'm not a criminal.'

'Ye sud ha'e taken the twenty thumps wi' the Colonel.' MacTavish rapped Pico on the head.

Ere long papai's complexion turned a shade of green as we pitched about on the sea, and he got sick over the side of the packet-boat. MacTavish positioned papai on deck near a pail, and each time papai got sick, so did the dandy next to him, and then the matron next to the dandy, and then the matron's portly husband, and so on, they each of them taking a turn at it – what an odd thing it was – until it seemed that most every passenger had sickened with this malady related to the sea.

I placed a rosolio drop on papai's tongue to soothe him, and he moaned his gratitude, his eyes half-closed. Then, abruptly, he reached for the pail, and the dandy next to him did the same with his pail, and the matron next to him, and you can guess the rest. I resolved to relieve papai's and everyone's suffering, and so, having told Wind to make haste and push us to Dover, I pressed my tiny hands on papai's forehead, praying with all my might. *Hola, ho! God! Please help my dear papai.* Que milagre! Like a miracle, papai's head sank upon his breast, and he snored for the remainder of the sea journey, as did the dandy and then the matron, &c.

The sun now being low in the sky, we sighted the British shore and the lofty white cliffs. 'Huzzah! Old England for ever,' shouted a sea officer with pride and relief. 'Huzzah!' echoed MacTavish, rousing papai from his peaceful slumber. In a wistful mood, papai gulped down French courage from his flask. He, having noticed my curiosity, offered me some.

'Papai, I am not yet six years old,' I chided him.

'Humph.' Papai offered his flask to the dandy next to us.

'I dare say I'm more than six years of age.' With a whoop, the dandy gulped down the wicked liquor, and when he had done, he honoured us with a loud belch.

'Well, I never!' protested the matron next to the belching dandy.

I began to giggle, when papai covered my mouth with his hand to shush me.

'Papai, where do memories go?' I shan't ever forget this silly dandy, methinks.

He paused to reflect on the matter. 'Well, now, everyone has a sea of memories. Some memories sink to the bottom of the sea, where you hope they never resurface, while others you wish to keep afloat for ever, but they eventually sink as well over time, unless you go and fish them up.'

I do believe I gathered up many memories from my adventure on the continent – some of them joyful such as rope dancing with the gipsies, some of them frightening such as nearly falling into an abyss, some of them hurtful such as being told why my natural mother had abandoned me in a foundling turnbox wheel. Would they all sink inside of me, down to my toes, never to be thought of again by me?

Oh, how I longed to hold my mamãe Aggie and to recount my adventure to her before any of it faded from my memory. I imagined that she, being a forbearing and sympathetic soul, would understand why I had gone off, and she would deem my adventure a fortunate misfortune, because should not a child know from whom she sprung? If not for my quest to find a perfect moon world – a world that turned out not to exist – then I would not have discovered my natural mother and the truth of my mysterious beginnings.

We put ashore at Dover, cheered by the lingering rays of the setting sun, when a chaotic scene ensued with passengers and porters and customs-officers. 'My girl, I am quite recovered, now that I'm back on English soil, and I shall be reunited with my dear wife,' rejoiced papai, his eyes bright and shiny. 'They say you must quit your home to appreciate it when you return.' Determined to share in his happiness, for I wished to be at home once more in Scarborough, I straightened my majo jacket, and I flung my brown capa over my left shoulder in the way I had seen Señor Gonzalez do with his capa whenever he summoned up a manly resolve. I promenaded down the pier in a graceful paseo, rattling my castanets – ta-ria-ria-pi.

But then, the distant blare of an alphorn beckoned me, and I began to pine for the past, and it pained me to think that everyone I had met on the continent would forget me, for I surely would never forget any of them. I turned round one last time, imagining I could see far into a continent at the horizon now blurred in a vapour of violets and oranges and reds and yellows. Lo! There I am, dreaming atop the tower at Villa La Luna. There I am, riding a mule with my beau Oskar Denzler in the Gemmi pass. There I am, dancing the bolero with Doña Marisa at Casa Castiglione. *Enough,* I told myself, and with a sorrowful heart, I bid everyone and everything there adeus.

Finis

About the Author

Robin Elizabeth Kobayashi writes about love and the eccentricities of life in a historical context. She takes delight in the sublime and the ridiculous, the extraordinary and the everyday, the magical and the mystical, and the wisdom that can be extracted from it all. Her current passion is reimagining the lives and destinies of some of the peripheral characters from Jane Austen's world, including here, the curiously evasive and opaque character of Colonel Fitzwilliam from *Pride and Prejudice*. During the day, in her more serious moments, she works as a senior legal writer and editor for a leading global publisher and provider of information and technology committed to advancing the rule of law around the world.

Visit www.facebook.com/freedomandmirth.

Send inquiries to freedomandmirth@gmail.com.

92486351R00130

Made in the USA
Middletown, DE
09 October 2018